KINGS OF
PETALING
STREET

Dear Nat

Thanks for
being here,
and for
everything!

Wai
(Eng)

ABOUT FIXI LONDON

>———————<

FIXI LONDON WAS ESTABLISHED TO PUBLISH
URBAN CONTEMPORARY PULP FICTION FROM
SOUTH EAST ASIA.

KINGS OF PETALING STREET (2017) IS OUR FIRST BOOK.

READERS AND WRITERS ARE WELCOME!

DO FOLLOW US:

FB.COM/FIXILONDON
TWITTER @FIXILONDON
INSTAGRAM @FIXI.LONDON

JOIN OUR MAILING LIST AND CHECK OUR WEBSITE

WWW.FIXI.LONDON

KINGS OF PETALING STREET

WILLIAM THAM WAI LIANG

First published in Great Britain in 2017 by
Fixi London
Unit 15, Grosvenor Way,
London E5 9ND

Kings of Petaling Street
Copyright © William Tham Wai Liang 2017

A CIP catalogue record for this book is available from the British Library.

Paperback: 978-0-9955558-0-8
Ebook: 978-0-9955558-1-5

Printed and bound by Clays Ltd, St Ives PLC
Design and typeset by Teck Hee
Consultant Lyana Khairuddin
Cover Photograph: *Chronicles of Crime: Last Supper* (2006)
by Wong Hoy Cheong

For my family

"Kalau saya punya dua tangan tidak jem,
saya sudah tembak. Lu nasib baik."
*If I could shoot, I would have done so.
You were just lucky.*

—BOTAK CHIN,
upon his capture in 1976

PROLOGUE

8pm. A motorcycle drew to a halt outside a coffeeshop in Cheras. It was the kind of place where old men, gamblers, businessmen and occasional counterfeit sellers gathered for late-night Hokkien mee and Tiger Beer. The rider dismounted and entered the restaurant with its rain- and mud-stained tiles without bothering to remove his helmet or lift his visor. He made his way inside, past the Indonesian servers holding bowls of soup and kway teow, through the clouds of kretek smoke, and walked to the back of the restaurant where a man with a shock of wavy blond hair sat in front of an altar of the deity Kwan Yin. The blond man was known as Ah Fung the Phoenix, for reasons everyone had forgotten. He was an enforcer for a group of loan sharks who controlled Petaling Street, intimidating even the most errant of fake beggars into abiding by the rules that they had laid down.

"Ah Fung?" the motorcyclist demanded, causing Ah Fung to turn around. His eyes were watery from too much drinking and too little sleep. Witnesses later said that he had been involved in an extortion incident in Kepong just hours before and probably had been eating a quick supper before heading to the nightclubs.

"Boss sent you, is it?" Ah Fung snapped. He tapped a cigarette on his palm.

With that, the motorcyclist drew his gun and shot the gangster in the head. There was a spray of blood and everyone was screaming as they dove under the plastic tables. There was blood and brains in the soup, splattered on the walls and on the altar. The motorcyclist turned around, reholstered his gun, and walked out of the restaurant back to his motorcycle. He was gone before anyone could call the police.

Detective Ramalingam knew all of this because he had recently been assigned to the Homicide department at the Ampang Police Station. He had made it through the traffic with Sub-Inspector Kassim, and they'd sealed off the restaurant while other officers, roused from their television sets, rounded up witnesses. But almost everyone, even the workers, had made a run for it. They were too afraid to be part of the investigation. Ramalingam tried not to look at Ah Fung's mutilated head, lying face down in the soup, flies already settling on the gaping wound, while Kassim interrogated the owner, who replied in broken Malay.

"And then the motorcyclist shot him. Like that. And then he ran away," the owner faltered, trying to wipe blood off his spectacles with the cloth that he usually used to clean the glasses.

"And the motorcyclist didn't remove his helmet?" Kassim asked.

"No, boss. He just came in, fired the shot, and walked out."

Kassim sighed and looked at the dead body crawling with flies. "And this fellow?"

The owner began babbling about the gangs and made it a point to denounce Ah Fung. "They say he even dealt drugs," he concluded.

Ramalingam waited as Kassim painstakingly wrote down the details. The owner was more than happy to cooperate, spinning colorful details of Ah Fung's daily routine. He ate there at least once a week, being a huge fan of their Hakka Mee. He lived in an apartment somewhere in Balakong, or so the owner gathered. Ah Fung was happy enough with other people knowing that he was a gangster, as long as they didn't bother him. Waiters fawned over him at restaurants, not because he gave generous tips but because he had a foul mouth and trigger-happy fingers.

Around midnight, the owner was allowed to leave, and he gratefully put on a clean shirt and fled in his beat-up VW while the police carried Ah Fung's body away in a black bag, destined for the overflowing morgue. Only Ramalingam remained, waiting as SI Kassim put his peaked cap back on and ventured outside. Ramalingam waited as Kassim lit up a Marlboro. Only after a few puffs did Kassim look Ramalingam in the eye.

"You're not too disturbed, are you?" asked Kassim.

"No, sir."

"Don't bluff. I was watching you when we first entered the restaurant. You were looking anywhere but at the gangster's corpse."

"I will try to look next time."

Kassim laughed, exhaling thick billows of smoke from his blackened lungs. "You need to be tougher than that. How old are you now? You must be in your early twenties at the most. When I was your age, I was in the army. They took us into the jungles to fight the communists. I killed men there. I came out of there a different man. Killing was second nature to me. In there I met other boys who came out of Kelantan and God-knows-where-else. They all went in, their uniforms dangling from their skinny frames, and they all left as killers. Those years changed my life. Perhaps tonight will change yours."

Ramalingam was quiet, momentarily fiddling with his bootstraps as he squatted on the concrete steps outside the restaurant.

Kassim regarded him with pity before patting him on the shoulder. "Come now," he said. "Get some rest. I will see you in the station at the usual time tomorrow."

>———————<

The man who ran the Yew Hua Coffeeshop on Jalan Sultan had been a comrade of Kassim's during the Emergency. They had served in the same unit, but while Kassim had risen through the ranks, Yew hadn't been as lucky. He had been crippled and left for dead during an attack on a communist camp, and survived by using his elbows to drag himself through the jungle. Yew now needed crutches to get around, using his pension to pay the rising electricity bills. From what Ramalingam heard, Kassim had contracted him as a police informant by paying off his gambling debts. Ramalingam had only been to the coffeeshop once, during which Kassim and Yew had chatted for hours about random things, from the political crisis in Singapore to the Indonesian Konfrontasi. But now it seemed like Yew had noticed something amiss.

"Yew told me," Kassim wheezed as Ramalingam entered the station the next morning, "that one of the young men who lives down the road from him has recently been acting strange. He has also obtained a motorcycle. His name is Wong Kah Lok, I believe. We don't know anything else about him. No criminal record; not even a speeding ticket. And he was out late last night. Yew saw all of this and told me everything."

"So where is this Wong now?"

"In custody. A squad car picked him up at Yew's coffeeshop an hour ago. Come with me. We'll question him now."

Ramalingam had never been in the interrogation room before. He looked at Kassim. Kassim's face was blank, but his trembling hands told a different story.

The interrogation room was exactly as Ramalingam pictured it. It was bare, painted white, with only one fluorescent light flickering in the dimness. They took their seats at the plastic table and waited. Kassim said nothing. The door opened again and Ramalingam looked up to see a police officer shoving a man through it. The man was Chinese, with hooded eyes and a mustache, his hair lank and untrimmed. He looked straight at Kassim as he was pushed into his chair. That was the first time Ramalingam had ever seen a prisoner look back with such contempt.

"You are Wong, aren't you?" Kassim growled. "Wong Kah Lok?"

"Yes, I am."

"Then you know why you are here. You have been arrested on the suspicion of committing murder."

"I did no such thing, officer."

"Don't lie." Kassim was on edge now, leaning forward. "Last night, a motorcyclist killed a man in a coffeeshop in Cheras. My sources told me that you recently acquired a motorbike. And last night, you were out at the time of the murder."

The man blinked. "So I was out. But that doesn't mean that I did anything. I borrowed a friend's motorbike. So what? I am sure many of your officers also have motorbikes. Even children know how to ride them!"

"Don't get cocky, Wong. You are here because you are our prime suspect."

"But you have no proof! You say I shot a man. But I have no gun. Tell me if you can find one person who can prove I was there!"

Ramalingam watched as Kassim flexed his fingers. "I don't care," he spat. "I am the law here. We can easily throw you into jail. You might never leave."

The man was silent for a while. Was it out of fear? No. It was something more complicated than that. "Throw me in," he challenged them. "But I have friends who can back me up. They were with me last night, down at Bukit Bintang. I swear, officer, that I was nowhere near Cheras."

Kassim stood up suddenly, and for a split second Ramalingam thought that he was going to reach for his revolver. But he didn't, although his hand hovered over it for a moment. Then he stormed out. Ramalingam looked back at Wong, who was gazing at the floor.

Ramalingam followed Kassim outside. Kassim had already lit up a cigarette. He was quiet, sitting alone at the table where the other officers took their breaks.

"So what now, tuan?" Ramalingam asked.

"Damn all this, I miss the communists," Kassim swore. "We can't do what we like any longer, now that we are in a democratic, perfect country. We can't beat him up or throw him into the jungle to die. We have no proof. We'll get laughed out of court with no evidence."

"Surely there must be something! A witness, one of his roommates or something…"

"We have to let him go," Kassim said, sounding defeated. "I cannot go to war with such a man. He's with one of the big Chinese gangs, or so Yew tells me. They rule the city, these kings of Petaling Street. If there's no evidence we can't do anything. This Wong fellow knows how we work. We can only hold him for so long, and then we have to release him. If not we'll have war on the streets. Don't forget, the Commonwealth soldiers are still in the country. They are watching us to make sure we act like obedient puppets. Our hands are tied."

"So we let him go?" Ramalingam was incredulous.

"Yes, I suppose so," Kassim said. And for the first time since Ramalingam had known him, Kassim put his face in his hands and began to cry.

1
DEATH COMES TO KL

Restoran Klasik blazed with light. Sometime ago, the huge dance hall in the middle of the restaurant had been filled with covered tables, men in three-piece suits and women in imperial gowns. Chauffeured BMWs and Porsches drove to the front doors with their doormen in elegant Baju Melayu. Back then, the guests would walk on the red carpet into the grand dining room, taking their places as a French chef (originally from Algiers) emerged from the kitchen, recommending the plat du jour to the diners, while, in a corner, musicians played lively pieces from Bach and Chopin (never mind that they were just music students from Universiti Malaya).

But those days were long gone. Restoran Klasik was now divided into two sections. One still served European food, but with less flair, and the other became a bar of some sort. By eleven, the tables were moved to one side for the dancers to gyrate to pop music after having overpriced beer and fish and chips. Half-nightclub and half-respectable establishment, it was so out of place in Bangsar Baru.

Gavin sat in the office on the second floor overlooking the restaurant's dance floor. His mind, restless as it was during the day at Yohan Eng College, hummed even faster that night as he tried to force himself to look through the records again, to make sure that the accounts were balanced. Worse still, Crazy Foo had not turned up for the third night in a row.

On the first night, Foo had accosted Gavin as he ate silently at his usual table in the corner. Foo was drunk after a few bottles of Sapporo.

"Eh, Gavin ah, you can help me to take over for tonight or not?" he asked. "I have to go see my girlfriend and I forgot that tonight got shift."

"You don't have a girlfriend," Gavin mumbled as he chewed on his fries.

Foo was desperate. "Look, I know that you are boss's son and all, but please-lah help me. I will pay you, OK? Double salary. You just help me jaga the office."

Gavin was no stranger to the office. He had spent most of his afternoons there growing up under the watchful eye of Crazy Foo. He sat in front of the monitors, where cameras peered down at the till and in the kitchens, while Foo left to gorge on a private stash of Hup Seng biscuits. It was like that each afternoon. Gavin neglected his homework for his new job as Crazy Foo's unofficial assistant, and Foo began to pay him. It was peanuts, but enough to buy extra hours at the CC and a succession of new handphones. Over time, Foo taught him other things: how to spot pickpockets and thieves, how to order new supplies of Bintang Beer at cut-rate prices from the Indonesians, how to bribe the health inspectors when they showed up to check for dead rats and *Aedes* mosquitoes on the rooftops.

It had gone on for years. Foo had become even sloppier and often showed up for work drunk. Once, Gavin considered telling his father and getting Foo fired, but Foo had stopped him with an irresistible promise: "You keep quiet, and I'll show you all about our world."

"I know all about the syndicate," Gavin, aged seventeen, shot back. "I'm not stupid, you know."

Foo laughed, swaying as he spoke. "Well you don't know everything, OK? You know what it's like when you kill a man? Do you even know how to fire a gun?"

And he brandished his own revolver, slamming it down so hard on the office table that Gavin, despite his anger and bravado, jumped backward. "Can you... show me?"

"Eh, use your head. Your father don't want to teach you. But I can teach you a lot of things," Foo said, his lips parting to reveal a smile like a crocodile's, with sharp little teeth that threatened to snap off Gavin's fingers.

So Gavin began to step into Foo's place, letting the old gangster roam the nightclubs, gambling dens and massage parlors that only opened at night. He showed up once or twice a week, collecting Foo's paychecks. Once he scraped through school into college, he began to take Foo's place more often.

On the third straight night that Foo hadn't showed up for work, Gavin sat in the office. He sometimes ate his meals there, preferring not to be disturbed. He was sick of the crowds who dreamt only of wasting the night away. There was a time when he'd been willing to be one of them, dancing closely with everyone until the dance floor appeared like one gigantic creature with many limbs and a single spaced-out mind. But not anymore.

A message on his phone. It was an SMS from Chee Fong:

Eh, you here ah? We downstairs already.

Gavin sighed. He had been half hoping that none of his college mates would show up, but there they were. He could see them from the office, huddled in a corner. He looked at the nearly illegible accounts and overflowing letter trays and left. The office could do without him for one night.

"Gavin!" Chee Fong called out as soon as Gavin approached them, wearing a checked shirt over his singlet. Chee Fong's face was already red and he was wearing sunglasses despite the dimness of the restaurant. Beside him, Robert looked slightly uneasy. Sure, they had all gone out for drinks together, but those were in other places where even Gavin was able to blend into the crowd. Restoran Klasik was Gavin's turf.

"Hello, Chee Fong," said Gavin, as Chee Fong wobbled on his feet, embracing him.

"Brother, I thought you ditch us," Chee Fong slurred. "Thought that you were emo and stuff."

"Are you OK?" Robert asked.

"I'm OK." Gavin managed a wry smile. "No big deal, right? We are all men here. We can handle small things like that."

"Yalah, I guess so," Robert mumbled. "I mean, things like that happen all the time. You saw Aidan and Jess. Broke up after how long? Something like six years what. Cheer up."

Gavin kept smiling.

"Aiya, be more like me," Chee Fong said. "I lost my scholarship and I come back from Canada to study here. No big deal what, carry on only."

Robert snorted at Chee Fong's response. "Bro, don't listen to this guy. You still have us. We should go out for drinks or something. That will make everything better."

"We are already having drinks here. Don't be so awkward, lah," scolded Chee Fong.

Gavin let his friends argue among themselves. He was in no mood to talk. Just a week before, Danielle had told him that it was over under the Moorish domes of the KL railway station, that she couldn't see him again before she transferred out of Yohan Eng. He wanted to scream, to run after her, and kill himself. The next few days had passed, with the pain dulling somewhat, but it returned to stab at him when he thought he could finally get their break-up out of his head. Chee Fong and Robert now insisted on trying to cheer him up.

Half an hour later, Chee Fong was properly drunk and Robert had stopped trying to be polite and was openly disparaging Danielle. "You know, her father is good friends with Chancellor Zahid. No wonder she could get in," Robert said. "I bet she's been doing 'other stuff' to pay for her fancy apartment too!"

"Eh, Gavin, don't be so emo can or not?" Chee Fong mumbled as Gavin forced himself to keep paying attention to them. "Look over there, that leng lui. The one with the damn short skirt. I think she don't have a boyfriend. Go try with her lah!"

"How would you know that?" Gavin sighed, without bothering to turn his head.

"Look, she's been soloing the whole evening, wah lao! Look at her dance!"

Gavin was about to raise his hand to signal for a bouncer. He'd had enough of the night and was ready to have all of them thrown out of the restaurant. Never mind his reputation at the college, which was already in tatters. Never mind that they were pretty much the only people outside the syndicate that he could talk to with some semblance of honesty.

A man began weaving his way past the dancers and waiters. Gavin was stunned as Crazy Foo reappeared, seemingly unconcerned that Gavin was slacking off work, sitting with his friends in a corner of the restaurant. "You, boy, come with me," he panted.

Gavin was about to tell him to sober up when he realized that Foo's red face wasn't not a sign of drunkenness, but of blood and adrenaline pumping through him—his gaze was keen and more focused than Gavin had ever seen.

"Sorry," Gavin said, pleased for an excuse to leave. "Got some business to do."

He followed Foo as the old man raced for the doors, without even pausing to stare at the women in his way. "What is it?" Gavin asked as he loosened the collar of his shirt.

"There is some guy, he's called Maut, and he's come to KL," Foo gasped.

"'Maut'? As in 'death'?"

"Ya, ya, aren't you listening? Now come with me!"

2
THE SYNDICATE

Foo explained the situation to Gavin in increasingly broken English as they pushed past the front doors of Restoran Klasik to where he'd parked his modified Datsun.

Foo had been at his usual karaoke bar—where a string of "girlfriends", mostly poor students and migrants who'd ventured out of the remote villages of Johor and the east coast, had bled him dry before dumping him for wealthier patrons. He had been mourning the loss of his latest fling, whose name escaped him, with a large glass of Poison (a blend of guava juice, vodka, chili flakes, slices of ladies' fingers, all mixed together with diabetes-inducing lumps of sugar) when a group of men walked in. Luckily, Foo was wearing a fedora that night (ostensibly to look cool, in reality to hide his bald patch). He was well hidden from the men in the darkness of the room. He recognized them as the hired thugs of Chang Kok Chye, the Seremban gangster.

There was Ah Fung II, an assassin who had worked with Chang after his uncle was supposedly murdered by the elder Wong. The others were younger but Foo vaguely recognized them as Nasiruddin and Leonardo Goh, two of the gang's top lieutenants.

Foo was glad that it had been some time since he'd been out in the field, long enough for the younger members of the gang to not recognize him. The bartenders had left after handing the drinks over to the men, who were already drunk when they entered. Foo debated whether to run or to stay, but he elected to remain in his seat, hoping to hear some insider intelligence.

The men didn't even look at him, preferring to talk to each other in loud, drunken voices. They talked about football and the MRT project, but a few drinks later, Foo realized that he was on to something big.

"Who caught Maut?" Ah Fung II had mumbled. "That guy can really run!"

"Forgot liao," Leonardo Goh said. "Luckily he didn't have a gun that time. He's damn scary when he has one!"

"Eh, stop it lah," Nasiruddin warned them as he lit up a cigarette. "We're supposed to keep quiet about this."

Who was Maut? Foo had wondered.

"So I went undercover for two days," Foo said as he started up the car engine. "To find out who is this Maut. And when I found out, wow! We must get this guy."

"You mean Chang's gang is holding him prisoner? And you want to rescue him from them?" Gavin asked.

Foo slammed his foot on the accelerator, freeing the gears and racing through the night, along the highways and out of the city. He dialed his usual lieutenants, bellowing orders as he cut corners and ran red lights, zipping through traffic without fear of arrest.

Gavin had never seen his father looking as impetuous as Foo. His father had always been distant, preferring to watch rather than to talk or even touch Gavin. Gavin's earliest memories had been of his father quietly seated in the living room of their Cheras hillside mansion. While buildings had sprung up like mushrooms after the rain, the hillside remained almost untouched, one last sanctuary from the city that spilled in all directions. Gavin had known nothing outside the grounds in his earliest days, and certainly almost nothing of his father. While he played with Lego bricks and watched television, his father was dressed neatly in his work shirts. His hair was combed back so that the gray strands were hidden before he left in the blue Mercedes-Benz driven by Boon. Once, Gavin, tired of the grounds, had tried to sneak out, but he was caught by the Nepali security guard and locked up in the mansion.

His father had come back, and, in a rare show of anger, slapped Gavin. "I told you," he said over Gavin's protesting screams, "never go outside! Don't you understand? It's dangerous out there!"

And so Gavin continued growing up within the walls and grounds of the mansion on Cheras Hill, receiving a tutor until he was old enough for school. When he thought about it, he realized that, somehow, he had always known about his father's work. His father had said almost nothing about his involvement in the syndicate, preferring to refer to it as "the business": both Restoran Klasik and the Laksamana Hotel. Much of his time was spent donating to temples and charities.

Gavin recalled the time when they were both walking in Petaling Street, accompanied by a bodyguard. An old toothless hawker had come running up to them in his battered Fung Keongs. Ah Leong, who was their bodyguard, had rushed forward but Wong stopped him. The man broke down, embracing Gavin's surprised father, blubbering about his magnanimity or something, but eventually they had to leave.

"Who was he?" Gavin asked naively.

"Someone I helped once." Wong seemed nonchalant, but Gavin could tell that he was pleased. It was one of the rare times his father showed a hint of emotion behind his stern mask.

Eventually the true nature of the syndicate revealed itself. It had been just before he sat for his UPSR exams. He heard a scream at midnight and sneaked downstairs in morbid curiosity. He peered from behind the banisters on the stairs at the scene below. Blood. More blood than he could ever have imagined, staining the Persian carpet and white marble tiles. His father was there, in his vest. The Nepali guard and a few of his lieutenants surrounded him. Uncle Foo was stretched out on the table, while another man in an apron was carefully rolling up Foo's shirt.

Gavin almost retched. Foo's torso was coated in blood, and it had started congealing, while fresh blood still pumped out of the wounds stretching across his belly. The people around him were shouting in a myriad of dialects: Hokkien, Teochew, Cantonese and what Gavin suspected to be Hakka. The man in the apron clumsily emptied a bottle of antiseptic onto a crumpled ball of tissue, and was dabbing it on the wound while Foo shrieked in a horrible, high-pitched voice.

"Boss, he needs a doctor," the medic (or was it Ah Leong?) said. Wong presided over the events stoically despite the panic around him.

"Not yet," his father said, his voice barely audible above Foo's protracted screaming. "We can't send him to the hospital with a bullet piercing his stomach. We need to get it out first. Tell them that it was a car crash or even a monkey attacking him, but get the damn bullet out of him first."

Gavin watched in horror as the medic reluctantly lifted a pair of forceps and inserted them into the gaping wound. He turned away, sickened, and retreated to his room, covering his ears with his pillow as Foo's screaming continued. Eventually Foo fell silent and the doors opened downstairs and closed. Gavin rushed to the window and saw twin headlights cutting through the darkness, heading down the hill and back toward the city.

He heard footsteps coming down the mahogany-lined corridor. Was it his father? He listened as they drew near, eventually terminating outside his door. Did his father know that he was there, watching the makeshift surgery? The footsteps picked up again and Wong Kah Lok was gone, retiring for the night.

The next real brush with the syndicate came two years later, when Gavin was a student at Methodist Boys' School. He was out on the field, skipping classes, dribbling a football down the pitch under the blazing sun. Eleven in the morning and he had been running since eight, completely unchecked, when he saw the discipline master hurrying toward him across the pavilion. His heart sank. Mr. Singh was a former policeman from Klang who wasn't to be fooled with. Singh carried around a rotan that he used to whack unsuspecting rule-breakers. But that day, even Singh looked nervous.

"Boy, you follow me," he said.

Singh took him to the canteen, where Crazy Foo, wearing an ill-fitting shirt and trousers, waited with a cup of kopi-O. "Ah, thank you," Foo said to Singh. "Sorry ah, have to take my boss's son back early. Got some urgent stuff."

Singh didn't press further, looking apprehensive at the thought of talking with the plump gangster.

"Boy, faster," Foo mumbled as they exited the side gates and went to Foo's ancient souped-up Datsun.

"I don't understand," Gavin said as he got into the seat beside Foo, who struggled to start up his engine.

"No need to understand, you just keep quiet, OK? You got see anyone try to catch you or not?" Foo asked.

Gavin shook his head, confused, and Foo managed to get the engine started. They raced away from MBS to join the choking traffic. Gavin couldn't feel the air-conditioning and his school shirt was sticky and damp with accumulated sweat from the morning's football. They squeezed past the cars near Dataran Merdeka, passing under the LRT tracks and into the older parts of KL, away from the gleaming skyscrapers and toward the gray-flaked, moss-covered concrete mid-rises that loomed over Gavin.

They arrived at the Laksamana Hotel. Gavin had never been there before and began to suspect that he was part of a kidnapping plot. He was surprised that he wasn't scared but curious. At last, he could see the inner workings of his father's syndicate.

"Out," Foo ordered, and Gavin stepped on to the burning road, the heat radiating through the rubber soles of his white Batas. "In."

They were walking through the Laksamana, past the seedy reception, the receptionist ignoring them as he leafed through the day's *Nanyang Siang Pau*. The hotel was empty save for them.

"Why isn't anyone staying here?" Gavin asked.

"Don't be so blur," Foo scolded him. The gangster was agitated, shifting his weight from one foot to another as they entered the old lift, creaking as it slowly took them up to the seventh floor, the doors opening equally slowly.

A short walk down a corridor with paint peeling off its walls took them to the deluxe suite, where Foo knocked on the twin doors. When the doors opened they stepped in.

His father embraced him. The hug was rare and Gavin was taken aback, wondering what was happening, but there were too many men talking at the same time, each trying to outdo the next.

"Boon is already waiting for them near the school…"

"Should we call the police, boss?"

"It's time to do this now. 'Day of Judgment', Mr. Wong. You've been delaying this for so many years…"

"Not yet," Wong said. The room was bare, with no beds or wardrobes. The only furniture was a Nyonya armchair and desk with a few landline phones and cabinets that overflowed with excess papers; men hurried past with guns in hand.

"You need to understand," Ah Leong began. "You have waited for at least ten years. Now is the time. They have given you an excuse."

"What weapons do we have left?" Wong demanded. "The police stopped Boon on the SPRINT highway for speeding. He was carrying eight pistols and a few parangs with him, and three cases of ammunition. They confiscated those but then Boon escaped."

"Boss," Foo said, holding a Nokia to his ear. "Boon says that he can see Chang's men approaching. He has his own gun already. Give the order. Then we can start an attack on Chang. He's at a coffeeshop in Jinjang right now."

Wong was quiet. Gavin was holding his breath as Foo and Ah Leong waited, fighting the urge to give orders to kill and shoot.

"Too late," Foo mumbled, still pressing the phone to his ear. "They have driven away already. We can't do anything now."

Wong let out a sigh of relief, while the other men looked disappointed.

"Foo, make a police report. Give them the license plate number of the kidnappers," growled Wong. Foo left, leading the quiet men into the corridor, closing doors and leaving Gavin and his father alone in the room. For a while, Wong was quiet again, looking out of the windows at the ruined streets below him, teeming with cars, crows and discarded plastic bags He turned to Gavin, squatting down to face him. "Gavin, are you OK? Did you see anything suspicious?"

Gavin shook his head.

"That's good," Wong said, more to himself than to his son. "At least you're safe."

After that, Boon was ordered to bring Gavin from school straight to Restoran Klasik, only returning to the mansion at night. At the first opportunity, Gavin was transferred out of MBS to an international school with armed security guards and a fence that extended twelve feet underground. That was how he came under the direct supervision of Foo, who took him under his wing and showed him the syndicate.

Foo drew to a halt in Puchong, killing the engine. It was late and the restaurants were all closed as they waited in a back alley. "We can't do this," Gavin said. "There's so few of us, and you want to attack Chang's men? Are you drunk or something?"

Foo laughed. "You are scared. Are you a man or not?"

Gavin said nothing. Outside, another car drew to a halt. Gavin looked out but the windows of the other car were tinted.

3
FOO

Gavin was Wong's second son. The first was called Gerald, but he was dead, along with his mother. Gavin was too young to remember any of it happening, so his father dutifully filled him in when he was much older.

That night, Wong was in a three-piece suit, slightly uncomfortable despite the air-conditioning. His wife sat opposite him, with Gerald. Gavin had come down with a fever and was left behind at the mansion. They were sitting in a corner of the restaurant and music was playing. Wong remembered it was *The Four Seasons* by Vivaldi, and by the end of the night the music veered off into Strauss's "Blue Danube".

"One of Chang's men was there," Wong told Gavin. "He had a gun and shot at our table, hitting your mother and brother, but they were only trying to kill me. Since then I've been trying to get revenge. They have also hit back, many times. Your attempted kidnapping was just the latest incident. I need to make sure you're safe."

Wong said no more to Gavin. Instead he retreated into an impervious silence, not moving from his favorite armchair. Gavin suddenly remembered that talk when Foo briefed him on what had happened.

Chang had recently hired Maut, an assassin who came out of nowhere. Maut was probably from the lawless north of the country, the gray area at the Malaysian–Thai border. He had proven to be a worthy killer, skilled with guns and other weapons. But for some reason he had gone rogue, attempting to kill Chang.

"My contacts, they told me ah, that Chang was threatening him or something so Maut tried to kill him," Foo said quickly as he killed the car's engine. "But it went wrong and Chang survived. Maut got try to run away but he was caught by the other men. They lock him in a house. It's just near here only. But now they want to kill him. The people I got talk to, they say he is questioned for last few days. When they get correct info from him, they will execute him!"

"So how do you know he's still alive?" Gavin asked. He was sick of Foo's rash plan and was tempted to get out and flag down a taxi for the relative peace of his apartment. He had long since moved out of the mansion on Cheras Hill.

"I don't know," Foo said, shrugging. "But we must try and get him for sure. Cause this guy maybe can help us. Now, you stay in the car and call me if got any police or danger."

"I'm not part of the syndicate," Gavin said, panicking. "I want to get out now."

Foo flashed him a snarky grin. "Sure or not? You are practically begging to join us, Gavin. No need to lie to me. If not, why you still come with me? Better you report me to your father straight away, right?"

Gavin said nothing as he grasped the door latch. After several seconds he let go of it and Foo relaxed.

"Now then," Foo said, in his best imitation of a bossy tone. "To work!"

>————<

Foo was his father's chief lieutenant. True, he was a gambler, drunkard, and a serial womanizer, and were it not for his father's charity he would be languishing in a prison cell or in a back alley with a handful of used syringes. But Foo knew how to get around. From his long, boastful stories, Gavin had guessed that Foo was a smuggler as a teenager—bringing sacks of rice from Indonesian sampans on the beaches to Port Dickson—before joining the syndicate. Foo was a man who, despite his social awkwardness and bluster, was as ruthless as the other assassins. But better than that, he was able to see plans where nobody else could. Gavin supposed that he saw something like that in Maut.

The syndicate attracted people from all over the peninsula, plus stragglers from Indonesia and Borneo. They were men on the run, who were desperate for cash and willing to do anything for meals or women. Those were the shadowy details that Gavin had picked up from Foo—while his father refused to discuss anything.

Foo had mumbled about the thrill of running through the streets with the police in pursuit. He talked at length about his first assassination, which took place on the tracks of the KL railway station. He said all this at the Iwamasa-san Japanese restaurant in Bangsar, which he had treated Gavin to on his fifty-fifth birthday. Gavin had wondered why Foo chose to invite him and whether it was really his birthday. But he was happy enough to let Foo pay for the extravagant order of sashimi, chicken yakitori, and endless cups of sake.

Eventually Foo grew tired and leaned back in his seat. They were sitting in a large private room, with paper sliding doors and a window overlooking the bright lights outside, but it was just Gavin and Foo that night.

"I got invite your father to attend," Foo finally said, his eyes bloodshot. "But he don't want to come. He wants to stay in his house."

"Doesn't he still go to Laksamana Hotel? You could have just gone out for a beer or something."

"Ha! He never go to the hotel already. He wants to stay in. Dunno why. Maybe he's scared or something."

"He always looks very calm. What makes you think he is scared?"

Foo laughed unexpectedly, wheezing. "You should have seen your father when he was a young man. That time he was seriously damn terror. He was one of the best assassins that ever worked in KL. Everyone was blown away, boy."

Gavin had just started college, and the thought of his father running through KL with a gun in his pocket struck him as comical. "I didn't realize that he ever got his hands dirty."

"Ya, he did. You think he got to the top without doing any dirty work, is it? Everyone last time had to kill people. Not that we liked it, but what to do? It was life, man!"

But Gavin suspected Foo secretly reveled in the assassinations he carried out.

"But," Foo continued, raising another porcelain cup to his lips. "Sometimes I think your father only changed after your mother was killed. OK, so he was always quite quiet. Never says a lot. But after that he started hiding in the house more. I have to do his work for him! He hired that Nepali security guard and got Boon to drive him around. He is seriously paranoid now. You know ah, one time he said to me, 'If we can… avenge!' Yes, that the correct word. He say if we kill Chang and avenge your mother, he will retire."

"Did you know my mother?"

"Oh. Ya, I got meet her a few times. She was very nice person," Foo said. "Where was she from? Somewhere in the south, is it?"

"Malacca."

Foo looked quite guilty as he downed his drink. "Eh, Gavin. Let me ask you a question: do you miss your mother?"

Gavin was taken aback at the heartfelt question. He looked straight at Foo and saw that his eyes were unfocused. He was drunk, and he would definitely remember nothing of it the next morning.

"No."

"Your father does," Foo slurred. "He got talk about her sometimes. And he is scared that something like that will happen to you, so that is why he don't want to tell you more about the syndicate."

*That explained thing*s, thought Gavin. He sat back and let Foo ramble on, recounting his brushes with death. Each moment in the life of an assassin could be the last one, which was why they were paid so well. But there was always a market for them. Businessmen trying to bump off their rivals, politicians trying to get rid of blackmailing prostitutes, and even rich men's sons trying to snuff out their parents for their inheritance.

>————<

Gavin followed Foo out of the car. He recognized the other assassins who emerged from the vehicle next to them. They were Ah Leong and a man called Gunner, short for Gunasekaran. He met them several times before, usually at the Restoran Klasik or his father's New Year parties. It was comical to see these hardened men dressed in starched red shirts, looking uncomfortable among lavish surroundings without the usual aura of violence around them. They looked at him in surprise, and Ah Leong raised his voice at Foo in rapid Cantonese, which Gavin didn't speak but could certainly understand.

"What is boss's son doing here?" Ah Leong said, fuming.

"Relax, relax," Foo said. "Tonight we're going to have some fun."

4
YOU WANT TO BE ONE OF US?

Foo outlined the plan. From the intelligence he'd gathered in the last few days, Maut was being held in a two-story semidetached house just two streets down from them. He was being guarded by two of Chang's gang members: Nasiruddin and Leonardo Goh. The house was perfectly ordinary but it had been soundproofed and there were reinforced bars on the windows. It was like breaking into a fortress.

"So I have this." Foo produced a hacksaw from inside his backpack. "We cut the grille and go in. I will go first. You two will cover me. Those two gangsters inside, they are probably relaxing and smoking ganja because they think they are safe. So, this should be easy only."

Gavin listened uneasily as the men discussed their plans.

"Then this boy leh?" Gunner gestured at Gavin. They all sat inside Foo's car, which started to reek of their collective sweat.

"He will help us jaga," Foo said on Gavin's behalf. "'Cause if the gangsters got backup, then we need someone to tell us. He will call my handphone if got anyone come."

"Can trust him or not?" Ah Leong asked. "You know that you never discussed this with boss. Are you sure he's not spying for the old man?"

They still spoke in Cantonese, unaware that Gavin could understand them.

"Him?" Foo said. "He don't know anything about the syndicate also. I trust him, OK? Anyway, I thought he might want to see what we do."

Ah Leong looked unconvinced, but he unzipped his briefcase. From inside it he drew out a revolver. Gavin felt himself breathing faster.

>————<

A year earlier, Foo had showed him his new gun.

"This is a Stech-kin." Foo had struggled to pronounce the Russian name. "I got this from my friends in Hanoi, and it's fucking expensive. A present for myself!"

He removed the stubby revolver from his holster, fully loaded with the safety catch on, and laid it on the office table. Gavin picked it up with trepidation, the weapon heavy in his hands. It seemed so natural in Foo's grasp, but in his it was clumsy and awkward.

Foo sighed. "Tell you what. Later I take you outside the city, OK? Teach you how to use it."

Gavin wondered if it was better just to stay in the restaurant. But the gun eventually swayed him, and he was in Foo's car later that evening, while elsewhere in the city the other students were cramming for exams.

There was a text from Danielle on his phone. He unlocked it and read the message. It was a reply to his earlier message. Hey, want to go for supper later tonight? he had asked. And she had replied back at last.

I'm free. What time? Maybe you can give me a lift.

Sorry, something just came up, Gavin texted back, feeling a twinge of guilt. He had spent so long trying to get a date with her but now he found himself locked in a car with Crazy Foo, about to fire a gun for the first time.

They eventually stopped by the roadside. They were alone and Crazy Foo got out, his pathway traced out by the weak lights from the road. Gavin followed. They cut through a graveyard full of headstones engraved with ancient Chinese script faded by the rain and the heat, and then over a fence before walking into a clearing where Foo finally turned a flashlight on. In front of them was what looked like a mining pond, a relic from the old days when mining dredgers sifted through the mud for tin ore. But the machines were long gone and the pits were abandoned, left to fill with rainwater, creating ponds that were so deep people drowned and vanished when swimming in them.

There were some abandoned oil drums lying on their sides. Foo paused to wipe the sweat from his forehead, slapping at his elbow and leaving the bloodied stain of a flattened mosquito.

"There," he said, pointing at the oil drums. "Good place to practice shooting. Here got no polis, no jaga. No houses either because there is a graveyard and people very superstitious. Very quiet." Gavin took the gun from Foo, who said, "You cross your arms over one another. If not, when you shoot, the gun got recoil. Now, you let go the safety… Fire!"

When Gavin fired his first shot, the recoil hurt more than he imagined it would. The gun made almost no noise, but there was nothing else other than the rustling of branches in the jungle.

"You missed," Foo snapped. "You try again, more properly!"

Gavin closed one eye and fired again. This time there was an echoing thud and the bullet blew a hole in one of the drums. He turned around to see Foo looking delighted. "Good, good," he said. "Try again!"

Each time Gavin fired he tried to imagine Foo out in the field, shooting at other men, covered in bloodstains but never flinching from incoming bullets. He thought of the mines his father had warned him about.

"There are things called penunggu," he said. "There were stories from my village when I was young. The penunggu wait for children to go swimming in the ponds. And then they drag them down where they would drown. Don't go there."

Had his father told Gavin those stories because the ponds were where his men practiced shooting?

"I very surprised that your father never teach you how to shoot," said Foo once Gavin had emptied the entire magazine. "I thought he is very worried about you. How come he doesn't teach you how to use gun in case you got kidnap?"

"Maybe he just doesn't want to get me involved in any of this," Gavin said. "My father never told me anything about the syndicate. I learned everything from you."

"Ya, I am actually good teacher." Foo beamed with pride. They were walking through the graveyard and toward the car. "Tell me, you want to learn to shoot someone?"

"What for?" Gavin wondered if he had heard Foo correctly.

"You can be like us. All of us are brothers here. All you do is point the gun then you shoot. Easy?"

The way Foo said it, it was as if killing a man was as simple as flicking a light switch. Both times, something went out, but whether it was a lamp or another person's life made no difference to him. Foo was a man who had lived for so long in a world of death that other people were walking ghosts to him.

Gavin didn't reply. They returned to the car and were once again returning to the city. It was long past midnight, and the graveyard and the mines vanished into the jungle as if they had never existed. He listened as Foo rambled on and on about the gun's specifications and its drawbacks, but his mind was elsewhere.

We can still go out tonight if you're free…

Danielle's message had been sent two hours before, but Gavin hadn't seen it, his hands still shaking from the elation of holding the gun. He tried to reply but couldn't think of anything to say so he set the phone aside, watching in detached silence as they traveled down the highway.

>————<

They reached the house. There was some lalang growing out of cracks in the cement, but apart from that the house was untouched. It was sturdy, solid, and unremarkable. Foo parked just down the street, away from the windows. Gavin watched as the men loaded their weapons, carrying extra rounds in their pockets.

"Quick one, OK?" Foo said, yawning. "I don't want to stay here too long. Then, after that we burn the house. Pretend it's an accident."

The other men responded with precise nods.

"Stay here, Gavin," Foo instructed. "If you got see anyone, call my handphone."

Gavin quietly watched them. The three men left the car and he sealed himself inside, behind the tinted windows. The three men ambled toward the gate, and they climbed it as if they were schoolboys. Gavin could no longer see them; they were hidden by the overgrown ferns in the garden. Why didn't the neighbors call the police? He looked at the two buildings beside Number 18— they seemed uninhabited. Did they all belong to Chang's gang?

He felt as if he had walked into a film or painting that he had no right to be in. Nothing but silence. Then there was a series of faint cracks, as if fireworks or car tires were exploding in the distance. Gavin held his breath.

And then there was a message on his phone, from Foo:

Come in!

Gavin got out of the car, locking it with Foo's keys. He hauled himself over the gate and toward the door, its locks cut off and the grille hanging open. Carefully, he pushed his way past them and opened the wooden door, which had been shut.

Inside, the lights had been turned on. There was practically no furniture inside, the floor was dusty and curtains covered the windows.

"Up here!" Foo called from upstairs. Gavin took to the parquet stairs, hurrying up them and leaving footprints in the dust.

Up on the second floor, he found himself recoiling. There was a body slumped in an armchair. There was another one on the floor a few feet away. *Was that Maut?* Foo was squatting in front of the two bodies, sweating heavily and looking his age for once.

"So this is what we do," he said calmly, despite his sweat. His gun was grimy and he was wiping it with a wad of tissue. "I give you a chance to do something. That guy down there, you see him? That is Nasiruddin. We only hit him in the back. He is still alive but soon he will die anyway."

Gavin saw what was coming. "You want me to shoot him."

"Ya, ya," Foo said impatiently. "Take my re-vol-ver. Shoot him dead."

Gavin wasn't thinking as he accepted the gun from Foo. He walked over to the gangster, who had managed to turn his head toward him, eyes blossoming red with broken blood vessels. There was a pool of blood spreading out from under him in intricate arcs, seeping into the cracks in the parquet.

"Shoot him," goaded Foo. "You want to be one of us, issit? Then shoot him! Faster la!"

All this was being said as if they were boys playing a game. The gun was in his hands. He was about to kill a man.

"He is dying already," Foo said. "More painful if we leave him like that. Even if you call the ambulans, they will sure send him to the polis station, not the KLGH. Shoot."

Gavin forced himself to look into the face of the dying man, whose eyes were almost closing. It would be an act of mercy.

"Faster!" Foo barked. "If polis come and catch us then it's your fault!"

He raised the gun like Foo had taught him, and squeezed the trigger. There was almost no sound, just a wet thump, and the body was still.

"Mr. Foo!" It was Gunner, his voice coming from downstairs. "It's Maut. We found him. Ah Leong has poured petrol on the floor already. Now we need to go!"

5
JUST AN OLD FRIEND OF YOUR FATHER'S

Gavin returned to college, attending the classes he had so often skipped. He did so not out of a desire to continue his studies, but because of a stern warning from the chancellor's office. Zahid had written a short note, threatening Gavin with expulsion if he didn't show any improvement.

He'd been at the college for about three years and had just passed the second year exams way behind schedule. The classes were no preparation for a world where desperation and violence went hand in hand. He still remembered his father speaking to the chancellor just before the first day of classes while he sat with them inside the office, unable to look Zahid in the eye. It was a few years before Zahid joined the government and started canvassing for votes. Back then he was a businessman who had just become the chancellor of Yohan Eng College.

"He is a difficult boy, but I'm sure he'll do well," Wong had said, leaning on his walking stick.

"Hmm, I suppose we can make something out of him," Zahid conceded. Zahid was well built, and his suit fit him like a second skin. But his expression hinted at a concealed vindictiveness.

Wong's smile remained unchanged. "So you'll be able to get him into the sciences, right?"

"It's not a problem," Zahid replied. "It only depends on whether he can cope."

Both men shook hands; the transaction was done. Wong placed a hand on Gavin's shoulder and they left the office. They fell into an uneasy silence on the way out, which Gavin eventually managed to break: "You and the chancellor sounded like good friends."

"I've had some business with him before," Wong said. "He owes me a favor." His father didn't elaborate and Gavin kept quiet as they were whisked out of the sprawling grounds and back to Cheras.

Gavin had attended a few classes here and there, but his heart had never been in it. He had been contemplating leaving, to work in the restaurant or something, collecting Foo's paychecks, when he met Danielle.

>———————<

It was at a friend's party in his first year. Gavin had driven there in his secondhand Sorento. He drove past the construction site of the new Istana, up more roads and into a mansion in Duta Hills. He was taken aback at first. The massive mansion belonged to a Datuk in the import–export industry with a minor role in the government.

He parked his car next to a fleet of Ferraris and Porsches, and was greeted by the host.

"Gavin!" said Azhari, who was red-faced. *Had he been drinking?* "Alhamdulillah, you were able to make it. Come in, come in!"

Gavin followed him down the path and toward the house. The sound of pop songs and dubstep blasting from speakers inside the house was already making his head spin. Next to the sheer opulence of the mansion, his father's own place on Cheras Hill was nothing. As he entered, Gavin caught sight of the swimming pool, lit up as if for a competition, surrounded by other students and barbecue pits where sausages and air-flown New Zealand steaks were grilling away.

The inside of the house looked like it had been lifted out of a catalog. Gavin adjusted his shirt as Azhari mumbled about the architecture.

"Is this your party or your father's?" he asked.

"My father? Good God, that old fart. He's on his honeymoon. Yes, you heard right, second wife. Divorced my mother sometime last year, she's gone back to her kampung in Perlis. He's with that leatherback turtle activist… Erra, yes, that's her name, in Dubai right now. You know that seven-star hotel they have there? That's the one they're staying in. While he's overseas, I'm giving myself a little treat."

Azhari had read law in the UK until earlier that year, when he had been expelled and forced to enter Yohan Eng College. "My father is chums with Chancellor Zahid," Azhari said, accepting a kebab from one of the catering staff who wandered about. "That's how I got in."

"Funny, that's what happened to me too," Gavin admitted.

"Of course, this was way back before Zahid started working with the party."

"What, he's a politician as well?"

"You're a bit slow!" Azhari chuckled. "Zahid doesn't have a parliamentary seat yet, but he wants one in the next election. That's why he looks so religious lately. Have you seen him at the mosques? What a joke. Everyone knows his only friends are gangsters."

They reached the dining room, where a boy, who bore a striking resemblance to Azhari, played the guitar for his groupies, ignoring the food in front of them.

"Eh, Nus, that's mine," Azhari said impatiently as he left Gavin. Gavin watched him laughing away, swigging from a bottle on the table, before wandering off. He passed the imitation old masters on the walls and the chandeliers that illuminated the snooker players. He wandered past the other youths who climbed out of the swimming pool, drying off their smartphones, and steered clear of the lovers hidden in the immense garden, out of sight and earshot of everyone else. He accepted a plate of steak and wandered back indoors, looking for a place to sit. Unable to see any familiar faces, he gave up and stopped at the living room where a television was beaming the latest match from Manchester. People milled about vaguely, some yelling their hearts out and others watching disinterestedly.

He started eating, when somebody interrupted him. "Excuse me, but you're Gavin, aren't you?"

He turned to face the speaker. It was a girl he didn't recognize, wearing a fashionable dress that hung loosely from her slight frame. "Yes, I am," he said, surprised. "And I'm sorry, but I don't know you."

"My name's Danielle. I'm friends with Chee Fong. He told me that he had a friend who would be here tonight."

"Small world. Are you a friend of Azhari's as well?"

She laughed. "I haven't even seen him this evening. I've met him before but he was the friend of a friend who got invited here tonight, if that even makes any sense. She's here as well, but she just met some guy and they've been busy all night. So I've been on my own."

"Well, at least there's somebody you know here. I only know Azhari, but he's gone and ditched me. How did you recognize me?"

"Chee Fong of course! He showed me your picture after he found out we were both coming to this party."

Gavin smiled. Chee Fong was always keen to introduce everyone he knew to each other. "You're a student at Yohan Eng as well?"

"Yes, I am. Psychology."

"I'm in biochem. I've never really been interested though…"

"Shall we go outside? It's a bit noisy in here."

They walked outside. They took a bowl of ais kacang each and found somewhere to sit. He found himself talking easily to her, yet being careful not to mention the syndicate. It was something he had become very good at over the years.

"You're not used to big parties like this, are you?" he asked her.

"How did you know?"

"You've been on your own all evening, haven't you? Just like me. Plus, your dress."

"What about it?"

"It's not yours, is it? It's too large for you, and the way you walk and hold yourself, it's as if you feel you don't belong here. I guess you borrowed it from your friend, the one you came with…" Gavin stopped, feeling that he was talking too much. "I'm sorry, I didn't mean anything by that."

"No, it's really not important. But yes, you're right. My family's not rich and I got in through my dad's connections. But at least you're used to all this," she said, indicating the bright lights of the house behind them.

"No," Gavin admitted, surprised at how honest he was. "I've just been good at pretending all evening."

"It looks like we have something in common then."

They talked all night, until some of the partygoers began to leave.

"I need to find my friend again," Danielle said, turning toward a gazebo on the opposite side of the swimming pool. "She's supposed to give me a lift back to my house."

"I can give you one," Gavin offered.

She laughed. "I've only just met you! Thanks, but maybe another time. It was really nice to meet you here tonight."

"It was nice to meet you too."

"Do you want to exchange numbers or something?"

He saved her number. Gavin waved goodbye and turned to walk back toward his car. Azhari had retreated after falling into his own pool and was somewhere inside the house, dancing and drinking, but Gavin wasn't thinking about him as he got into his car, turned the engine back to life and drove toward the city.

><──────────<

Classes had ended. Gavin left the lecture theater and checked his phone. There was a message from Foo. Ever since the incident with Maut, Foo insisted on texting Gavin daily.

```
I give you lif go Laksamana today. After your 2 o
cork class.
```

Gavin thought he would be tormented by guilt, or at least feel a twinge of horror, as he had killed a man just a few days ago. But it didn't happen. It was as if someone else had pulled the trigger. What did Foo want now? No doubt it had something to do with the prisoner. Gavin frowned as he recalled the other texts Foo had sent:

```
Faster wash your hand, if not maybe polis can
trace your fingerprint.
```

```
Don't tell your father abut Maut.
```

```
If anyone got ask you tell them that night we
want clubbing at nouveau. And also you delete
your text when read finish ok?
```

Gavin reached the stairs leading down to the college compound. He brushed past some people on the way, when an old man came through the doors, forcing him to stop on the steps.

"Good afternoon," he said pleasantly. "You are Gavin Wong, aren't you?"

"Yes," Gavin said cautiously, trying to take in the man. He'd never seen him before. He was easily over fifty, perhaps the same age as his father, Indian, with thinning but neatly cut hair. Gavin could decipher nothing from his calm expression.

"My name is Ramalingam," the man said, reaching out with a calloused hand. "I hope I didn't startle you."

Gavin returned the handshake tentatively. "I'm sorry, but you are—?"

"Just an old friend of your father's," Ramalingam said. "I would like to talk to you."

Something seemed amiss. Gavin had only been part of Foo's plans for less than a week and already strangers were asking to see him. He wished he had a knife or even Foo's gun. But the old man standing in front of him looked harmless.

"What would you like to talk about?"

Ramalingam stepped aside as a gaggle of students hurried past. "I've been reading the newspapers recently," he murmured.

"There's a lot of crime these days. Assassinations too. Regrettable, isn't it?"

"I guess so."

"There was a nasty accident in Puchong. Looked like a fire burned down two houses before the firemen showed up. A few people got killed there."

Gavin flinched, and the man named Ramalingam's smile widened. "Of course, the police know that it wasn't an accident."

"You're a policeman," Gavin said.

"Yes, I am. We don't have hard evidence, but we have learned to connect the dots over the years. We can tell, for instance, that your father was linked to the Bangsawan Heights incident about twenty years ago, even if nobody talked and forensics didn't turn anything up. There are patterns that even hardcore criminals fall into which we can trace very easily. It's just a matter of time before we have enough proof to send your father to prison."

"My father is an honest businessman. A good man. He has nothing to do with crime."

Ramalingam kept smiling. "Or that's what he likes to pretend. But we both know better, don't we, Gavin? Please pass him a word of advice because we don't meet each other very often. All his crimes, his murders, they can't continue for much longer."

"Are you threatening him?" Gavin was more astounded than angry at Ramalingam's audacity.

"I am, I'm afraid," Ramalingam said. "Have a good day. I must be off."

With that, the old policeman limped away, down the steps and on to the sweltering streets, mirages shimmering in the background. It took Gavin a moment to compose himself before he shouldered his backpack again and hurried down the steps. Ramalingam was nowhere to be seen, but Foo's car was. He crossed the compound, past the jaga and under the boom gates. He opened the door and Foo grinned at him.

"You want me to go to the Laksamana?" Gavin asked.

"Ya, ya. That guy Maut, the last time you saw him he was un-con-scious. Now he wants to talk to you, direct. Don't let the old man find out. It's a secret for now. Remember, he don't want you to disturb his business."

And the car was racing off again. They passed mosques brimming with people performing Friday prayers. Gavin wondered what it was like to step inside one of the prayer halls, surrounded by people seeking blessings and salvation—wondering if any of them, like him, had ever killed a man.

6
MAUT

Laksamana Hotel was a hive of activity. Small-time drug peddlers and businessmen with their escorts paid to stay in its rooms, giving them a dubious full occupancy rate. Even Gunner, the freelance hitman who sometimes worked with the Penang and Ipoh gangs, stayed the night in the hotel's creaking rooms when he was in KL, as did Crazy Foo when he was too drunk to drive back to Kajang.

Gavin felt uncomfortable in the office. The only times he'd been there was when his father was around. But Old Wong was still in the Cheras mansion, refusing to show up. Crazy Foo had already taken a seat next to the executive chair where Gavin's father usually sat, which made Gavin more comfortable—until Foo insisted that Gavin sit in his father's place: "Boss's son, sit in boss's chair lah."

So he sat down in the chair, taking in the sparseness of the room and the notebooks by his side, written in an old-fashioned, barely legible Chinese script. He had no idea where his father had learned to write. As far as he knew, his father had barely attended school when he was young, turning to the streets early in his life.

"Why do you need me?" he had asked Foo as they cut corners and ran red lights on their way to the hotel.

"Boss is still not supposed to know," Foo warned him. "The old man, he very soft already. Doesn't even want revenge anymore. Last week, I got tell him that it's very important we attack Chang.

Next month he got hold his birthday party. That is the best time to kill him, because we have guys who can dress up as caterers or something. But no! Your father just drinks only. Doesn't want to fight at all."

"So how can this Maut help?" Gavin asked. "I mean, if my father doesn't even want to fight, what is the point of hiring Maut?"

"Cis! Shut your mouth first. I am doing the old man a favor. He is old already, he don't know what he wants. He will appreciate this. Don't forget, Chang killed your mother," Foo said.

"Here he is," said Ah Leong as he entered the suite, followed by Maut.

Gavin was disappointed. Maut looked as uncommunicative as the night they had rescued him from the Puchong safe house. His hair was lank, and his skin, tanned by years under the sun, looked like old leather. His body didn't bulge with muscles, unlike Gunner or the notorious Ah Fung II. Maut's frame was slim, a man who was good at disappearing into the shadows. He looked like the farm laborers that Gavin had seen in Perak and Pahang, or the construction workers who picked up bricks and poured concrete into the foundations of upcoming skyscrapers. Only one thing set him apart from them: his eyes. They burned with silent determination.

Maut sat opposite Gavin as Ah Leong brandished a pistol.

"So, Maut, where are you from ah? That night, didn't get to talk to you, you were unconscious," Foo drawled in bad Malay.

Maut said nothing, staring back at Foo. Foo repeated his question in English, wondering if Maut was Filipino or Thai instead. Still, he received no response.

"He's a quiet man," Foo said to Gavin. "Go on, make him talk."

"We heard about your work, Maut," Gavin said. His Malay had worsened after his years in private school. All he could do was ask for directions, order food, and make small talk. It sounded strange to give praise in a language he wasn't comfortable with. "You try to kill Chang. Hard to approach him. Even harder to kill him. Congratulations."

Maut opened his mouth to speak. "Thank you."

Gavin frowned at his accent. He couldn't place it. Maut spoke just like his teachers had, slow and deliberate, but his voice sounded raspy, as if he wasn't used to speaking at all.

"The bastard never even opened his mouth when we talked to him," Foo whispered in astonished Mandarin.

"Why did you do it?" Gavin asked.

"I wasn't happy working for him," Maut continued. "A bad boss."

There was a long silence, during which Maut gazed blankly at him. Gavin began to feel there had been a mistake, that they must have captured the wrong man. Even Ah Leong was starting to look furious. But he was no match for Foo, who got up while holding up his gun.

"We are the syndicate. Impossible you don't know who we are. Chang sure have mentioned us before. We are assassins. I don't care who the hell you are, and if you don't want to talk I shoot you here. We can cripple you and then shoot you in the head. This is a big hotel. Lots of places for body. We can lock you in a fridge; the only way someone find you is if the electric cut off. But if you do not… co-ope-rate with us, you will die for sure. So what you want? People normally don't get to choose their own death."

Maut said nothing, his face still expressionless.

"This is boss's son." Foo gestured at Gavin, still waving his revolver. "Show respect, fuck you!"

"Enough!" Gavin said, staring at the gun.

"What do you want me for?" Maut asked.

"What you mean?" Foo demanded.

"I am an assassin. I kill people. You rescued me from the house and you will not kill me now. What do you want me to do?"

Gavin and Foo exchanged looks but Gavin couldn't think straight. He was now facing a man who had killed people without any remorse, and he was discussing the details of his father's business in the same chair that his father normally sat in.

"How did you do it?" Gavin asked, more out of curiosity than anything else.

"A bomb," Maut said. "I stole one from Chang's office. He has a car. You know, a Ferrari. I was asked to accompany him and some of his men to a nightclub near UTAR, where he extorts money from the owner. They left me to take care of his car. I unlocked the boot and left the bomb inside. Timed it for twenty minutes. Chang would spend about ten minutes inside the club, then he would come out. I would be gone by then. After that he would go back to his house in Tropika after sending people to look for me. Then on his way back the car would explode and he would die."

"So why didn't that work ?" Gavin asked.

"The car bomb exploded but I timed it wrongly. Chang spent too long inside the nightclub. The Ferrari was destroyed but he was safe. After that, Chang's men caught me at the LRT. They tortured me."

Even Foo was struck by the audacity of Maut's plan. "You try to kill him with a bomb?"

"Yes."

Foo turned to Gavin. "This fella is either a genius or completely siau. A bomb! We only use handguns."

"Tell me," Gavin said, ignoring Foo. "What do you know about Wong Kah Lok? I am sure Chang has mentioned him before."

"That he is their enemy. I don't know anything else, except that Chang wants Wong to die."

"My father will not be at peace until Chang is dead," Gavin said. He and Maut looked at each other for a long time before Maut spoke again.

"You are his son. Gavin Wong?"

Gavin nodded. "I have an idea right now. You are clever, Maut, I can see that. My father is old. I look at him and he is tired of assassinations and the syndicate. If Chang dies, he will be at peace."

"What are you doing?" Foo asked Gavin, alarmed. Gavin ignored him.

"You want me to kill him?" Maut asked.

"Can you do that?" Gavin felt a growing excitement in his voice, a wild, burning sensation.

"Yes."

7

RAMALINGAM

5pm. Anwar had just arrived, putting on his spectacles.

"So what now, Inspector?" he asked. "You've told me everything already. There's nothing left to talk about."

"I haven't told you about the Bangsawan Heights murders," Ramalingam muttered.

"You have," sighed Anwar. "You have forgotten. Please, try to think. Is there anything at all you haven't talked about?"

The blue-and-white police station at Ampang Jaya was quiet that afternoon. Inspector Ramalingam had just returned from Yohan Eng College, driving his old Vauxhall Viva, which he'd lovingly maintained since buying it from the late Supt. Kassim Muhammad. He was sweating. The sun was too hot in the cloudless sky. He dabbed at his forehead with a handkerchief as he hobbled into the station, past the police cars parked in formation like battle tanks. He needed his walking stick. It had been a mistake to forget to bring it. He climbed the stairs into the reception, where errant motorists fanned themselves with their tickets, cursing the slow speed of the electric fan, the slow receptionists on lunch breaks, the police, and the government under their breaths. Nobody paid him any attention, an old Indian man in a tattered shirt and used trousers, and nobody noticed the shiny police boots that he wore. He passed them and went back upstairs.

The policemen and office staff nodded at him when he walked past. He had been at the Ampang Jaya branch for so long that everyone could recognize him the moment he entered the station, whether in or out of uniform. Even policemen who were stationed back at Ampang Jaya after postings in Johor Bahru and Butterworth were amazed that he still looked the same even as the years passed.

"Tuan, Samad hasn't reported back yet. We might need to make a report soon," his secretary said as he approached the office.

"Thank you for telling me. We'll wait and see if he shows up. Damn the man, he's never on time." The trembling in his knees was worsening. Fuck it. He needed to go to the doctor. He would have to write that down.

"And the IGP sends his regards. There is a birthday card for you; I placed it in your office."

Ramalingam felt a fleeting confusion that he managed to mask with a weak smile. "I will look at it. Thanks again."

The secretary took his seat again and Ramalingam entered the office. *Amini, that was the secretary's name, wasn't it? No that was the name of the previous secretary, from ten or twenty years ago. Was it Saiful? No, that was the clerk from downstairs. Was it Abbas? It was probably Abbas.* He would have to remind the man to wear his nametag.

His uniform hung from a clothes hanger on the wall. Ramalingam felt it absent-mindedly. For several years he had kept the uniform, along with all his old ones in his house. Even when it started tearing at the seams he got it tailored. He thought of the last time they had a full inspection, the last time he went out in public in full uniform.

>————<

Independence Day. He had been down at the Dataran with the other inspectors with their shiny medals, and he adjusted his beret as his own team came down the road, marching in time to the music. They were flanked by the army and their battle tanks in camouflage paint, and after they went past he retired to the seats that had been set up for VIPs and other guests, who watched in boredom as a military band played. Across the street were cameramen and news reporters.

In the midst of the forced festivities the inspector general arrived, smiling with porcelain-white teeth and shaking hands with his subordinates. Eventually he approached Ramalingam.

"Why, Inspector Ramalingam! You're still looking as healthy as ever!"

Ramalingam smiled uncomfortably. "Well, I try to be, sir. Age is catching up with us."

He resented the fact that the IGP was five years younger than he was, yet he was still only an inspector at a quiet station outside the city where there was little action. It was the perfect place for him—he wouldn't be a nuisance to the force again. They had long memories, those men in power. They didn't forget what he had done, and they were determined that he wouldn't be given the opportunity to make a mistake like that again.

"Eh, same uniform ke?" the IGP reacted. "I recognize that patch right there, on your shoulder! You were wearing this last year at the parade, weren't you?"

"I am attached to it. Good material, Tuan IGP. It has served me many long years."

"It has. But not long until retirement kan? One more year at the most, right? By the way, I want to introduce you to someone..."

Ramalingam followed the IGP to a table where diluted rose syrup was served in wine glasses. There was a man there. Ramalingam frowned. He vaguely recognized the man, but from where? *One of the government ministers? An ex-policeman?*

"This is Chancellor Zahid," the IGP said. "Of Yohan Eng College, and soon to be MP. Tan Sri Yunus Ishak's son! The chancellor was just hired by the MACC! A real big shot. One day this man may even be our PM!"

"And it's so much work! Some of the things I see, you will not believe!" Zahid sighed, turning away from the drinks. "Tuan IGP! It's good to see you again. How is Nora? And your son... Fadzil, right? I haven't seen them since last Raya."

"They are fine. Haven't had the chance to hold a feast yet. Busy year. Lots of cases, and also all these 'Democracy' protesters. Adoi! They are distracting us from the assassinations and motor hooligans and drug dealers. We will need to come up with a better way to stop them from rioting!"

Ramalingam watched as the two men laughed. The chancellor turned to face Ramalingam.

"I believe you must be Inspector Ramalingam," he said, shaking his hand. "The IGP has said a lot about you. A true hero. You were there at the Bangsawan Heights murders, weren't you?"

The old inspector tried to hide his wincing. "Yes, that was me." He wasn't sure if Zahid noticed. Ramalingam would not forget Bangsawan Heights. Each night it returned and preyed on his dreams.

Zahid kept smiling. "You're a good man," he said, as a squadron of MiGs deployed colored smoke above them in red, blue, yellow and white, a Jalur Gemilang in the sky. "And I would like to learn more about you. Why, for your efforts you should be promoted!

Being an inspector is an insult to a man like you. Ya Allah! Why are you still in Ampang Jaya? Nothing happens there. Tough man like you should be stationed at Bukit Aman or something!"

"There's a long story behind that, and, frankly, the details would bore you." Ramalingam made up an excuse on the spot, but Zahid seemed to see right through it.

"Tell you what, Inspector. Tonight, I am meeting with a few of my colleagues at the Mandarin Oriental for our private Merdeka celebration. Why don't you join us? No need to attend the open house at the PWTC. Trust me, the PM's aide himself told me the food is quite frankly disgusting this year. My treat, Inspector."

Ramalingam looked back to see the other inspectors, all of them looking bored to death by the spectacle despite their respectful gazes, and found himself saying yes to Zahid's invitation.

>————————<

He buttoned up the uniform. He was resplendent in blue again, the epaulets gleaming under the sunlight that came through the slits in the plastic blinds. But whenever he caught sight of himself in a mirror, he felt like an old man in fancy dress. He shuddered whenever that thought came into his mind, like a warning. *Time to leave soon, Ramalingam. Time to retire and collect your pension and live quietly.*

He'd been reading reports all afternoon, and now he had to write his own. His hand paused several times as he sought the right words. He translated them from English to Malay. It was getting more and more difficult for him these days.

"Sir," the secretary said, opening the door. "Doctor Anwar is here to see you."

They chatted for a while. He was like the other psychiatrists who came and went, called to the office through favors. *Oh, there's this Dr. Ng who graduated from Australia, who treated someone with PTSD after he came back from Bosnia... How about Dr. Arumugam? He's a new one. He was treating bomb victims in Bali before this...* But all the would-be miracle workers couldn't produce results, leaving Ramalingam to continue suffering, burying his misery in his pillows each night. Anwar was just like the rest of them.

"Please, try to think. Is there anything at all you haven't talked about?"

There were so many things, Ramalingam thought desperately. Things that Anwar, with all his certificates and qualifications, couldn't even begin to imagine. He was tormented by all that he knew, so tempted to let everything out in a cathartic outpouring, but he couldn't. He willed himself to forget. Forgetting was easy, erasing from his mind people and places that he never wanted to see again.

"I don't remember," he insisted.

Anwar sighed and Ramalingam escorted him to the door.

"Please find someone to talk to," the psychiatrist said, as he buttoned up his blazer despite the heat outside. "It's worse if you keep quiet."

Ramalingam thought of the time he went to Bangsawan Heights, when he saw the bullet holes in the stairwell, blood flowing down the stairs, but they were more real to him than Anwar, to whom he bid goodbye through a haze of cigarette smoke.

He returned to his office. He was ready to resume work. The secretary greeted him with more news.

"Sir, it is Samad, the bastard finally picked up the phone. He says he can finally report to you. Yew Hua Coffeeshop, the usual time."

Ramalingam nodded, feeling ill. He closed his office door behind him and sank into his chair. He was tired, so tired, but as he looked around he could have sworn he saw a flash of blue: Old Wong's Mercedes-Benz, passing down the street. He blinked and saw nothing outside. No car or assassins, nothing. But there was something else that he had forgotten, something his secretary had mentioned…

It was the birthday card from the IGP, next to his inbox. He ignored it. He was going to forget that he was getting old. In time he would even forget who he was and what he had done, and what had been done to him.

8
NOT THAT KIND OF PERSON

Several weeks later, Gavin's pencil shaded in his answers on the exam answer sheet, trying to recall the principles governing inflation and the banking system. It had been a year since he switched from science to economics, but it had been another disaster. There he was, sitting for exams he was sure to fail, because at the back of his mind he thought of the quiet man named Maut and the house on the hillside where his father still lived in seclusion. Once in a while his father would give him a call, but they would have nothing to say to each other and each call would end after a few minutes of awkward conversation.

Halfway through the examination he stopped for a rest, his brain wrung out like the sponges the hawkers used at the coffeeshops to wash out their grease-encrusted woks. He remembered that it wasn't too long ago he had vigorously read his books, ready to take on the world, in the few short weeks after he first met Danielle.

They had met up often after the party at Azhari's house, while Azhari had quit school to become a clerk in his disappointed father's department in Putrajaya.

They went for movies at the old Indian theaters after bak kut teh in Klang, where the speakers would sometimes burn out and the film reels on the projectors snapped, where there was nobody but them and the few old Indian men who chewed nuts and asam as they watched celluloid dreams from Hollywood. They also went skating, Gavin tripping over his laces while Danielle raced ahead, sometimes laughing and teasing, other times showing him how to balance on the rapidly melting ice while other skaters zoomed past like multicolored fish. They went for drives in the countryside, the headlights of Gavin's car bobbing in the darkness, sometimes drawing to a halt as monitor lizards dragged themselves across the roads like confused snakes.

Gavin remembered a short surge of hope in his free-falling life, looking forward to something other than a dead-end job after he (someday) graduated. He thought about Danielle, studying hard as she aimed for the elusive scholarships that Zahid had introduced, passionately telling him about the day she would be able to afford to continue her studies abroad. Both of them studied at the library late into the night, and for the first time Gavin felt like everyone else.

But that feeling of hope was gone when Gavin was in the exam hall, scrawling out half-baked answers, wishing the end would come soon.

"So how was the exam?" Robert asked, turning around in his seat once the exam scripts were collected. Gavin shrugged. Robert had been doing well in his studies, and he would probably graduate early. Gavin knew he wouldn't see Robert again after that day.

They were walking out of the examination hall when one of the lecturers, who had been observing the students, called out to Gavin.

"Gavin Wong." Mr. Lim looked up from the exam scripts he had been collecting. "Chancellor Zahid wants to see you."

"What for?" Gavin asked, but Mr. Lim had no reply for him; instead, he began stacking the papers in front of him. Gavin waved goodbye to Robert and went to Zahid's office.

>———————<

As they saw each other more often, Gavin sensed that Danielle knew exactly who he was. He had laughed about his father, telling her about the old man's idiosyncrasies: his days spent refusing to leave his mansion and their awkward reunions whenever Gavin felt the urge to leave the chaos of the streets, where people swirled like ants and cars clogged the streets like plaque in arteries. But he never mentioned what his father did for a living.

"A businessman," he told her once. "He owns a hotel and restaurant. Nothing fancy."

But in college, it was common knowledge that Gavin was the son of Wong Kah Lok, the feared King of Petaling Street. Nobody ever mentioned it, not even the perpetually drunk Chee Fong, but Gavin could sense their reluctance to talk to him about the subject. Even the lecturers treated him with unease, as if he was a museum specimen or an escaped wild animal.

One night they went dancing at a nightclub. It was supposed to be a night to relax after a hard week of cramming for their assignments. A boy in a singlet, with rippling biceps and a Mohawk, came up to Gavin on the dance floor as the strobe lights flashed and the cigarette smoke hung around them despite the "No Smoking" signs.

"You… Gavin Wong," sneered the boy. Gavin recalled seeing him somewhere in college, but the name escaped him.

"Yeah," he replied, struggling to be heard above the thumping bass. "What do you want?"

The boy gave him the middle finger. "Get lost from this place. It's not for scum like you and your shit father," he said above the screeching songs from the speakers.

Gavin struggled not to lose control, but it was already too late; he had a few drinks in him and he swung at once, clobbering the boy in the face. He stumbled backward with blood spurting from his nose, before crashing into the cocktail waitress. There was a brilliant flash of light; for a second Gavin could see glasses and empty Heineken bottles in mid-flight. Then there was scuffling and yelling and screaming.

A bouncer at least twice Gavin's size emerged. "Out!" he shouted, raising a huge fist. "Or I call the police."

Gavin ran out, his shirt stained with someone else's drink. He left so quickly that he was surprised to see Danielle hurrying after him. The music immediately died down once the doors closed, and they were back outside the shopping mall. Friday night. All the students from the colleges had converged in the clubs under the massive concrete lion's head at the Pyramid. But now Gavin didn't see any of them, they were all indoors. Nearby, there was Arabic music and the sweetened whiff of shisha, and an Arab family that seemed oblivious to the chaos inside the clubs, eating couscous and kabsa.

Gavin and Danielle sat next to each other for some time, not saying anything. There was a slow breeze wafting against their faces. Eventually the Arabs left and the restaurant closed. Behind them, past the palms and the faux-Egyptian obelisks, cars filled the highway as the late-night revelers attempted to get home.

"So it is true ?" Danielle asked. "You're Wong Kah Lok's son?"

"He is my father, yes."

"I was wondering about that for a while. Not just from… you know, what happened inside."

"Then you should know that I'm a dangerous person to be with," Gavin said with the ghost of a smile. "You should go hang out with Chee Fong instead. He may be a drunk but his parents are decent enough."

She touched him on the arm, her fingertips cold in the balmy air. "You're not that kind of person. I can tell."

Gavin thought of the times with Crazy Foo, where Foo would talk long into the night about shooting and violence and mayhem. "Perhaps not yet."

"You don't have to do what your father has done."

"I'm doing what he wants me to do," Gavin admitted. "He wants me to stay out of his work."

Danielle looked at him. "Then you should."

He took her hand, his mind burning with renewed clarity of purpose. They stayed under the streetlights for a long time, neither one ready to let go.

>———————<

The lights in Chancellor Zahid's office glared down on Gavin. The colors were too bright, almost garish, as Chancellor Zahid poured two glasses of water for the both of them. Those sharp little teeth smiled back.

"You don't look very well, Gavin. Pockmarks, some pimples, your face is pale, like you never see the sun even though we live in a tropical country. Exam stress?"

Gavin felt uneasy, as if Zahid knew exactly what he'd been doing in the time he was meant to be studying: spending late nights at Laksamana Hotel with Crazy Foo as they looked through papers, while Maut, like a shadow, stood behind them, listening as they went over the logistics. Gavin didn't know what was happening, but Foo explained the details so well it was as if Gavin was the one who'd planned it all.

"Do you have any more exams?" the chancellor asked, as he set the glasses down in front of Gavin with loud clinks. Gavin shook his head, but he was still thinking of the night when they would put the whole plan into action, where everything they had hidden from his father over the last few weeks would finally come together. That night, Maut—after spending most of his days holed up in Laksamana Hotel for his own safety—would return to the house in Tropika where Chang lived.

The chancellor sighed. "You've been here for three years already, and you show no sign of improvement. Your father has helped me tremendously over the years, but I'm afraid I cannot help him any longer, especially when I look at your grades. The lecturers have been complaining to me. They say that you're a delinquent and you are not proving yourself. I have to warn you that if things do not change, I will have no choice but to expel you."

Gavin couldn't think straight, as if he had been punched in the gut.

"It depends on your final results, of course," Zahid continued, his brows seemingly knitted together. Behind him, Gavin saw the photos of Zahid and the Prime Minister, and Zahid meeting the Tourism Minister in a far-off Western country. His father had told Gavin that Zahid wasn't content with being a chancellor. His real aspirations were higher.

"The results should be out already," Gavin said. "I had my first paper three weeks ago. You must know."

Zahid's smile didn't falter. "Yes. And you have not made the grade. I can offer you the chance to retake some of them. After all, your father and I go way back."

Gavin stared at the photos of Zahid, wondering how his father and the would-be minister were connected. It was one of those strange links between the men who lived in the city, where everyone was a friend or an enemy or somewhere in-between.

"In that case," Gavin found himself saying, "I withdraw."

"You are leaving the college?" There was no alarm in the chancellor's voice, just suppressed triumph.

"I'm afraid so," Gavin said, the day's events spinning out of control faster than he could have imagined. "It was a pleasure, Chancellor. But I am afraid I have to leave."

"You are following in your father's footsteps, aren't you?" Zahid didn't make the effort to be polite. His eyes narrowed, unblinking like a snake's.

"Perhaps," Gavin said. He got up and left as quickly as he had come in.

In his pocket was his phone, brimming with messages, including the latest one from Foo:

```
Tonight confirmed. Maut kill Chang later.
```

9
TROPIKA NIGHT

Tropika was just out of KL, somewhere in that indeterminate area between the kampungs and planned townships. Boon sat behind the wheel wearing a red shirt, the type he only donned for New Year celebrations. Ah Leong accompanied him, wearing a shirt under a dinner jacket that he was constantly pulling at. In the back sat Maut. He was dressed entirely in black, down to his vest. His hair had been trimmed and all trace of his mustache was gone, and there was a pistol in a holster under his vest.

Boon drove through the pothole-ridden holes of a squatter village, where the houses blazed with light from their flat-screen TVs. Eventually the squatter houses thinned out and they were driving past plant nurseries and makeshift farms, where placid brown cows slept among overgrown long grass. The roads were quieter and there were fewer streetlights. For a moment it seemed like they were driving through the countryside.

Out of nowhere, white cement walls rose over the parched grass, while tall palm trees and cempakas grew behind them, lit up by the European-style lamps that topped the fences. Tropika, the rich people's township. Ah Leong prepared the notes as the Mercedes-Benz pulled up closer to the arches and guardhouses nestled there, boom gates preventing their entry. The car slowed to a stop and Ah Leong inspected his unnaturally combed hair.

They drew up to security, and Ah Leong rolled down the window. The captain of the guard, the least skinny of the three

Indian men who manned the security checkpoint, adjusted his cap and peered at them.

"Where are you going to, sir?"

"Ah, hello," Ah Leong said. "There's my cousin, his son has a Full Moon celebration tonight. His first full moon, you see."

"OK," said the guard. "Address?"

This was one of the security measures. Fortunately, one of Crazy Foo's regular drinking partners was one of the cleaning staff at the Tropika Clubhouse, and he always complained over cheap toddy about the rich men, women, and children as they dined in their overpriced restaurant, bowled in their private bowling alley, and splashed for hours on end in their swimming pool while he mopped up their spilt drinks and vacuumed expensive European carpets. Foo paid for his drinks while the man let slip trivial but important details about Tropika.

"It's number nine, Jalan Effingham, Tropika," Ah Leong said. "You want his name also? Jackson Yip, and his wife Amelia Pang."

The guard nodded. "Identification Card or license?"

Ah Leong grumbled in Hokkien to Boon, who said nothing. He produced an IC bearing the name of Hector Soong, of Taman Maluri. It was one of Old Wong's tricks.

The guard took the IC into the hut and jotted down the number. Then he returned it to Ah Leong. "You know how to go?"

Ah Leong nodded. "Yeah. Down there, right? After the clubhouse?"

"Yea, boss." The boom gates lifted and they were driving through.

The arch and the hut disappeared into the darkness. They drove past the sweeping golf courses while Maut watched. Even the grass was different: it was foreign grass, not the scrubby patches of weeds that scrabbled to survive by the roadsides.

They skipped the turning to Yip's house. They were racing further up the road, where the houses were bigger and situated further apart, bearing glamorous names like The Gardens, The Conservatory, The Palace...

They arrived at The Decadent. The house was vast and sprawling, the fences painted black and topped with yellow spikes, and the car drove around its perimeter and through the open gates. Cars were lining the sides of the road, Ferraris bumper to bumper with gleaming Maseratis. The Mercedes seemed modest in comparison as they motored up the driveway to the mini roundabout by the front doors of the elegant building.

The guests walking along the driveway laughed and gossiped so loudly that Ah Leong could hear them through the windows:

"You got see the old man?"

"Damn ham sap, right?"

"I know it's his birthday but he is surrounded by all those women..."

"You remember the plan, Maut?" Ah Leong said. He saw Maut nodding in the rear-view mirror. "You remember how to get around?"

Maut looked different from the time they had first found him. His hair, now short, had given him the look of a normal man, not one rescued from the streets.

Music blasted from the open doors, which were constantly blocked as people bustled in and out; some of them headed out to explore the grounds while others hurried in with empty glasses, hoping for a refill. Boon brought the car to a halt and Ah Leong and Maut exited. Ah Leong felt out of place there, and his eyes started to dart around the place. Chow Kit and Petaling Street he could handle, but parties were a whole different matter.

Maut followed as he entered the house. There was an invitation that Foo had somehow obtained and passed on to him, but there was nobody around to check and he mingled with the guests, becoming part of the crowd. Maut had already disappeared, looking for Chang, as Ah Leong somehow found his way to the atrium, where a small fountain gurgled, and the men around him were laughing about politics and economics and the price of goods in the Malaysia stores. He hoped that Maut would find Chang quickly so that he could call Boon and get out before security was alerted.

Maut pushed his way through a side door and went up a flight of stairs to the second floor, where Chang lived. Maut had only been there once, due to Chang never trusting him enough, but he hadn't forgotten the layout. That was long before he tried to kill Chang.

Not much had changed. No extra security guards or anything. For all Chang knew, Maut had probably got killed in the burning house. There were usually guards patrolling the grounds and guard dogs leashed to their handlers, prepared to tear intruders limb from limb. But they were swamped by the well-wishers, associates, and other guests that Chang had invited for the birthday celebration.

The corridors were empty. They were usually one or two guards wandering about, but security seemed to have become inebriated by the free flow of alcohol and not even a single guard appeared. The waiters downstairs had tried serving Maut wine, as if he was a VIP, but he'd refused as he threaded his way toward the bedroom. He had seen no sign of Chang anywhere else, and with Chang's reputation, that was the only place he would be.

Portraits lined the wall. They traced the life of a man from infant to kingpin. A baby boy in a studio photograph, his family so poor that they had jewelry painted in. And then the photos jumped forward a couple of decades, and there was a plump young man in a shirt, scowling as he tried to force a smile, outside the Yup Hong Mill in Negeri Sembilan, the Chang gang's original base of operations before encroaching into Kuala Lumpur. In another photo, an older Chang posed with a wife and sons. The wife had divorced him and gone off to marry a mat salleh, while the sons were now embroiled in a bitter struggle to force their father to update his will.

In the past year, two lieutenants had plotted to wrest control from him. Maut had been tasked to kill both of them. He killed one in a nightclub, spiking his drink with rat poison. The other died after his motorcycle was sabotaged, sending him crashing into an oncoming car. Chang's position was secure, or so he thought. If Chang died the gang would fall to pieces, with its Ipoh, KL and Negeri Sembilan factions fighting each other for control.

Maut paused, withdrawing into the shadows. Somebody was coming. Maut crouched in the darkness as the assassin Ah Fung II marched past in an embroidered jacket. He waited as Ah Fung II paused by one of the banisters. Ah Fung II was now a bad shot due to his damaged eyes, but he was a terrifying man who displayed no fear.

Ah Fung II had been Maut's rival when he was still in Chang's gang. And it had been Ah Fung II who managed to hold him face down in an alleyway as he tried to escape after the bombing attempt, breathing down his neck with a desire to kill.

Maut waited. He didn't have much time. He'd managed to get so far, after he had taken care of the CCTVs tucked away in every corner. He had found his way into the security room, unlocked as usual, where a bespectacled man was playing DotA on his gaming laptop instead of watching the monitors. Maut strangled him before he could tear his eyes away from the shifting graphics. When it was all done, Maut found his set of keys and locked the door before leaving to rejoin the party. With all the loud music, the drinking, and with nobody to raise the alarm, he would be safe for the time being.

Maut waited, and eventually Ah Fung II grunted and trooped back down the stairs, presumably to get more drinks. When he heard the faint click of the door, Maut continued approaching the bedroom where he would find Chang.

>———————<

Downstairs, Ah Leong was sweating in his jacket.

"Are you all right, sir?" one of the servants asked him as he passed with a tray of éclairs.

"Ya," Ah Leong mumbled. "I drank too much already."

He checked his watch. Maut had been gone for twenty minutes. Dammit! He needed a cigarette but lighting up in the middle of the crowd was out of the question. Any second now, someone was bound to notice him loitering at the back of the dance hall, where men, abandoning their wives and girlfriends, were dancing with the girls that Chang had hired for the night. The deejay looked like some runaway American college boy, and he was blasting music over shouts of "Happy birthday, Mr. Chang!"

He had dealt with killings for the last ten years, during which he had progressed from being a Malaccan Catholic school dropout to a VCD seller, before finding his way into the syndicate. Initially he had started out at Restoran Klasik, serving drinks and moonlighting as a bouncer, until he confronted a parang-wielding robber who broke in late one night, after he'd slashed one of the security guards like a hock of meat. Ah Leong hid behind the bar counter as the parang man tried to break open the safe. He broke cover and grabbed a bloodied Mauser from the dead guard's hands. He shot the parang man in the head. Wong noticed his usefulness and Ah Leong was promoted to gun-running. Ah Leong became a master at befriending customs officers and policemen, eventually becoming third-in-command, below Crazy Foo.

But now he was scared stiff. He was alone in a house crawling with Chang's men. He had heard enough of their reputation to know that any moment could be his last. The boss's son (prompted by Crazy Foo) had promised him a handsome reward if Chang died, a bonus that would keep him in his rented room above the karaoke joint for another year at least.

He headed to the drinks table and downed a Carlsberg in a few gulps. Maybe the beer would calm him down. But he dropped the bottle and it shattered. People nearest to him turned to look. "Sorry, tipsy," he said, hurrying away. He turned back again. It was Ah Fung II.

The assassin looked ridiculous in his mandarin collar, especially on a dance floor where people partied to pop music, but Ah Leong knew that he would be armed. He hadn't bargained on Ah Fung II entering the room. They had never met, but an assassin could always recognize another assassin. There were obvious signs, and Ah Leong knew that Ah Fung II would come for him if they even made eye contact. Ah Leong grew more uncomfortable. Fuck the last few drinks! They would give him away.

Ah Fung II moved deeper into the crowd, giving Ah Leong a chance to escape. He made his way to the front of the hall and turned back again. Ah Fung II had seen him after all! The assassin was pushing past people as he strode toward Ah Leong. As calmly as he could, Ah Leong hurried past the drunken crowd and the front doors, to where Boon sat in the Mercedes with the engine idling, reading a car magazine.

"Where's Maut?" Boon asked as Ah Leong entered the car, sweating.

"Just drive!" Ah Leong spat, and Boon kicked the engine into gear, and they sped down the driveway, away from The Decadent.

Ah Leong flipped open his phone, typing out a message to Maut.

```
They've seen me. We are leaving now. He will come
for you.
```

>———————<

Maut read the message but it hardly mattered. He was there already. The doors were locked but he had the keys from the dead security man. There was the master key, nestled in his hand. He inserted it into the lock and turned. The door opened without a sound.

He heard Chang's laugh, accompanied by that of a woman, softer than his and sounding nervous. Maut closed the door behind him. From the outside, nobody would hear anything. The room was soundproofed. He was behind a Japanese paper wall that separated the room from the door, allowing Chang another layer of privacy. Maut removed the pistol from his pocket, double-checking the silencer. Then he pushed open the sliding doors.

Chang and his escort stared up in shock for a split second. Chang, his gray hair recently dyed, was in the process of unbuttoning his dinner jacket, and the woman in the tight black dress had already slipped off her stilettos. Chang swore and leaped off the four-poster, sending a champagne bottle smashing to the floor as he tried to reach the panic button. But Maut had already taken aim and fired. The bullet grazed Chang's skull and he screamed, crumpling to the carpet, writhing. The woman was paralyzed with shock. Her eyes followed Maut as he strode toward Chang, who held a feeble hand to his bleeding scalp, his eyes wide with fear.

"You were supposed to be dead... the fire..." he gasped, choking out blood onto his carpet.

There was no need for words. Maut lowered the pistol, and, like a machine, fired once more. Chang rolled flat on his back and didn't move again.

The woman watched fearfully as Maut approached her next, still clutching his gun.

"Please, don't kill me," she whispered. What was she? Thai? Burmese? It didn't matter.

"You will not talk about this," Maut said softly.

"I won't... I hardly know him..."

Maut pistol-whipped her. She fell unconscious onto the duvet. She wouldn't wake for an hour at least.

There was a commotion from outside, a man banging on the door. Maut stood up quickly. Only one man would dare to disturb Chang.

Maut acted, before Ah Fung II could alert the entire house.

He hurried to the door and unlocked it, and the assassin swung it open. Ah Fung II stumbled in and Maut fired, the man collapsing before him. He ignored the man's shallow gasps as he nudged him behind the door, locking it shut. The sounds of the party still reverberated through the building. Ah Fung II had been quiet, trying not to alarm the guests. But Maut couldn't be sure who else he had told. He needed to leave, quickly.

He hurried to a window and pushed it open. There was a tree just outside, its sturdy branches strong enough to take his weight. He climbed out of the window and swung forward, gasping as he managed to get a grip on the branches, and in a moment he was down on the ground. He brushed slivers of bark from his bleeding hands and ran through the grounds, past the waiters and merry guests.

He reached the driveway, to where the cars waited. He didn't have much time. There was a young man just up ahead, half-drunk and trying to unlock his car door. He eventually got the Honda's doors open, and Maut held the gun to the back of his head.

"Give me the keys," he said.

The man obliged, dropping them into Maut's outstretched palm. Maut struck him, dragging his body behind the hydrangea bushes. Then he got into the car and drove away. He didn't stop until he reached the first traffic light, having gone past the guardhouse and Number 9, where a child's birth was being celebrated.

10
LAKSAMANA

It was almost morning and the city was waking up. Half the businesses were closed and the remaining workers on Saturday shifts were still in bed, even as an orange glow replaced the opaque gray clouds. There was a hint of haze in the air, its burning odor like the Hell notes burned in Chinese temples for the lost souls in the underworld, released during the Hungry Ghost month.

Gavin had been at the Laksamana all night. He slept in the executive chair, with Foo on the armchair opposite him. Ah Leong briefed them about the night's events at two in the morning. He talked about Ah Fung II and how Foo had been followed before escaping with Boon. They waited in the shadows for half an hour, waiting to see if Maut re-emerged, but there had been no sign of him. Convoys of cars had swept past their stationary Mercedes, signaling the end of the party. They had been forced to leave, surmising that Maut had been captured.

Foo handed out payments to Ah Leong and Boon. The assassination failed, so both men made do with RM150 apiece, not even enough to cover their costs for petrol and new shirts. Gavin didn't go home to his empty apartment. He preferred the office in the Laksamana instead. When he woke up in the morning, he saw the text from Ah Leong.

> I just heard from Maut that Chang is dead. Maut say he will come in the morning.

Maut made his way through the crumbling corridors, past the departing guests and their escorts who gawped at the man with a Glock still nestled in its holster as he limped to the deluxe suite. Ah Leong let him into the deluxe suite, slightly awed by Maut's reappearance. The assassin said nothing as he faced Gavin and Foo, who demanded his story.

Maut gave them an account, and it ended with: "I got rid of the Honda on the way. And I also called the newspapers. There will be a report in all the papers this morning."

"Go get copies from downstairs," Foo called out to Ah Leong, who left the room.

"So now he is dead," Gavin said. He didn't feel a sense of relief yet. Chang was his father's problem. "We will have to tell my father."

"He will be happy," said Foo, already typing out a message.

"Don't tell him I helped you," Gavin said quickly. He hadn't spoken to his father in a while, at least not since reporting his last exam results. The gulf between them had widened into a chasm. "This was all your idea after all. You take credit."

"OK," Foo said. He wasn't complaining; the rewards for him would be enormous. But he knew Old Wong had forbidden Gavin from ever becoming a part of the syndicate.

"I trust you to keep him out of it," Wong had said to Foo ten years before.

But Foo had been unable to resist and now Gavin was embroiled and there was no way he could explain things to the old man. He would just keep quiet about it. He sent the message out to Wong.

"Front page!" Ah Leong returned, clutching three newspapers. A trio of lurid headlines screamed for attention.

NOTORIOUS SEREMBAN KINGPIN MURDERED
DEATH IN TROPIKA
ASSASSINS TO BLAME FOR VIOLENT MURDER?

Gavin snatched one from Ah Leong while Maut watched, unperturbed, and Foo reached for the moneybox under the counter.

The notorious Chang Kok Chye, 53, long believed to be the head of illegal operations ranging from narcotics to murder, was found dead in his mansion in Tropika early this morning. Mr. Chang died from a gunshot to the head in the bedroom of his home at approximately midnight. According to witnesses, he was holding a birthday celebration at that time.

His chief of security was also found murdered, leading to suspicion that the assassination was an inside job. Several other people were injured, including a security guard, the son of Datuk N. Mahadeva, who was a guest at the party, and a woman who declined to be named. The assassin, after killing Chang, reportedly stole a car and fled the scene.

Chang rose to prominence in the last two decades by importing and exporting biscuits and other grain products under his family's business, Yup Hoong Products Sdn Bhd. However, he was also believed to be involved in the criminal underworld, and had ordered a string of assassinations over the past decade to secure his dominance over the Klang Valley's crime circles. He leaves behind a divorced wife and two sons. Chang's relatives are now calling for increased police involvement in protecting them, as they fear that the parties who killed Chang may target them next.

A police investigation is underway, led by Inspector K. Ramalingam. Inspector Ramalingam was unavailable for comment at press time.

Police are currently on the lookout for the murder suspect, who is believed to be between 30 and 40, dark-skinned and possibly foreign.

Gavin could hardly believe it was all for real. He looked up to see Foo handing over a stack of banknotes to Maut, who carefully put them into his pockets and his backpack. After so many years, his father's struggle was over.

Foo whipped out his phone.

"It's your father," he said, reading the message. "He wants to see Maut. And he wants to see you as well."

"Does he know about me?" Gavin asked.

"No. He just wants me to pick you up from your apartment and update you. And he wants all of us to be there as soon as we can."

11
ON CHERAS HILL

Wong Kah Lok had been awake since morning with his usual coffee, looking through the syndicate's records. The walking stick lay beside him, its curved handle nestled on the table. Letters and words ran through his head, a lifetime as an assassin now reduced to a string of figures. Through the windows, the rising sun lit the city in a soft glow, with the haze that drifted over the straits softening the sharp glass outlines of the skyscrapers.

He recalled the first time he entered the house many years earlier, right before the wedding. He hadn't needed the stick then; it was before the hospital visits became commonplace and before he became a broken old man. It hadn't been a subtle change: he morphed from assassin to pensioner in the few days after the shooting at Restoran Klasik.

>————<

"This house, I think you'll like it," the alcoholic businessman named Balasingam said as Wong walked around for the first time. "Very nice architecture," Balasingam continued, smelling of nightclubs and beer. "I think you will like this house, Mr. Wong."

Balasingam had been taken aback when Wong offered to buy his Cheras mansion, which he used as a holiday retreat, but his reservations soon dried up after a few glasses of brandy in the sitting room.

"You are getting married soon?" Balasingam asked Wong.

"Yes, I am," Wong said with a hint of pride.

"Congratulations," Balasingam hiccupped. "You sir, are human after all. You know the stories they spread about you?"

"I have heard some of them."

"Well, they seem to be painting the picture of a different man. They call you the King of Petaling Street, The Butcher of Cheras. The last I heard, they've started comparing you to Botak Chin. Did you ever know him?"

"Unfortunately no," said Wong, sipping the brandy. "We moved in different circles."

"Hmm, I see," Balasingam mumbled. He grew morose and the talk turned to business. "If I were half the man you are, I would still be in business."

"Perhaps I can help you. What's your problem?"

"I'm a developer," Balasingam said, puffing out his chest. "My family's from Singapore, my uncle was developing all those HDB flats. You know, the ones where—"

"I know what a HDB flat is, Mr. Balasingam."

"Well, I've been trying to build an apartment block near Mont Kiara. That was supposed to be a place for the rich, you see, near the golf courses and stuff. But guess what? My partners disappeared! They withdrew their funds and left me. I didn't have the capital to continue the project, and my own relatives refused to support me."

Wong looked at Balasingam. The man was filled to the brim with alcohol, and probably drugs too, but underneath the defeated façade he was offering the syndicate the space to expand its operations.

"Let me tell you something," Wong said. "I can help. I have a few friends here and there, and they might be interested in the construction business."

"But you're an assassin," Balasingam said. He was obviously drunk, bringing up topics he had been too afraid to broach before. "You don't know the construction business."

"But you do," Wong said. "We can help you, Mr. Balasingam. Trust me. We have the capital."

Balasingam hesitated, but Wong knew what sort of man he was. He was like his father: a person who had big dreams but failed. No matter. With a bit of cash, Balasingam would be able to dream again while another front opened up for money laundering. A few minutes of discussion later, it was all set. Wong left with the house, free of charge, while agreeing to fund Balasingam's project.

"What is it called?" Wong said as he bade farewell to the drunken developer, returning to the Mercedes-Benz with Boon at the wheel.

"Bangsawan Heights," Balasingam answered.

>————<

So many things had changed from the first time Wong stepped into Kuala Lumpur. He was still a teenager, fresh out of school.

Wong, when he was still Kah Lok to the neighbors, had grown up in a small town. The town was long gone—razed by developers in an attempt to build a city after it had been abandoned over the years—but back then it still had a name.

Salamat. What a strange name, as if it was a fortress or a temple where people could find salvation. But Salamat was just a small collection of huts, shophouses and a police station that often doubled as a post office, all along the same street.

His father had come from KL as a failed businessman. Kah Lok had wandered through the town in his slippers, playing football in the village fields with the other children, some of them too poor to afford new clothes. He knew nothing of the world outside of Salamat, smack in the middle of competing rubber estates. Kah Lok had watched some of the other boys his age leaving school early to help out in the estates, under the supervision of the Chinese and Indian barons who took over from fleeing Westerners as the British left Malaya.

But his father wasn't like the other men.

"You know, I came from China when I was only a few years older than you," he said to an enthralled Kah Lok in Hakka. "But I built myself up! I worked in the mines, and after that I went to Kuala Lumpur and started a sundry shop. Everything I have, I've built with my own two hands."

But at the only coffeeshop in town, Salamat Kopitiam Ltd, Kah Lok heard a different story by Old Man Gun, whom the boy helped in running the char siew stall.

"Your father ah, he is very bad businessman," Gun said. "You look at him! Cannot survive in KL, so he come here." Since Old Man Gun was rumored to be an ex-convict who broke out of Paya Besar Prison, Kah Lok never dared to talk back to him.

Kah Lok listened to stories, of course, but most of them were from his mother. She read out old legends to him each night, from a precious collection of books written in ornate script, rescued from another place. She talked about Chang'e, the Moon Goddess, banished to live on the moon for stealing the elixir of immortality.

"I was never from Salamat, originally," she said one night. "I was from Penang. I met your father there. He was an adventurer, who had come all the way from China to make a fortune. He was like all of us, but he didn't succeed. So we were forced to come to Salamat. It's nothing compared to the cities out there."

She would tell him about Ipoh, George Town, Johor Bahru, Kuala Lumpur and Singapore, cities so large that he could disappear inside them, to emerge again a different person. Cities where one could go to make a living. Kah Lok listened as he tried to imagine a world bigger than Salamat, and perhaps even Yong Peng, where his father had once taken him. Kah Lok went to the only school in Salamat, where there were only three teachers for the twenty pupils. They used secondhand schoolbooks obtained from Muar, but he was never interested in books, preferring to work for Old Man Gun or sometimes sitting with the other kids, smoking kreteks on the peripherals of the town behind the fishmonger's where they spent the afternoon in the company of feral cats that picked at tiny discarded fish-heads.

Kah Lok sometimes ventured to the building site of the proposed cinema in town.

Cinema—what a word. His father had described the theaters he frequented in Kuala Lumpur. They had huge balconies where people fought for the best seats, first and second and third class, chewing groundnuts as they watched dreams unfolding before their eyes.

"They will come," his father said, as if he was a young man again, on the tramp steamer that would take him from the Port of Hong Kong to the South Seas. "They will come from Seri Medan and Parit Sulong and Parit Yaani. This will be the first cinema in these parts!"

And Kah Lok believed him, never noticing his father's graying hair or his parents arguing late into the night. They were living out day after day among the rubber estates in the shadow of the hills and the mudflats of Johor.

On the day when everything changed, Old Man Gun accosted him while he was smoking behind the fishmonger's.

"Eh!" Old Man Gun shouted. "Kah Lok! Your parents, I think they've been beaten up by the loan sharks. I saw one of them; he was driving to your house a few minutes ago."

"What loan sharks?" Kah Lok asked. It was a hot day and there were no clouds and he had skipped school like he always did.

"The ones that your father borrowed money from to build the cinema!" Gun said. "The cinema that can never be built. Why you think he so stressed now? Because he cannot pay for it. They don't want to lend him any more money. So now they want to kill him!"

At the mention of the word "kill", Kah Lok panicked. He was running, even as Old Man Gun hollered for him to stop. Kah Lok ran up the slope to the house. There was a fancy sports car parked outside the house and he stopped, trying to catch his breath as he hid in the shrubs.

A man appeared, dressed in a sharp suit. Kah Lok noticed his hair was dyed a vivid blond. He held a gun. Kah Lok found himself breathing faster as the man entered his Lotus, the engine screaming to life as it roared down the dirt road.

"Pa! Ma!" Kah Lok called out as he raced into the house. He saw the bodies and it was too late. He backed away, stumbling down on the road, too dazed and shocked to do anything else.

Old Man Gun arrived at the house later, out of breath and still calling out to Kah Lok. He seemed to know what had happened.

"They are dead," he said. "And there is nothing you can do. They will come for you next. Now listen to me, boy. You need to get out of this town. There is nothing here for you."

"Where can I go?"

"Anywhere," Gun said, his hard face softening a little. "Just as long as you're not here. The loan sharks might find out you are the son and kill you as well, just for the hell of it."

"I have no money." Kah Lok tried not to sound weak in front of the stern old man staring down at him.

"Go into the house. Take anything of value."

Kah Lok did as he was told, trying not to look down at the floor, quickly ransacking the cabinets and the drawers, but there was nothing. The loan sharks had taken everything, even his mother's old schoolbooks. The only things he had were a few dollar notes he'd pilfered from his father's wallet that morning.

He packed his few clothes into his schoolbag and then he was outside again, where Old Man Gun was waiting. There was a trace of pity on the old man's face.

"Look, you are just a boy and this is not your world. I would like to help you but I cannot. I must take care of my family. And if I take you in, I will be in danger next. Those loan sharks are dangerous men. I have heard they were fighting in the jungles with the Commies, and they have killed many people, even children and grandparents. You must leave. I know, because I was one of them."

"Where do I go now?"

"Anywhere. Try Kuala Lumpur. You can become a new person once you get there."

Old Man Gun gave Kah Lok a lift to Yong Peng, racing out of the rubber estates to the bus station. A bus was there, bound for Kuala Lumpur.

"Get on!" Gun shouted over the chugging of the motor. As Kah Lok got out, the old man thrust a bundle into his hands.

"Take this money. So you don't think I am a cruel man. But I have no choice."

And before Kah Lok could say anything, Gun ran off, vanishing down the road. Wong Kah Lok bought a one-way bus trip to Kuala Lumpur, and fled Johor, Salamat and the loan sharks, bound for a new life.

>————————<

Wong's landline phone rang and he answered it. The Nepali guard spoke quickly: "Boss, they are all here."

Wong steadied himself as he finished his coffee. A few minutes later, Ah Leong entered, dressed more sharply than Wong remembered. Crazy Foo came in next, followed by Gavin, looking gaunt and pale.

Finally, Maut walked in. Wong took a good long look at the killer and was disconcerted. This man had nothing to show, as if he was just a shell of a human being.

"It is an honor, sir," Maut said, stepping forward.

"Thank you," Wong said, suppressing all emotion. "Thank you for what you have done."

Maut displayed no reaction.

"For the longest time, I have wanted nothing more than to see that man dead. Now it's over."

Crazy Foo was fiddling with his phone. He was angry, not just from lack of sleep but from the fact that Wong hadn't said anything to him. He was the one who'd come up with the plan, for God's sake. Now Wong was lavishing praise only on the assassin, a man with the vocabulary of a child, who had walked out of the jungle and into the city. He listened as Wong questioned Maut about what happened. Maut gave him the details. Wong listened with rapt attention, his beady eyes concentrating hard, while Foo wondered if he had the courage or the madness to remind Wong about his own contribution.

Gavin hadn't been in his father's company for a long time. They had spoken over the phone several times, mostly birthday wishes and concerns about Gavin's studies, but it was always cast in the shadow of their last meeting during which Gavin had stormed out.

>———————<

He, Foo and his father had been in a private room in a Chinese restaurant, while fish in aquariums destined for their plates stared back at them. A policeman had been gunned down at a traffic light in broad daylight, but while Crazy Foo joked about it, his father said nothing. Eventually the talk turned to Danielle.

"She'll break up with me soon." Gavin poked at the tilapia.

"It's because of what I do, isn't it?" his father had asked, the crabs and prawns momentarily forgotten.

"Yes. It's inevitable," Gavin said, as if he wasn't in control of his actions. "She knows that being with me is dangerous."

"You aren't involved," Wong said as calmly as he could. "Anyway, I don't intend to work in this business for much longer." Their conversations were always rigid and formal.

"That's not true and you know it. You've been doing this your whole life. It's all you know. You're stubborn."

"That's enough." His father's face colored. "I don't know where you're getting all these ideas from."

At the end of the dinner, Gavin left without a word. His father hadn't said anything that could calm his mind, and his thoughts churned madly.

Not long after that, he and Danielle saw each other for the last time. She had just returned from a trip to Ipoh to see her grandparents when Gavin met her on the railway platform with a bouquet he had picked from a vendor in the market that morning.

"I've talked to my father," he told her as the Intercity trains passed them on the long tracks that ran up and down the peninsula. "He says that he will leave."

"Gavin, please," she said, her voice quivering. "You know it's not just about your father. It's about you as well."

"Me?"

"Yes. You're becoming like him, even when you promised that would never happen. Don't tell me that you haven't been out at night, with those gangsters, doing God knows what."

"You heard this from Chee Fong, didn't you? He only says nonsense, you can't trust him."

"I'm sorry, Gavin." And she left him at the old railway station, leaving him at a loss for words.

>—————<

Maut finished recounting his story.

"There is something I want to ask," Maut eventually said. "I want a job here."

"A job?" Wong asked, wondering if he had heard correctly.

"Yes. My old employer is dead. I need a job."

Wong hesitated, looking at Crazy Foo. Foo was taken aback too, but he nodded.

"Very well." Wong composed himself. "You know what it's like, don't you? We call you when we need you. We pay you based on the success of your work."

Maut just nodded.

"Good," Wong said. "You have impressed me, Maut. And I look forward to hearing more about you. Would you leave for a moment? I have something to discuss with Foo and my son."

Ah Leong escorted Maut out of the hall and to an adjoining room. When the door was closed, Wong turned to Foo at last.

"Where did you find this man? That was very rash of you, but I am glad at least it worked out."

Foo described what had happened, leaving out Gavin's part in the story, while Gavin waited awkwardly at the side of the room.

"And you think he is trustworthy? While you still know nothing about him?"

"He just risked his life to kill Chang for us, boss. Sure we can trust him."

Wong nodded again. "Take him back to the Laksamana. Give him a room or something, and a bonus. Personally, I'm disappointed that you acted without orders, but it paid off."

Foo bowed and departed, entering the side room—and now it was just Wong and Gavin, father and son. A moment's silence passed.

"How have you been?" Wong asked carefully. The memory of their last encounter still burned fresh in his mind.

"Fine, I guess," Gavin said. The number of things he wanted to tell his father multiplied in his head, but they remained unsaid. "So you will retire now, I guess?"

"I promised," Wong said. "And after what happened to your mother and your brother, I can say that I have had enough of all of this. We can start again."

He drew Gavin into a stiff-armed hug, and Gavin hugged back, but it was forced. Both of them felt a myriad of concealed emotions that they couldn't voice.

"I have to go now," Gavin said finally. "I'm sorry. There's something that I need to do."

"You must stay for lunch at least," Wong said.

"I'm sorry," Gavin said, wondering if his father was still angry with him for everything that had happened over the years—but he found himself thinking of Danielle instead.

"There's something that I must do. I will come for dinner, all right? Maybe next week or something?"

Wong, unconvinced, nodded and took his seat as his son hurried away.

12
MEMORIES THAT NEVER QUITE GO AWAY

Wong was back in Restoran Klasik. It had been a long time since he was last there, and it now struck him as being too vulgar, but that didn't matter. He limped across the parquet and to the grand staircase leading to the upper balconies. He passed by waiters laying out the plates and cutlery on the tables, and cleaners who picked up the residue from the dance the night before, including, for some reason, half a handcuff. The steps were too high and he just about managed. Down below, Boon was sitting at a table, occupied with the new Samsung purchased with his earnings from the assassination. Waiting for him in the office was Foo.

Foo, Crazy Foo. He remembered when Foo had been more reliable, but the man in front of him looked like he had a hangover and had just tumbled out of bed. But somehow, he kept the records impeccably up to date.

"So, boss, welcome back," Foo said in Cantonese.

"Hello, Foo," Wong said, sitting down, watching over the dance floor. The restaurant was due to open in several minutes. He would watch for a while and leave, heading back home. There were so many things he had to do. And he was going to tell Foo all about them, about the promises he had made to himself the night his wife died.

"So, what you want to talk to me about?" Foo asked.

"Retirement," Wong said.

Foo was quiet. "So how now?" he said at last.

"Well, we will need a new leader. Naturally, my first choice was you."

"Me, boss? I am very humble because of that," Foo said, trying not to hide his excitement.

He had dreamt about the chance to succeed Wong for years. The dream had started several years before, when he was with Wong in a pub not long after the shooting. He'd been forced to drag a despondent Wong out of the mansion. They sat in a place in Bukit Bintang which was owned by Ah Leong's relatives, and Foo had suggested how they could get revenge on Chang. But eventually, Wong pulled him aside.

"Listen, idiot," he said, gripping Foo by the collar, for he had been much stronger then. "I know that you sympathize with me as Xue is dead because of that bastard Chang. But I don't think I will ever get a chance to kill him. He is too cunning and I may get killed in the process. But I tell you what: you might be the one to do it."

"What you mean?" They were in the back alley, amidst the garbage bags strewn about.

"I might not live very long, and I need to take care of Gavin. He is the only family I have left. Everyone else is dead, and I can't spend too much time at the syndicate. I need you to start taking charge."

"Wah... your replacement, ah? I don't think I can do that."

"You have to," Wong said, his face clammy. "I need to stay as far away from Chang as possible. I can teach you all you need to know about taking over. You will follow me around. I will show you what to do."

And Foo had learned, seeing the syndicate from Wong's point of view. It was like a machine, and slowly he began taking over various portions of the business, starting with the Klasik, and later the Laksamana. Eventually he was running the day-to-day business.

And now it was high time for him to finally take over the syndicate.

"However," Wong said. "There is a problem."

Foo's smile faltered slightly. "What problem?"

"You have been reckless!" Wong snapped. "You took Maut in without my permission and kept it quiet for so many weeks. You lied to me all that time."

"I had no choice, boss. You will sure say it is too dangerous."

"You directly disobeyed me, Foo!" Wong raised his voice. "I am old, yes, but I will not tolerate insubordination. I've been checking on you for some time. You've been neglecting your duties, going to the nightclubs and leaving everyone to themselves. You show up here for work, completely drunk even when you knew I was coming. And one last clue: the paperwork. There's nothing amiss in this office. Nothing is out of place. I know you can't stand filing reports and accounts. I saw the accounts at Laksamana this morning. They were a complete mess. But this place is spotless. Why is that?"

Foo was sweating, but he didn't have to say anything. Wong already knew the answer.

"It was Gavin, wasn't it? Tell me the truth. You've been getting him to do some of this work?"

"He volunteer, not I ask him..."

"I told you, many years ago, not to involve Gavin in any of this!" Wong snapped. "I cannot let you take over this syndicate. You were not prepared then, and perhaps you never will be."

"Then who will?" The color was coming back into Foo's face now. He was furious.

"I will stay in charge," Wong said, getting up from the chair. "Until I find a replacement. Maybe Ah Leong, he's a good worker. Maybe Boon, he's responsible enough. But not you. I can no longer trust you."

He left Foo and went downstairs. His legs ached and there were people already entering and barking orders at the waiters. Boon came hurrying up the staircase to meet him.

"Boss, there's a man here to see you!"

"I'm in a hurry," Wong said. He wanted to go home, to try to think things through, to call Gavin if he had to.

"You don't understand, boss, it's the inspector."

"Ramalingam? He's here?"

"He booked a room. The Maharaja Lounge. And he wants to talk to you."

>————————<

Ramalingam waited inside the room decorated with imperial antiques. He was wearing a cummerbund and black tie, both of which he'd had no occasion to wear for years. And in a nightclub, of all places! Restoran Klasik had such a good reputation but it had fallen into complete disrepair. Yet, Wong and his cronies tried to keep up appearances. His secretary had prepared an exhaustive report on the restaurant for him.

"They still have formal dinners there," he said as Ramalingam peered at the report through his reading glasses. "Very popular with the old crowd. But they also have a dance hall, where the whole place becomes something like a nightclub. It's very popular with ministers who want to look respectable but party at the same time."

"Still, the reviews are quite good. I see the tandoori roast chicken is excellent," Ramalingam noted.

"Why does the chancellor want to meet you there?"

"He wants a change of location," Ramalingam muttered. "He wants to meet in a different place, even if it's in the lion's den itself. He likes to live dangerously. But he knows Wong Kah Lok, so it's not dangerous for him."

Wong wouldn't kill him in the Klasik, as far as he knew. The old man had never even tried. It was like an unspoken promise between them. But to be on the safe side Ramalingam packed his pistol with him. It was a Colt Python, the first gun he had received as a policeman. It was tucked into the cummerbund and covered by his black jacket before he drove to Restoran Klasik. There were two entrances to the restaurant: one for the nightclub and one for the east wing, where the old lounges were still in operation.

Ramalingam entered from the ornate front doors, while the clubbers went through the back-alley entrance. Wong limped into the restaurant. The old man looked less tired than he had been the last time Ramalingam saw him, as if a huge weight had been lifted from his shoulders. Ramalingam suspected that it was Chang's murder.

"Inspector," Wong said cordially. "It is very pleasant to see you again."

Ramalingam forced himself to shake Wong's proffered hand. He forced himself to not think of Bangsawan Heights—anything but Bangsawan Heights.

"So, what's the occasion?" Wong asked, taking a seat opposite the inspector.

"We have a mutual friend joining us. The chancellor. He has something to celebrate, and he invited me to dine with him."

"Interesting. I didn't know he was on the way."

"Well, he has been busy recently. You've seen the newspapers, of course. Running for elections and all that. But he wants to take the night off."

"No doubt he's here for the club. The Klasik still has a good reputation, after all. He can go in and enjoy life all he likes and nobody needs to know anything else. He still has to maintain his good name. They are calling him the Sheikh now, aren't they?"

"He is a controversial man," Ramalingam shrugged. "But he is very religious now. It's all in line with our government's policies nowadays."

"Trust me, we've had real sheikhs here," Wong said. "But you're not here for small talk, Inspector."

"You can explain your part in Chang's murder."

Wong looked unfazed. "You give me too much credit—this time it wasn't me, and that's the truth, for once."

"You two are long-time enemies," Ramalingam said, ignoring him. "And he has made several attempts to kill you."

"I did nothing to him. If you think I did, you are wrong. I have been quiet these days, Inspector. Enjoying my retirement."

"Retirement? We both know that'll never happen as long you're still the head of the syndicate."

"You've got nothing on me after all this time."

"This is your final warning. Since I'm close to retirement myself I intend to take you down before I leave the force."

"I'll be waiting," replied Wong. "In the meanwhile, enjoy the rest of your evening, Inspector. I recommend the fish and chips."

Wong left the room.

Ramalingam's blood was pulsing through his calcified veins. His hand twitched for a moment, almost reaching the gun under his cummerbund. Wong was too much. He was sick of the man's blatant lies. He didn't want to consult the IGP or his superiors any longer. He just wanted to end it, preferably by putting a bullet in Wong's skull.

Ramalingam tried not to remember the murders in the stairwell.

"Ah, Inspector Ramalingam!" The chancellor entered the room, followed by several others Ramalingam didn't recognize, although some were clearly military men. "You are here early. We were wondering whether you had arrived yet."

"I had nothing to do," lied Ramalingam. "Strange place for a meeting. I would have thought you would go to the Four Seasons or the Mandarin Oriental again."

"Too many reporters," the chancellor said, taking his place at the head of the table. "I can't really jeopardize my political future with all this social activity! All haram, kan?" He laughed, and the other men roared along with him.

The dishes arrived soon after and Ramalingam didn't touch his food, but he reminded himself that he was working with the chancellor now. He was starting to find the whole idea despicable, but he had no choice. He had agreed to everything and this was his punishment: to show solidarity with a man who would someday rule his life.

"And now, gentlemen, let me tell you a story I heard about the missing RMAF jet engines…"

>————<

Wong returned to the office, hoping to have another word with Foo, but Foo had gone for the night. *Where?* He'd neglected the office again and had probably hit the pubs after Wong reprimanded him. Wong thought of Gavin working there, and he felt numb. He should have known better than to trust Foo, but what else could he have done? Everyone was a possible traitor—just like the man who had betrayed him and his wife.

>————<

The Bordeaux wine bottle. The silverware. *The Four Seasons* playing in the background. Opposite him were sat his wife and Gerald. But under the bright lights, her façade had crumbled. She told him it was the end for them; she would have to leave. She couldn't cope with the pressure of his life any longer.

Wong wasn't going to budge, refusing to quit the syndicate, not while it pulsed with life, trapping him like a drug. She was upset, the strain of the last few years getting to her. She lived in fear, despite the cameras that Wong had installed at the mansion, and the hiring of Boon to ferry her around. He told her that everything would be fine, and that a dinner at Restoran Klasik, which he had just purchased, would improve things.

Wong turned to the doors, where the bodyguard stood in his blue vest. Wong didn't know his real name then, later finding out that he was the nephew of Ah Fung, the first man he ever killed. Masquerading as a poor farm boy from Kedah who needed a job, Wong had taken him in, and that night he was on security duty, Wong not knowing that Chang had bribed him already. The boy had poor eyesight but he was strong, and fearless once given a gun.

Gerald watched in alarm as the man who would be known as Ah Fung II made his way closer to them, already unsheathing his weapon as the "Blue Danube" started up. The child let out a shout, *Papa!* And Wong turned around just in time to see the assassin with his gun out for revenge.

And the firing began, one bullet catching Wong in the hip, and Ah Fung II raised the gun again, his boyish face streaked with malice, and his wife was running toward him, shouting for it to stop, as the musicians disbanded in panic and people ran for the exits. And the gun fired again, and Wong was screaming; his wife had been shot too, suddenly motionless; there was blood on his hands as he struggled to reach his own gun that had fallen to the ground. He fired once, shattering one of the lamps as Ah Fung II retreated, struggling with his gun. Wong pulled the trigger, sending out a volley of shots, one hand clutching his wife's wrist in a silent prayer for her to hold on. Broken glass was falling like rain, and Wong screamed as his face was cut, and then Gerald's cries were silenced. He glimpsed Ah Fung II running for the door, the murderer throwing his jammed pistol aside.

Wong wanted to run after him, to gun him down, and it would have been easy, but his wife and son were lying motionless and he knelt in a red puddle, not sure which way to turn, still holding his gun. It was over. He didn't move until the police, led by Ramalingam, arrived to take him away, where he knew nothing more.

13
EVERY DAY YOU MIGHT DIE

Gavin was in one of his nicer shirts as he drove toward Bukit Bintang on Friday night. People thronged the streets, jaywalking through the traffic that crawled like snails toward the city center. All around the lights blazed as if it were day, except that the businessmen and shopkeepers had been replaced by men in skinny jeans, sporting earrings and nose rings, and women in outfits so skimpy that even Crazy Foo, probably blind drunk in a pub right then, would have averted his eyes. He honked the horn as a group of drunkards passed in front of him, one of them mouthing swear words he couldn't hear above the ancient Simple Plan CD playing in his car. He wanted to be at the Mandolin at Changkat Bukit Bintang, with its refurbished shophouses that now served Irish whiskey and alfresco dining. He wanted to be away from the syndicate that night. Couldn't Foo allow him a taste of freedom?

He managed to fight his way out of the quagmire of Bukit Bintang, still angry with Foo. *Fuck that man!* He was about to reach the Mandolin when Foo called him. Gavin glanced around to make sure there were no policemen on the street before answering the phone.

"Gavin ah, I want to talk to you a while," Foo mumbled, half-drunk.

"Not now. I need to go and see Danielle."

"Please-lah. Come and talk to Uncle a while. I am at the bridge near Sultan Abdul Samad Building."

Gavin thought of Danielle, who was celebrating a friend's birthday at the restaurant, information that he had gleaned from mutual friends on Facebook. He made a sudden U-turn, trying to escape the streets, eventually driving up to the blurred outlines of the Sultan Abdul Samad's minarets, the flagpole and its fluttering flag almost invisible through the haze. He drove along the bridge and spotted Foo, bending over to stare at the muddy confluence on which Masjid Jamek perched, as if about to fall into the Klang River.

Gavin parked the Sorento in a side alley and got out. He ignored a Nigerian ticket tout and strode over to the bridge where Foo stood. It was unusual for Foo to be outside by himself, especially in a part of KL that was so deserted at night.

He reached Foo, who was holding a bottle of Carlsberg.

"Gavin ah!" Foo finally noticed him as he leaned next to the old man on the railings. "How are you ah?"

"I'm OK."

It had been three weeks since Chang's assassination, two weeks since Gavin had last seen Foo. In the meantime, with no prospect of returning to college, he had spent a lot of time online, ostensibly looking for a job. He made the effort to see his father, finally responding to the man's invitations to dinner. He had expected his father to change after the assassination. Wong Kah Lok was smiling more often, but he was still distant. There was and always would be a gulf between them. Eventually, Gavin made his excuses and returned to his apartment, most of his days wasted on random searches online for all sorts of distractions, the rest of the time spent at malls, in the food courts, watching families and friends and lovers walking past, wrapped up in their own worlds.

Foo hadn't called him back to the restaurant ever since Maut had announced Chang's death. He invited Gavin to drinks with Boon, Ah Leong and Gunner (but not Maut), and for the first time Gavin felt as if he was one of the guys as they sat under neon-blue lights while bar girls danced wildly and sang off-key. The men who sat opposite him, the same ones who wielded guns like the mismatched forks and spoons in their hands, laughed and joked about football and politics. For a while, Gavin even forgot they were killers.

But those social nights dried up and Gavin went back to living alone. Even the city had fallen into an uneasy silence. After three consecutive days of reporting rumors and other nonsense, the newspapers lost interest in Chang's case. The police hadn't come for him, his father or Maut.

Gavin hadn't seen Maut after the assassination. Maut declined to stay at the Laksamana and insisted on going home. They had dropped him off at Chow Kit, where the Indonesian traders set up their shops. Was Maut from across the straits? Gavin could never tell.

"You live here ah?" Foo had asked. Maut nodded. "OK. Now that boss hire you, he call you when got work. If none, then you just do your own business, OK?"

Maut nodded again and exited Foo's car. Within minutes he had melted into the crowd.

Gavin spent the nights awake, his head still ringing with the shootings he had seen and Maut's disappearance, wondering if there was a way he could get back into the world he had so briefly been a part of. He managed to distract himself by focusing on Danielle.

How long since they had last seen each other? A few months, but it felt longer. Each day he found himself paralyzed, unable to bring himself to reach out to her despite the fact that everything had changed. But while he no longer felt a burning desire to get back with her again, he wanted some closure instead. She'd blocked him online but he still had a dwindling number of mutual friends, from whom he tried to get a picture of her new life. She was about to leave Yohan Eng for Taylor's and she was happy. For her, it was a fresh start.

"So, you got see your father recently?" Foo was half-drunk, staring at the muddy river.

"Only once or twice. We had dinner, but he didn't talk about Maut or Chang or anything."

"He got talk about retiring?"

"No. I'm surprised. I thought he was supposed to do that. I mean, I brought it up once, but he didn't answer me. He just kept eating."

Foo laughed harshly. "He don't want to retire already," the old gangster grumbled. "Because he don't trust me."

"Why not?" Gavin asked bluntly. "You're his oldest friend."

"Aiya, that was long time ago. You know how long before me and your father came on top? And how our pay was like shit before we get promoted? I tell you, that time we were like brothers. We work together and everything. I even got save his life many times before. But now he say that I am not reliable anymore. That I am drunk and cannot run the syndicate!"

Gavin thought that his father had a point, but he didn't interrupt. Now that Foo had confided his secret he was speaking more quickly, sometimes slipping into street Cantonese.

"...He also don't want to do anything now! He wants to close down Restoran Klasik because for him got bad memories. He also want to shut down more of our side business. Maybe one day he wants to shut down the syndicate!"

"Why?"

"He never tell you before meh? Cause he says he feels guilty. He thinks when he die he will go to Hell because he is assassin. Damn fuck. Like that then how our men survive? Just because he is superstitious then all of us have no job, no protection."

"In that case you don't have a choice."

"Actually, I got." There was a glimmer of madness in Foo's eyes. "Day of Judgment."

"What's that?"

"Your father design it after your mother died. He says that it is a synchronized attack. We get all our men and attack Chang at one shot. The moment we do that, we wipe out his gang forever. They cannot recover. Some more, the police will investigate, and then they will be crippled for life. I was thinking, if I order Ah Leong and all to do it, then I will have more respect than your father. The men won't listen to him for sure. I mean, what does he do? I know he is the King of Petaling Street and all that crap, but seriously, now he doesn't do anything! He is useless as leader. Maybe I... I..."

Foo swayed, perhaps worried that he had talked too much.

"It's too late now I guess," Gavin said. "Chang is dead, and his gang has collapsed. And my father is still the boss. That doesn't change anything."

"Ya, ya," Foo mumbled again. He looked at his bottle and emptied it into his mouth. Then he flung it as hard as it could. The bottle sailed over the railings and smacked into the concrete pilings by the side of the river, shattering on impact, before the glass shards were washed downstream by the sluggish currents. Even the river was running dry, looking more like a monsoon drain than ever. It had been hot and the haze was coming back like an uninvited guest.

Foo began randomly recalling fragments of memories while Gavin listened.

"Life as assassin is very hard. Every day you might die. Did I tell you about my first kill? That one was an accident. I was supposed to beat up this one guy near the train station. I was going to whack him and then he saw me and we fought. I managed to throw him in front of a train. Of course he get hit. Walao! What a mess. I don't want to see that again—"

"Hey, you two! What are you doing?"

Gavin turned and saw a policeman walking toward them. His heart sank. They weren't doing anything illegal, they were just talking, but Gavin saw a sneer on the man's lips, probably ready to pounce on them for no better reason than boredom and there were two strangers loitering near the Dataran so late at night.

Foo turned around, his eyes glazed over. "Drinking beer."

"Asking for it, is it?" The policeman reached for his notebook. "Name and IC?"

Foo sighed, and then he pulled up his shirt. Gavin saw the policeman's eyes widen as he saw the curve of the revolver's barrel.

"Nah! You go! Run-lah!" Foo shouted, and the policeman hurried away, disappearing around the corner. "Faster go now," Foo said. "Otherwise he will call backup."

They ran from the bridge and the mosque, and Gavin approached his car, nervous about being seen in Foo's company.

"Gavin," Foo said before they left. "You want to come and help me with some syndicate stuff?"

"What kind?" Gavin tried to sound casual, but his heart was pounding like a drum.

"I dunno. But now you kicked out of college already, right? You sure got nothing to do liao. But there are a lot of things I can show you. Work at the moneychanger, come with me and trade guns in Thailand, maybe even go out for assassinations…"

Foo didn't stop rambling until they reached Gavin's car. Then the old man shut up for a while. He fumbled with one of the pockets in his cargo pants and withdrew a knife, sheathed in a leather case. He handed it to Gavin.

"Nah, I give you present for killing Chang," Foo mumbled. "That one is mine last time, now it is yours. I think that one day you will need it."

Then he was gone, vanishing into the haze.

>———————<

The Mandolin was fully lit up when he arrived. This was a place with kitsch appeal but good food, where women in French maid outfits served trays of imported sashimi. Gavin walked close to the windows, passing the alfresco diners on the five-foot way and peering in for a glimpse of Danielle.

Danielle was at a table near the long bar, surrounded by a group of other girls that Gavin recognized as her closest friends from Yohan Eng. He couldn't remember their names now, but he could see the remnants of a birthday cake in front of them.

He was tempted to rush in talk to her again, but it would be suicidal. He could never do it now; his world was too different from hers. He had to turn away and force himself to return to his solitary life.

A young man sitting next to Danielle got up and touched her cheek before he made his way to the men's room. Gavin was stunned, recognizing the boy immediately from his spiked hair.

>————————<

Chee Fong zipped up his fly and flushed the toilet. God, it was filthy. It had overflowed earlier that night and he fought back the urge to piss in the drain outside while one of the underpaid workers mopped it up. The door to the washroom was locked but he could still hear the strains of a J-pop song. The music got louder as someone opened the bathroom door. Chee Fong stayed where he was, peering at the manga strip that the owner had pasted on the door, about a boy with blades for hands chopping through mecha robots.

"Wait la," Chee Fong said when someone knocked on the door. He unlocked it and Gavin was there. Before Chee Fong could decide if he was angry or plain surprised, Gavin shoved him back into the cubicle, and he gasped as he landed against the cistern.

Gavin locked the door behind him, a deranged look on his face. *What the hell's going on?* Chee Fong imagined an impossible scenario from the contraband DVDs he and his friends had traded under their desks at his Ipoh secondary school. Then Gavin drew a knife out of his pocket and the nightmarish vision was complete.

"You shut up. Don't say anything," Gavin whispered. Chee Fong nodded, trying not to let his panic show. "What are you doing with Danielle? Huh?"

"You're not dating her already what," Chee Fong said, terrified. "She is very pretty, so I—"

Gavin snapped in disgust, "She deserves someone better than you!"

"Like you ah?" Chee Fong's fear was replaced by a growing anger. "Huh? What if I go out and tell her what you are trying to do? See if she will forgive you?"

"Tell her all you like, but she isn't going to believe for one second that Gavin Wong showed up out of nowhere, locked you in a toilet and threatened you with a knife. Now, get this in your head: you leave her alone, or I'll take this knife and…"

He pointed the blade at Chee Fong's trousers.

Gavin hated himself in that instant. There was Chee Fong, reeking of ganja, wearing such a pathetic expression of misery that Gavin felt guilty. Chee Fong was harmless, just an ordinary boy having fun—just like Gavin had once been, for a brief period.

"You listen," Gavin said. "You go out there and tell Danielle you are sorry for touching her. Because she needs someone better in life, someone not like you, not like me. I don't care how you say it, but I will be watching you. Then you stay away from her. Say you are sorry and never see her again."

Chee Fong nodded frantically. Gavin replaced his newfound knife in his pocket and left Chee Fong huddled over the toilet seat. Then he hurried out through the back door and was back on the streets.

14
THE BASTARD

Wong Kah Lok was in bed when the news reached him. It was midnight and he'd been unable to sleep, consumed by recurring nightmares. When the landline phone on his bedside table rang, it dispersed the violent flashbacks and gave him time to breathe and think.

"Boss," Crazy Foo said. "Got bad news."

"Why?" Wong said, still groggy.

"Boss, listen first: this all happened tonight. First in Kajang, there is one of our men. You know Kang, right? The Penang guy? He was out doing a job when someone killed him. Don't know who it is yet. At first I thought he just unlucky. But then, got some more news. In Ipoh, our other fellow Sudip was taking holiday. He got killed on the bridge going to the old town. And then there is a third shooting. Not sure how, but our regional manager in Jinjang got stabbed in his house."

Wong was silent.

"Boss, boss? How now? All these people are dying in one shot. I think it is the Chang gang."

"How can it be?" Wong mumbled, his brain still sluggish. "Chang is dead already."

"I dunno, but who else will do that? No one else will dare to screw us."

"But that's it for now?" Wong asked.

"Yes, yes. Everything else is OK for now. You want me to tell the other men to wait see a bit first?"

"Yes," Wong said firmly. "One more thing: go and see if there is any CCTV footage in the regional manager's house that we can use."

The next night, Wong was eating alone in his house again. Gavin had rung to tell him he was busy. The servants laid out the food in front of him and he ate in a house too big for one man.

The phone rang. Foo again. Wong listened as Foo regaled him with more bad news. Three men had been attacked in their flats in Seremban. A grenade had been lobbed at a car driven by the Jinjang assistant regional manager somewhere along a coastal road in Nilai as he drove to his superior's burial. At the graveyard, where some of the men and the regional manager's family had gathered for the last rites, two more bodies were found in an open grave.

"About ten people die in two days." Foo was trying to offer an explanation. "This is very serious already, boss. This time I am sure it is the Chang gang. A lot of the killings all in Negeri Sembilan, in their area. Plus, my spies told me, there is a new boss, Ah Fung II. The one who killed your wife."

Wong gripped the receiver. "Maut said that he shot him."

"Ya, but he survived. Not sure how, that man is like a tank. But it is confirmed he take over already. The men saw him going into Chang's old office in Seremban yesterday. So how now? We got evidence. We need to kill them all before they kill us. Let me suggest first, got one nightclub in Shah Alam that they own. How about we go there and—"

"No killings yet. Just keep everyone safe, see if this gets worse. Keep an eye on Gavin. Get Boon to follow him around, make sure he is out of trouble."

"But boss…"

"This is why I did not attack Chang," Wong said sternly. "This is a war now. Bad for business, bad for our men. Get the guns out of the safe and give them to the men. They need to know they are in danger."

"Boss, seriously, we must faster attack—"

"No. I will not let this escalate." Wong replaced the receiver, suddenly afraid and uncertain. He looked out of the window.

That haze was just like the one he saw many years earlier, on the morning after he first shot a man. He hadn't moved for a long time, listening to Foo's snores from across the room. He eventually turned to stare at the .22 snub-nosed revolver lying in the open drawer beside his mattress. He'd slept peacefully, despite his fears that he would be forever haunted by the sight of Ah Fung's exploding head. Instead, it was like watching a Shaw Brothers' film with cheesy special effects. He hardly remembered walking away from the police station after they had hauled him in from Yew's coffeeshop near Jalan TAR. The sub-inspector had cursed him and shouted at him, but he said nothing they wanted. Eventually they had let him go. He walked back through the streets, amazed that he had escaped.

He had already been in Kuala Lumpur a few years by then.

>————<

The bus from Salamat arrived late, breaking down several times along the way. They had been delayed by a police roadblock as policemen with rifles stood lazily in front of them, assuring the passengers that there were no communists hiding in the bushes. Eventually Kah Lok arrived at Puduraya station, confused by the chaos that was the capital city. The roads were packed with three people to a bike and trucks overflowing with famished chickens, the flags flying on buildings stained with grime.

The boy spent the first few nights on Jalan Sultan, sleeping on the streets and begging for money. Most of the passersby ignored him but the rest of them took pity on him, throwing coins into his hands. But his luck changed when he wandered into a restaurant, begging again as he vaguely stared at the washerwomen by the ditch and wondered if they were hiring. One of the fed-up hawkers screamed obscenities in Teochew as he raised his chopping-knife, but another voice rang out.

"Oi, stop that!" a large man in a polo shirt boomed. "If not I'll get your boss to fire you."

Before Kah Lok could run away, the man pointed at him.

"You, boy, come here," he ordered in bad Cantonese. Kah Lok obeyed, almost expecting a blow to the head. "You are begging here a lot. I saw you the last few days," he said, not unkindly.

"Yes, Uncle."

"Where are your parents? Dead? Otherwise no parent would let their children wander around like this. What is your name?"

"Wong Kah Lok, Uncle. I am from Salamat."

"Salamat? Where the hell is that? My name is Chang Yup Hoong," the man said, reaching into his pocket to pull out another cigarette. "And this is my son, Kok Chye."

The younger Chang was a fat boy who didn't even look at Kah Lok, preferring to peer at the BB gun in his hands. Every few minutes he would raise it as if he was a sniper in an action movie. The elder Chang sighed and turned back to Kah Lok.

"You are obviously new to this city. So am I. My family is from Seremban. We do business there. You know Yup Hoong biscuits? I own the factory."

Kah Lok wondered why the man was telling him everything. But the elder Chang was in no mood to stop.

"You want a real job?" the elder Chang asked.

Kah Lok nodded. The elder Chang laughed.

"Good, good! You follow me. Come, eat first. What do you want to eat?"

In the end, Kah Lok ate his first real meal in the city, a bowl of beef ball noodles that brought tears of joy to his eyes. "Thank you, Uncle, for the food," he said.

The elder Chang nodded dismissively. He was rummaging around in his bulging pockets for the key to a car.

Kah Lok followed the elder Chang and his fat son as they got into a sports car. In awe, Kah Lok took note of the brand: Alfa Romeo.

A fishmonger on Maxwell Road gave Kah Lok a job at a shophouse, stacking boxes and running errands. The work was hard but there was some money in it, giving him the chance to move into a room across the street. Years passed, with him stuck in the room smelling of cicak and stale rainwater. The other boys who shared the room said little and left one after the other, for better jobs in other places while he remained there.

Then Crazy Foo moved in.

Crazy Foo was sixteen as well, and he sometimes worked at the shophouse. He was forever going on about the gangsters who prowled the streets. At first, Kah Lok didn't speak to him, wary of the muscular boy with tattoos. But that changed after Crazy Foo rescued him in an alley from a drug dealer, with whom he had gotten into a fight.

"You really like to fight, is it?" Crazy Foo said to Kah Lok later that evening in their room, bandaging him up in the dim glow of a flickering electric light bulb.

"He stole my money," Kah Lok insisted, but Crazy Foo launched into a rant about guns and knives. He wasn't just another shopboy but part of the gang itself. Kah Lok had long suspected that Chang wasn't just an innocuous biscuit merchant. Rather, the large Chinaman was on the search for more lieutenants to join his expanding operation in Kuala Lumpur. Kah Lok asked more questions and Crazy Foo happily elaborated. He described himself as a member of the elder Chang's enforcers. They roamed the streets at night, beating up Chang's business rivals and sometimes serving as his bodyguards as he drove through town in his Alfa Romeo, picking up bundles of Indonesian rupiah, Singaporean dollars, and Thai-made guns.

"There was one time ah," Crazy Foo recalled nervously. "I killed a man."

"How?" Kah Lok asked.

"Mr. Chang told me ah, to go and whack one fellow who didn't want to pay back money to him. So I went to KL station. It was nighttime and there was only one more train going to Klang. I saw the man there and I went near him. But he saw me and we started fighting. I pushed him just as the train is coming. Splat! It squashed him. I was scared but what can I do? I ran away, and guess what?" Here, Crazy Foo's eyes widened. "Chang asked me to join his assassination squad."

Kah Lok laughed. "You're joking. That only happens in movies."

"No, I'm serious. Chang sometimes has a lot of enemies. Then he has to kill those bastards. He thought that I killed the fellow on purpose, and say that I have... err, po-ten-tial. So now I am an assassin."

"Is it a lot of money?" Kah Lok asked, unable to help himself.

"Yah! You want to join, is it?" Crazy Foo said. "Wait, when I see boss tomorrow I go and ask him."

"No! I was just wondering only," Kah Lok said.

But throughout that week, his conversation played on his mind. He thought about it as he unpacked boxes and repainted the back wall of the shophouse. He thought about it as he tallied the stock at the end of the day. Foo's life was so much more thrilling than his life as a shopboy. Foo lived in a world where money showered down like confetti. And there was the respect Kah Lok had never noticed before; he saw how people looked down in deference whenever Foo entered the shop. Meanwhile, Kah Lok had to be content with being spat on by irate lorry drivers, nagged by his supervisor, and once thrown out of a restaurant for not bringing enough cash.

It took him a few weeks to approach the elder Chang as he made his rounds, timidly asking for a job in the gang. Chang didn't bat an eyelid but simply offered Kah Lok the chance to join Foo on his nocturnal prowls around the city.

In a year, Kah Lok started to collect loans from defaulters. He mastered Foo's menacing stride and shrill cries, demanding that people coughed up what they owed before he lost his patience and fed them to their own dogs. He was richer than he had ever dreamed. But he was forgetting the past. His life in Salamat was fading away; he could no longer remember what his parents looked or sounded like. He thought of one day returning to the house, to find out what had happened since he fled. But he feared the moneylenders would find him. He had barely thought about them since that day. He had been too wrapped up in his own fears but they suddenly returned to his mind. They had turned him into an orphan.

He thought of Crazy Foo, who now carried a pistol taken from a dead Japanese general. When he went to sleep, he replayed the same thought. Of going down to Yong Peng where the moneylenders were from. Of going up to the man who had killed his parents, and shooting him dead.

He went to see Chang again. The son Kok Chye was now in his teens, but he sneered at Kah Lok every time they met. Kah Lok ignored the younger boy as he stared up at the elder Chang.

"There is someone I'm looking for," he managed to say. "He killed my parents a long time ago. He works for some Ah Longs in Yong Peng. An assassin. He drives a Lotus. Wears a suit. He has dyed hair, blond."

All the details were flooding back to him, as if he was thirteen again.

The elder Chang stroked his chin. Kah Lok wasn't sure whether the old man was going to punch him or ignore him. The elder Chang's behavior had become more erratic in the last few months. Rumors had spread about fighting between himself and some of his lieutenants in Kuala Lumpur. He even heard that some of the men wanted to break away from the Chang gang.

But at that precise moment, the elder Chang was composed.

"Very well," he said at last. "I will see if I can find out who this man is. And if I do find out, what will you do?"

"Kill him," Kah Lok said without hesitation.

Months passed. Chang, on his next trip to Kuala Lumpur, drew Kah Lok aside at the shophouse.

"My friends in Muar have found your man. His name is Ah Fung. You are lucky. He recently left his old gang and is now in Kuala Lumpur. He is still working for moneylenders. He still kills people who don't pay."

"I'm not scared of him," Kah Lok said fiercely.

"Then you are one of us now," the elder Chang said. "Foo is your roommate, I heard. I will get him to teach you how to shoot."

Every night for a month, Foo took Kah Lok to the tin mines outside the city on his new Honda motorbike. Kah Lok used Foo's gun, firing at makeshift targets at the abandoned mines. "Your aim is very bad!" Foo often scolded as Kah Lok tried to hold the gun straight. Loud bangs echoed from the ricocheting bullets through the open spaces, and Kah Lok was always afraid the police would hear them and come for them, but Foo assured him that they were too underpaid to care.

In the end, Kah Lok's aim improved somewhat, and Foo even brought him kreteks as a reward. The two boys sat by the rocks, smoking as they stared at the mining lakes.

"You know about the penunggu?" Kah Lok asked Foo.

Foo shook his head. Foo was the sort of person who never stopped to listen; he had been running around and wreaking havoc ever since he escaped from an orphanage in Kajang to smuggle rice on the coast with a bunch of Indonesians.

"They wait in those pools. Like ghosts. They wait until you are near, and then they grab you and drown you."

Foo blew out a puff of smoke. "Damn stupid story. There are no ghosts. Either you live, or you are a corpse."

One of the elder Chang's men had given Kah Lok a gun earlier that morning. It was a snub-nosed revolver. "Boss told me that tomorrow night Ah Fung has a job in Kepong. That he will go and celebrate at his favorite coffeeshop if it is successful. If I go there, I can find and kill him." He clenched his fist, feeling the cold metal of the revolver pressing into his flesh.

"Take my motor," Foo said. "And good luck ah. Kill the bastard."

The next evening, he was ready. He put the helmet on to cover his face as he waited. He rode past the coffeeshop several times, always hoping to catch a glimpse of Ah Fung. But he saw nothing, and felt nothing except impatience and desperation. He wasn't to be disappointed. He saw the Lotus approaching from his hiding spot across the road and his pulse quickened. How could he not recognize it? The image was seared into his skull, refusing to leave him. And with a wave of anger and revulsion he saw the ragged blond hair of the killer who sauntered out of his vehicle and into the coffeeshop.

Kah Lok watched. He put on his helmet and kicked Foo's motorcycle into gear, racing toward the U-turn and stopping in front of the coffeeshop. He felt for the gun in his pocket. He walked in as calmly as he could manage. The helmet felt ridiculous, making him sweat more than ever. He almost bumped into the Indonesian workers with their plates piled with kway teow. He then snuck up right behind Ah Fung. He looked up and saw the benign features of Kwan Yin on the altar. He felt the gun in his pocket again, wondering if he had the guts to take a man's life.

"Ah Fung?" he demanded, his voice raspy.

"Boss sent you, is it?"

Ah Fung turned, and Kah Lok saw resignation in the man's eyes, as though he knew his time was up. This was a man who had killed all his life, always having the upper hand. But that night it would change. Wong didn't hesitate. He drew the revolver before Ah Fung's cigarette lighter was out of its pocket, and he fired. There was a burning stench and a vivid red stain on his visor, and people were screaming. What was left of Ah Fung toppled into the uneaten food. Wong turned around, people still cowering from him. He didn't run; he walked away from the coffeeshop.

Two weeks later, the elder Chang congratulated him and told him that he would make a good assassin.

15
GAVIN

Crazy Foo watched from inside his beat-up car as Maut left the mosque. It was a Friday and he was sweating. The devotees in their songkok and Baju Melayu hadn't looked in his direction. The air-conditioner was running and nobody could see anything through the tinted windows, but Foo could see everything. He'd been tailing Maut all morning.

But Maut went nowhere suspicious. He just went to a mamak for breakfast. Then he went window-shopping, gazing at the electronics at Low Yat Plaza. Then Foo drove with the crowd of cars near the mosque where Maut went for Friday prayers. And that was it.

Foo eventually managed to leave the area, driving morosely back to the hotel. He wasn't even sure what he'd expected to see. But the fact remained that he couldn't trust Maut. His face was always blank. Beyond the money that Foo paid him after each job, there was no sign that he planned to stay with them or to betray them. But Maut did everything he had been asked to do without complaining. He was efficient. He kept secrets.

But a lifetime of being an assassin had Foo worried. Maut was too good. He could sense it.

The night before, Foo had called Wong again.

"What now?" Wong demanded. Foo knew that the old man was irritated. The afternoon before that, one of their vans had been shot at waiting at an intersection. Foo was supposed to have followed the van as an added precaution, but he was too drunk to wake up in time. The van had been fired upon at the red light; the driver and his colleague were dead by the time the light turned green.

Each week, somebody was dead or in the hospital. But still Wong refused to hit back. Foo couldn't believe it. There he was, being ordered to accompany the syndicate's men as if he was a fucking security guard, while Wong did nothing! He suspected that Wong was punishing him for his drunkenness.

"We cannot attack them," Wong repeated. "We don't have enough men, and they might come for me, or Gavin, or you."

"Boss, listen. If we don't kill them now, when can we do it? So far twenty people are confirmed dead, five in hospital. If by the end of the month we don't finish them, then they will outnumber us."

"You do as I say. Get the men to travel in convoys. Give out whatever spare guns we still have. Tell them to look out. But above all, do not attack first. I want all of you safe. Don't start a total war. Get Maut to help."

"Maut cannot be trusted. We don't know anything about him. What if secretly he is still part of the Chang gang? We must fire him. Notice, just after you hired him, all the killings started?"

"You're paranoid."

"No, serious. Maut comes and everyone starts to die."

"You're not being careful!" Wong said as he slammed down his receiver.

Foo continued working, taking calls from clients and running the operations from the deluxe suite of the Laksamana while the old man remained cooped up in the mansion on Cheras Hill.

Ever since the killings began, the old man had stopped talking about retiring. Chang Kok Chye's killing at Tropika was a hazy memory by now. The old man was now calling the office every day for updates. Each time Foo mentioned a death to him, the old man became more agitated.

He always mentioned Gavin. "Is Boon keeping an eye on him? The boy hardly ever calls me. I'm worried for him; he is on his own."

"That's why we must attack them, in case they kill your son," Foo would always reply. But Wong refused to consider the possibility.

Foo stayed at the desk for the rest of the afternoon. Violence was bad for business. They were defenseless and close to being wiped out by Chang's resurgent gang, even though its leader was long dead. He looked through the account books that Gavin had neatly annotated. A few more months of bad business would sink them. The syndicate was a huge part of Foo's life, and he wouldn't let it go without a fight.

He picked up the phone and dialed. "Hello, Gavin ah?"

>———————<

Gavin was up on the rooftop of the apartment. Evening was already falling and the heat was dissipating somewhat. He had long since run out of face masks but he simply stood there, watching the haze as it shimmered over the skyline. The light played tricks on him, the way it undulated and reflected off the haze itself, creating a hideous dancing pattern of shadows in the sky.

"What?" Gavin said, more irritably than he intended.

"It's Foo here. Is everything OK?"

"Yes. Boon is following me around every day. I see his motorbike across the road whenever I go out."

"Listen, come with me this evening. I want to treat you."

Gavin sighed, but not too loudly. Foo always had something up his sleeve. But that evening, he didn't want any part of it. He'd only tumbled out of bed a few hours before, drunk and feeling gutted. The night before, against his better judgment, he'd gone to see Danielle.

He had long toyed with the idea of seeing her again. Even after Boon showed up at his door, telling him that the Chang gang was slowly picking off their lieutenants, Gavin found himself wondering what had happened to Danielle, whether she was involved with Chee Fong, and whether she was worried about him, caught up in a gang war that was slowly making its way onto the pages of the newspapers.

"You stay inside!" Boon ordered Gavin. "If Chang's men see you, then how? Sure they will assassinate or kidnap you!"

It had been fruitless trying to argue with Boon, who even started bringing instant noodles and luncheon meat over. Gavin remained cooped up inside. He tried to bargain with the bodyguard, telling him that he needed to get out, but Boon refused. "If you don't like this, talk to your father!"

Gavin didn't want to talk to the old man. His father had only called twice since the killings flared up, both times issuing warnings against going out. The second time, he suggested that Gavin return to the mansion, but Gavin declined. Too much had happened over the years for him to return.

In the end, Gavin found out (after a call to the nervous Chee Fong) that Danielle was back at college one evening to file her request to transfer out of Yohan Eng. He wondered if it would be better for him to stay put in his apartment and leave her alone. But he had to see her again.

So he set off through the service bay, slipping past the garbage collectors, burned brown and wearing their conical hats. He had a cap and a pair of dark glasses. Then he hailed a taxi and was on his way back to Yohan Eng College.

He arrived there in the evening. He stepped back into the compound, past the security guards after flashing his student card at them. He saw her at the office, just as he was about to call her. She looked untroubled, free. He felt guilty as he strode toward the stairs that would take him up to the office. But he couldn't just turn back.

"Gavin?" Danielle said as she came into view, descending the staircase.

"Hello," Gavin said awkwardly. He forced himself to look her in the eye. "Listen, I'm sorry about what happened that day, at the train station. I hope you can forgive me."

"I'm sorry, too," Danielle said, her expression softening. "But even *you're* not safe here. I've seen the news. You should be home or even out of KL."

"Can you give me another chance? Please?" Gavin didn't know what made him say it. It was so false, so corny, but he meant it.

"Gavin, you don't understand. My parents are here."

"If you don't care about us any longer, I'll leave."

He was prepared to turn and run, to put everything behind him. But Danielle didn't look away from him. Gavin felt a surge of hope, as if the last few weeks could be erased, that he and Danielle could start over again from where they left off at the tracks of the old railway station.

Then the door to the office opened and her parents stepped out. Gavin had only seen them once before, when he gave Danielle a lift back to her house. She'd told him about her parents. Her father was a technician who worked for one of the smaller multinationals, and her mother used to be an accountant. They lived perfectly ordinary lives, as far as Gavin knew.

Too late, they were there, and Gavin was transfixed by their stares.

Danielle's father stepped up, in front of his daughter, and Gavin wasn't sure how to react. Neither of them spoke for some time.

"You are Gavin Wong," he said in the end.

"Yes, sir," Gavin said.

"You are in love with my daughter."

Gavin nodded. It was useless to lie to him.

"And you are Wong Kah Lok's son." Another nod. "Please leave Danielle alone."

Humiliation. Confusion. Anger laced with sadness. Gavin couldn't even bring himself to turn to see Danielle one last time. He went down the stairs, fighting the tears brimming in his eyes.

Back at his apartment later that night, he didn't do anything for a long time, preferring to sit watching the city slumber uneasily under the haze. Then he scrolled through the photos on his camera, hundreds of snaps from a happier time. Slowly, he began to delete them. They would never see each other again, even if they still cared for each other. It was too late. He was too involved with the syndicate now.

There was Danielle, next to him at the snow simulators in Shah Alam. There they were, at a park in the old town of Taiping, filled with all manner of trees pruned into exotic shapes. There she was at the bridge, the island shimmering in the background. And another one of them, holding hands. He deleted all of them. He didn't stop until dawn.

Gavin was still exhausted when Crazy Foo's Datsun pulled up in front of the apartment and he hopped in. Foo drove away, leaving Boon behind to guard the empty apartment. Foo said nothing. He simply handed a bottle of beer to Gavin.

They were meandering down one of the coastal roads. Gavin remembered being driven down one of these roads when he was much younger. His father had wanted to drive down to Johor then.

"There's a place down south, called Salamat. It's a nice town. That's where I was born," his father said. Gavin had been six. It was Cheng Beng, the day of worshiping the dead. They'd left the mansion at dawn and were driving past small kampungs on roads that wound their way through Johor's uneven terrain. They passed pineapple plantations, cows, and farm boys with their sticks.

"Remember to pray to your mother when we get there," his father said, his voice quivering. "And your older brother, OK?" His father was rarely religious, except on Cheng Beng, when everything became sacred for one mournful day.

But they never reached their destination. The traffic was crazy, even on the coastal road. Up ahead, a lorry had overturned, spilling coconuts on the road like severed heads. Gavin could see his father looking agitated, drumming his knuckles on the steering wheel of the blue Mercedes-Benz. Then he abruptly made a U-turn, as if he had lost his nerve. They returned to Cheras and never went to Salamat.

But now it was just Gavin and Foo, driving down the road, heading nowhere. "So what do you want to talk about?" Gavin finally broke the silence. Foo turned off the radio, the voices of Chinese pop stars abruptly cut off.

"Listen, I want to talk about all these killings that happen recently," he said.

"I'm listening," Gavin said, putting the empty beer bottle away.

"Your father, excuse me ah, he is a fool. He doesn't want to attack Chang, even though Chang's men are killing us like houseflies," Foo said angrily.

"He doesn't want the fighting to escalate," Gavin said, repeating his father's own words.

"Aiya, bluff! I know he is scared. He thinks we cannot win. He say that we should self-defense only. But self-defense, my ass! You think we can defend when every stranger on the road can be an assassin from Chang's gang, is it? Ah Leong, Ah Boon, Gunner, maybe me. All of us will die if we never fight back. Understand or not?"

"True," Gavin admitted.

"Which is why," Foo said, businesslike, "I need your help now. You know, my friends are getting very frustrated because your father never do anything. They want to fight already. You got remember the Day of Judgment, right?"

Gavin remembered the night that he and Foo were standing on the banks of the Klang River, with a drunken Foo blurting out the details of the plan to take down Chang's gang.

"One shot," Foo said with glee. "One shot and we destroy those bastards. We send ten men to their office in Seremban with pistols. Kill them all. At the same time, our other men will stalk all their bosses and shoot them. We know who they are and where they are. Then we will win!"

Gavin immediately pictured the newspaper headlines.

"But you see ah, your father knows it will be effective. But he say I siao liao!"

"You can always tell my father yourself." Gavin interrupted Foo, who then missed a left turn.

"You think I haven't tried yet, is it?" Foo snapped. "Every day I tell him, but every day he never orders the men to kill Chang's people. They are angry. That's why I need you to help us."

"How?" Gavin said blankly.

"Use your head! You are boss's son! You take over from him!"

"Are you mad?" Gavin said, alarmed.

"Eh. Let me tell you something. Gunner and Ah Leong, all of them, they damn respect you wei. After all, you are the mastermind. You got Maut to kill Chang."

"That was nothing."

"Aiya! Better than your father, right?" Foo fumed, swerving messily on the road. "If you tell them to attack, they will obey for sure. Last time you gave order and we won!"

A throbbing began in Gavin's head. It wasn't fear. It was sudden elation: an understanding that everything was in his hands. Somehow, impossibly, their future was in his hands.

"Why can't you order them to do it?" he said, despite his excitement.

"Eh, I will get fired. But you can do anything! Don't pretend you don't want it." Foo momentarily took his eyes off the road and frowned at him. "You're not that innocent also. You shot that man in Puchong."

"He was in pain already, and you made me do it."

"And you ordered Maut to kill Chang."

"That was different. It was so my father could finally get peace."

They were interrupted by glaring headlights up ahead.

"Fucking shit wei," cursed Foo, fumbling in his breast pocket for a pair of sunglasses while Gavin squinted.

Then the firing began.

"Look out!" Gavin shouted as he heard a bullet pierce the Datsun's chassis, and another. Crazy Foo was swearing, cutting his own headlights to lose the shooters in the approaching car.

"Get off the road!" Gavin screamed, but Foo had already done so. He made a sharp turn and was speeding past the trees, down a narrow road. From behind, the car slowed as it made the turn. They had the lead, but the Datsun was old, and there was no telling how long it would take before the car sputtered to a stop and they were obliterated by the snipers.

There was another wild burst of gunfire from behind them, audible even above the roar of the Datsun's stressed engine. Gavin turned around and saw the car's headlights increasing in intensity.

"Where are you going?" he shouted as Foo swerved his way along the road. Foo shouted something incoherent, but Gavin could tell the old man had a plan. Foo swung his steering wheel hard and they were amidst the trees of an oil palm estate, vanishing through the undergrowth, up and down over the rutted paths, and suddenly Foo killed the engine. The headlights were off and Foo wound down a window. Both of them waited in the car with bated breath, while, silently, Foo drew his Stechkin revolver from the glove compartment.

There was a rustling from ten, twenty feet away, as the powerful engine of another car drew to a stop. Gavin tried to peer out from between the fronds of the nearest oil palm, but it was no use. Then he heard the men shouting out in Malay.

"Where's the car?" one of them yelled.

"Samad was supposed to help us," another grumbled. "That one real useless."

"Careful, Zul. That old Chinaman maybe has a gun."

Gavin stared as Foo stuck the barrel of his revolver out of the window of the Datsun. The men were illuminated by the glow of the moon, although the Datsun remained hidden between the trees.

"Shh," Foo whispered, taking aim, while the men were fumbling with something, probably their torchlights.

He fired. Gavin heard screams of agony and then Foo threw the door open, firing again and again. More screams, and then Foo was running back, slamming the door shut. A moment later, there was another bang as the back window shattered and Gavin yelled, crouching in his seat as glass shards sprayed them.

Foo gunned the engine. The Datsun roared to life and he was turning the wheel, bringing them out into the open. Gavin saw one man lying on the ground, another groaning next to him, and the third pushing the door of their car open, the xenon lamps already blazing. Foo didn't hesitate; he rammed right into the open door, which crumpled instantly, cracks forming in the windshield. Gavin saw the bloodstains on the windshield as well, but didn't look back as they fled the estate for the city.

"Three men," Foo breathed at last, when he was sure they were not being followed. "We beat them all."

Gavin's heart was still pounding.

16
JUSTICE, A SMALL CONSOLATION

Grasping his cane, Ramalingam's hand shook as he hobbled past the security guards and toward the office at the end of the corridor, somewhere in the warren of the Malaysian Anti-Corruption Agency in Putrajaya. That was where Chancellor Zahid worked when he wasn't tending to Yohan Eng College. Samad, in his dark blue police uniform, followed him wordlessly. Ramalingam still felt uncertain about Samad. He'd hired the new man without consulting Chancellor Zahid. But for some reason he trusted the quiet man he'd rescued from obscurity.

><------------<

He was in Johor at the time, escaping the media after a group of elite policemen were slain in a shootout. He toured several of the smaller police stations, even though it was a weekend and he was on holiday. But the district policemen were thrilled to have K. Ramalingam, the famous crimebuster of Kuala Lumpur, visiting, and they showed him their guns and records and prison cells, which looked suspiciously spick and span.

But Ramalingam was there for one reason, and he made it clear to them over tea in the station canteens.

"I heard a lot stories about a man," he said, stirring milk into his Boh tea. "He's been incarcerated in the Paya Besar Prison. That's not too far from here. Apparently he's the only prisoner who hasn't tried to escape."

As always, the Johor police superintendents would squirm in their plastic chairs. "No, Tuan Inspektor, there's no such man. Not that we know of. And nobody ever escapes from the Paya Besar Prison."

They all knew better, of course. Paya Besar Prison was one of the older jails in the state. It had been built by the Japanese to house communists, whom they tortured each day. After the war, the prison was appropriated by the British to jail even more communists. But the prison fell into disrepair over the next decades, eventually opening again when a crime wave surged through Johor, filling up the other prisons. But renovations were costly and the wardens were too underpaid to keep their rowdy prisoners in check.

There was an old joke among the Johor police that if one's father/mother/brother gets arrested, send him/her to Paya Besar. Being sent to Paya Besar was like being in a Monopoly jail. Some of the more corrupt wardens had devised their own "Get out of Jail" system. Two thousand ringgit for petty thieves, five thousand ringgit for rapists and homosexuals, and ten thousand ringgit for convicted murderers. Prisoners constantly entered but were usually discovered to have mysteriously disappeared after several days. Sometimes they were said to have committed suicide, but the bodies were always buried in the prison cemetery by the time anyone launched an investigation. Paya Besar Prison's notoriety was thus ensured.

But there was one man who refused to try. Ramalingam heard the story from a young policeman in Kluang, who'd once been ordered to escort a prisoner to Paya Besar. The occupant of Cell 72 refused to leave, despite the chief warden hinting that it would cost only a few thousand to get out. It wasn't like he couldn't afford it; he was captured with at least RM1,500 in his pockets when the police caught him in Kuantan. Surely he had family members who could bail him out! But Prisoner No. 72 consistently refused to contact his relations, or to discuss the subject of payment. Wardens made successively lower offers to him but he always refused, claiming that it was his fate to remain in prison. The wardens feared and despised him in equal measure.

"What sort of devil is that?" the young policeman muttered. "It's madness to stay in Paya Besar. At night, the stronger prisoners beat you up, or even—"

"Can you take me there?" Ramalingam asked. "I want to see this man."

He was still the famous K. Ramalingam. What he was doing wasn't strictly sanctioned, but there was no disobeying the orders of a superior officer. Ramalingam was driven over rutted tracks in a 4x4 that afternoon. They passed orchards that merged with the rainforests, and entered the lowlands. Down the slopes and into a clearing ringed by hills. The walls and barbed wire fences of Paya Besar Prison came into view. While it was built as a maximum security prison, housed in the drained swamps of a valley to make escape more difficult, Ramalingam saw no guards on patrol.

"Hasn't anybody launched an inquiry as to why there isn't a single guard here?" Ramalingam demanded.

"Can't, tuan," the driver of the 4x4 said, as the prison gates opened. "You know how it is. The policeman who is officially in charge of the jail is the brother-in-law of Datuk X. Nobody dares question him."

Once inside, Warden Hussein, who looked like he had just woken up from a nap, greeted him. "You want to see number seventy-two?" he said skeptically. "What for?"

"He seemed interesting," Ramalingam said nonchalantly. They walked down several flights of stairs with empty cells all around them, eventually arriving at a locked door scrawled with graffiti.

Warden Hussein banged on the door. "Samad! There is a visitor for you."

He turned back to Ramalingam. "Fella's completely harmless. I'll give you some privacy. Shout if you need any help. I'll be around the corner."

Ramalingam waited until Hussein was out of sight, and then opened the door. He entered the cell, which was dank and smelled of stale urine. Samad sat on the bench, barely moving. His dark eyes followed Ramalingam as the inspector took a seat on the opposite bench, still clutching his cane.

"I am Inspector Ramalingam," he said shortly. "I heard a lot about you."

Prisoner No. 72 didn't flinch. He just stared back.

"I heard you were arrested at a hospital in Kuantan. Apparently you were on the run. They found a revolver on you. There were no bullets left. You are surely a criminal. But still, you refuse to leave. Why is that?"

There was no reply for some time. Eventually Prisoner No. 72 spoke. "It is Allah's will. I must atone for what I have done."

"A pious killer, huh? You're a rare breed. And your accent… From Kelantan, kan?"

Samad nodded, looking exhausted. Ramalingam looked at him for a few minutes, before finally speaking again.

"I am looking for a lieutenant. Someone to help me out with a special task. The problem is that what I'm doing is not strictly sanctioned by the IGP or his people. I'm working on my own, and I need men I can trust."

"And you trust me? I am a murderer," Samad said.

"You are a religious man. I need people with principles. You see, I'm also a victim. Have you heard of Bangsawan Heights? No? Perhaps someday I will tell you about it. But the gist is that I am doing something to avenge someone I failed. I am an old man now. I am losing my memory and I may be forced to retire soon. I want some justice, a small consolation, before that happens. I can't turn to my own officers or even my bosses for help. That is why I want you."

"So, what do you want me to do?" Samad said at last.

"Whatever it takes," Ramalingam said simply. He stood up, grasping the cane. "Now, you can stay here and serve the rest of your ten-year sentence for possessing illegal firearms and attempted assault. Or you can leave today and help me. I will give you ten minutes to make up your mind."

With that, Ramalingam hobbled into the corridor, staring at the curses scribbled on the walls by seventy years' worth of prisoners. In the end, he heard the door creaking behind him as Samad emerged from the cell.

><

That was a few months ago. Now Samad had his own uniform, a surplus set from the supplies office. He did as he was told. He was loyal to a fault. And Ramalingam trusted the ex-hitman. Together, they sat in a minimalist waiting room in the MACC office, adorned with pictures of Zahid in Mecca and some hibiscuses in a vase. Ramalingam hated Putrajaya. The administrative capital was devoid of life, as if it had been freeze-dried and put on for display, emptied of everyone except for government ministers and armed policemen.

Ramalingam was exhausted. He lost track of the numbers of the dead and dying as each day passed while reporters hounded the IGP for answers. His secretary (Abbas or Amini?) had shown him a webpage where thousands of users threw abuse at the police for allowing the crime rate to spiral out of control. But Ramalingam tried to keep the bad press and criticism out of his head.

The door to the office opened and Zahid stood there, in an Armani suit.

"Come in, Inspector!" he boomed. His eyes squinted in displeasure as he saw Samad lurking behind Ramalingam, but he remained civil nonetheless.

Ramalingam took a seat opposite Zahid's sparse desk. There was little on it except a framed photo of Zahid with a group of Pakistani mullahs at a religious conference. Zahid resumed his own seat. Samad remained standing.

"How are things, Chancellor?" Ramalingam asked pleasantly.

"Please, nowadays they call me the Sheikh!" Zahid boomed. "I must keep up my religious appearances. It will help bring in the votes. Elections are coming up, you know."

"They still don't know you drink, do they?" Ramalingam nudged the desk with his cane.

Zahid rolled his eyes, as he looked at his drawer. "What to do? You can't expect me to waste good brandy!" he said, laughing. "You've done well, Inspector. I congratulate you."

"You're welcome, Chancellor," Ramalingam said. He didn't mention his unease about how things were going too far.

"You've done incredibly well," Zahid insisted. "I feel that in a few months all this nonsense will be wrapped up. Then you can go back to being an inspector again. Or better still, promoted! I can talk to Tuan IGP—"

"That is fine, Chancellor," Ramalingam said, cutting him off. "All I need is a chance to do what is right. I don't need anything more."

"Are you sure? If I ever become Prime Minister, I would want someone like you as my chief of police!"

"You are too kind. But perhaps I should read you my report…"

Zahid listened as Ramalingam gave him the details. He reported to Zahid once every two weeks, telling him about the measures and tactics that he and Samad had come up with. But Zahid always looked impatient. He just wanted to know how many possible threats were left.

"We must get rid of every loose end," he always repeated. "We can't have a single witness left."

Ramalingam noted that whenever Zahid said that, he looked directly at Samad, as if threatening him.

Their meeting ended. "I have to go now," Zahid said, donning a songkok. "There's a new religious school opening in Precinct 7, and they invited me to the opening ceremony. I'm afraid that I cannot miss it. There's something I want to tell you first, though."

He looked at Samad. "Can you leave first?" he demanded. Samad bowed and exited the room. Zahid turned back to Ramalingam. "Get rid of him. I can tolerate everything you do except for the fact that you keep trusting this man."

"Why? He's one of the best men I've worked with."

"He's the lowest of the low," Zahid said. "A savage. He's a simple mercenary, Ramalingam. He will ruin our operation."

"I trust him," Ramalingam repeated. "If I don't work with him, I'm afraid I cannot cooperate with you."

Zahid sighed. "In that case you win," he said. "Come back in two weeks. Hopefully there will be a bit more progress by then. May God be with you."

"And Allah with you," Ramalingam said, leaving Zahid in his office.

17
IN THIS LIFE OR THE NEXT

Wong used to have a tattoo on his back. It was now only a few faint lines, but he remembered what it looked like.

>————<

It was a stylized version of Chang's name, long black vertical lines snaking between Wong's shoulder blades. The tattooist was also one of the elder Chang's lorry drivers, and the painful process took place in a salvaged Japanese army truck, Wong gasping as the needle pierced through skin while cars honked outside the tarpaulin.

But now it was done and he was one of the men.

As part of the gang, he roamed the streets at night with Crazy Foo, carrying his gun and keeping an eye on Chang's many businesses. He looked out for the massage parlors cum brothels, the cars full of drugs smuggled from across the Golok River, and the trucks of illegal Indonesian migrants fleeing the purges after the failed Gestapu coup of 30 September 1965. He sometimes had to manage errant gangsters from the rival 88 Gang and the Kugirans and the Mini Coopers, either gunning them down as they strolled down the roads, or setting fire to their cars at junctions with Molotov cocktails made out of Tiger Beer bottles. But despite the higher pay, working with the elder Chang was a hazard.

Chang could charm other men. He spoke of money and dignity and trust as he wheeled and dealed with politicians, policemen and rival gang bosses. Wong could see the elder Chang's gang was expanding. It spread from Negeri Sembilan to the capital. Men from the east coast were already pouring in, speaking the Kelantanese dialect, battle-scarred from their fights across the Thai border. There were Hokkiens from Penang who took cannabis-laden biscuits from the shop back to George Town. Once, Wong saw a group of Sabahans in the shop, demonstrating the assembly of improvised bayonets and bakakuk—home-made shotguns that were good for hunting and killing—to the awed gangsters.

He was also violent. Like the time one of the men failed to stop a defaulter from skipping town: Chang didn't listen to his excuses, but struck him in the face and knocked his teeth out. The man collapsed in a heap, but Chang calmly turned to Wong.

"Whip him," he said, as if referring to an irksome dog. "And stuff some paper in his mouth. I don't have enough money to pay off the police each time someone has to be disciplined."

And in the courtyard behind the shop, Chang watched the punishment with a malicious grin. Wong raised the whip that was stashed in the bathroom and brought it down on the debt collector. The man couldn't even scream but Wong could see him convulsing with each blow. He hated himself for it. When Chang called for him to stop, Wong and Crazy Foo cut the man's bonds loose, but he couldn't move, lying on the sunburnt tiles with his back raw and bleeding.

The years passed. Being a gangster was all that Wong knew and cared about. But there were times when he stopped by the temple to make a prayer. He'd forgotten the right mantras but he lit his joss sticks with fumbling fingers, feeling uneasy as he prayed alongside shopkeepers and fishmongers and pet-shop owners. He felt contaminated, as if he didn't deserve to kneel before Kwan Yin and Buddha.

Then came the night he was nearly killed.

He was at the Feng Li Benevolent Association as usual. Every Friday, the volunteers at the association provided food for the homeless. Wong often joined in, despite the fact that he had saved up enough money to get his own room, while Foo continued drinking heavily into the night and frequenting the brothels.

Wong was chewing on a stale dumpling when a group of Malay village boys wearing bandanas rounded the corner. Wong had seen enough since the May 13 riots to know that they were not out for a stroll. Not yet gangsters, but not mere delinquents either, he had seen the group making its rounds through Chinatown. He could hear them already, screaming obscenities at the crowd.

"Go back to China!" he heard their taunts. "Back to China!"

Normally, Wong would ignore them. They were just bored out of their minds and fed enough bile by their political masters to curse every Chinaman. They were nothing compared to the horrors he had seen on the streets at night. But that changed as a man stepped out of the Association, bespectacled, wearing a singlet and an apron.

"Hey!" he said. "We are just eating. You cannot just come and—"

One of the boys lifted the man's spectacles from his face while another brandished a switchblade. The boy, his hair shaved off and his face pockmarked, laughed.

"Get back, Chinaman," he sneered, and snapped the spectacles in half before the man's petrified face.

Wong had had enough. Setting his plate aside, he marched up to the leader. "You leave now and no one gets hurt," he declared.

Behind him, the Chinese man scurried back into the shop, presumably to call the police. Wong stood there, while Shaved-Head gaped at him, wondering what to make of this interloper. Wong stood his ground, eyeing the boys. So far, it looked like only the one with the switchblade was armed. He didn't have his gun with him, it was under his pillow, but he knew that if a fight started, Chang's men would come forth.

"What can you do, chink?" Shaved-Head challenged. "There're five of us."

Wong didn't hesitate. His fist flew out and Shaved-Head was clutching his throat, gasping, before falling to the ground. The crowd started edging away, a hundred nervous eyes watching expectantly. The other boys were unsure of what to do next. The street was silent.

Then Switchblade Boy screamed and lunged but Wong was ready, grabbing him in a headlock and sending him careening into a pillar on the five-foot way. The blade flew out of the Malay boy's grasp. A mass of bodies fell on Wong, and he kicked and punched whatever he could reach. He dealt one boy a blow between his legs and kicked another in the face. Already, Shaved-Head had crawled away and was running back into the shadows.

There was a blow to his side and he gasped, his hands coming away crimson. Switchblade Boy had come to his senses and fled the scene, his blade dripping red. The other boys followed while Wong crumpled to the ground. He could hear the crowd. Before he passed out he saw the fuzzy outline of Crazy Foo running down the road, punching the boys who got in his way.

It turned out that Foo carried him all the way to the hospital. None of the taxis would take the blood-soaked Wong;

even Chang's men refused to drive. "The little bastard is dead already," one of the truckers spat.

Foo would visit—when he wasn't too busy at the brothels. Other than Foo, there were hardly any visitors—not even elder Chang, who was away in Macau on a gambling holiday. Kok Chye had been sent to boarding school in Singapore. But news of the fight had spread. Some of the men in the hospital offered to wash his clothes out of respect. Others promised to get him a proper job in companies where their sisters-in-law worked as junior clerks. An elderly cripple at the end of the ward, who spoke to nobody else, not even the nurses or doctors, once gave him a packet of pork floss that Wong devoured while waiting to be discharged.

But the most surprising visitor was a girl. She came into the green-tiled ward while Wong stared at the television set, watching the war in Afghanistan.

"You are Wong Kah Lok, aren't you?" she said.

"Yes," Wong said, trying to place her. He was sure he hadn't seen her before. She wasn't one of Crazy Foo's girlfriends or Chang's relatives. He knew nobody else outside of the Chang gang. "Sorry, but who are you?"

"I am Xue," she said. "My father was volunteering at the Benevolent Association last week. The gangsters broke his glasses and almost hurt him, until you stepped in. It has taken me a while to find out which ward you were in." She held up a tiffin carrier, and Wong could smell sambal. "He wants to give this to you as a gift."

"Thank you," Wong said, embarrassed. "But I was simply helping."

"You are in hospital because of that," said Xue sternly. "It is the least that we can do."

She waited while Wong tucked into the rice packed into the aluminum container, a definite upgrade from the watery porridge the hospital served each day.

"It's delicious," Wong said as he finished, leaning forward to hand the empty carrier back to her. He winced as he pulled one of the stitches in his side; he was afraid to start bleeding again.

"Does it hurt much?" The girl pointed to his side.

"It is fine, thank you."

All of a sudden, he felt tongue-tied. He was furious with himself—but somehow, the girl made him feel foolish. He tried to think of something to say, but he couldn't. So they said goodbye and she left, leaving him to stare at the television screen again.

To his surprise she was back the next day, and the day after, with the same tiffin carrier. This time, they talked more. She told him she was a student in her last year at the local convent, trying to decide if she should continue her studies at Universiti Malaya. Her parents were Peranakans, Malacca born and bred, but they had left their home to work in the capital, in one of the kitchens in a foreign hotel. And he, in return, said some things about his own life, and when he finally felt comfortable enough, mentioned how he got recruited into the gang. She didn't say anything, and there was an uneasy feeling as she left. Wong didn't expect to see her again.

But still, she returned. She was there until the day he got discharged, limping out of the hospital. She too lived near Petaling Street, in an ex-hotel once called the Imperial, overlooking the teeming streets. And he told her some stories about the places he'd lived in since arriving in the city. He talked about the time he was fourteen, selling tikam to schoolchildren to supplement his meager earnings from the shophouse. He mentioned the first room he stayed in, which overflowed with cockroaches at night and was now converted into a snooker place. He spoke of the first time he was out on the streets after joining the gang, and how it felt so natural, and how he felt so secure amidst the gloom of the city.

They parted at Jalan Sultan, but she touched him on the elbow. "You can leave all this behind."

He gave her a sad smile. "I cannot. I am and will always be a gangster. There is no redemption for me in this life or the next."

He extended a hand, but she hugged him instead and then she was gone, vanished into the mass of people.

When he returned to his flat, he laid out his possessions. One of the thugs had stolen his wallet, and he would have to buy a new one. He searched for the keys to the shop and a comb. And then he found an unfamiliar scrap of paper and unfurled it. He stared. She had slipped him a note with an address on it. Was it hers? He felt a sudden, fluttering feeling, and allowed himself to smile for a minute.

>———————<

"You *love* her ah?" Crazy Foo said a week later. Wong had just been taken aside by the elder Chang, who screamed at him after he failed to stop thieves from stealing some of their supplies. For a week Wong had been unable to concentrate on anything. He thought of Xue each day, and the work he did became steadily less appealing. Especially the gun—he hated it there, lying next to his bed each night, reminding him he was bound to Chang. In the end, he pulled a drunken Foo away from a karaoke joint to talk to him.

"Yes, I do," he said in response to Foo's incredulous question.

Foo sighed and lit a cigarette. "Like that, better if you go," he said. "But you sure ah? If you run away, boss is going to kill you.

They say ah, last time got one man who try to resign. Boss cut him into little pieces and made him into meat biscuits."

Wong stared at the shelves of biscuit tins lining the shophouse. "I will run away then. To Penang or Ipoh or even Kelantan if I have to."

Foo sighed. "If you go, you cannot change your mind. Sure?"

Wong nodded again, more certain than he had ever been.

"OK," Foo said. "Good luck ah. Hope you can escape from this hell."

They parted ways, Wong not even leaving a note for the elder Chang.

>———————<

In a small Thai town in Songkhla, Wong winced as the tattoo-remover completed the painful procedure. He tried not to scream the whole time the man carried out his work, and it had taken a bottle of stout at the stalls outside to calm his nerves. But it was done. The tattoo was gone. He was a free man again; nothing could hold him back. He paid up and left.

He passed the rickshaws and roadside stalls bearing the portrait of the King of Thailand. He hailed one of the rickshaws and was soon heading toward the bus that would take him back to Penang, his new home, and to the woman who had come all the way north with him, who would someday be his wife.

He didn't know why she had agreed when he asked her to leave with him, at the doorway of the old hotel where she lived, and she would never tell him the answer. Was she tired of her life in a suffocating city, or did she love him as he loved her? She asked no questions. All he knew was that they were runaways together.

18
BANGSAWAN HEIGHTS

The killings continued. Ramalingam had long since given up on remembering the details. He focused on his own name, about how it was brought up in the papers so many times.

"Have you heard from Samad today?" he demanded of the secretary on his way back from 7-Eleven, carrying several newspapers after lunch break.

"No, tuan," said the secretary as Ramalingam prepared to lock the office door. "But he left a message. He says there might be a big kill coming up soon and we need to prepare ourselves."

Samad sometimes disappeared for days on end, and often Ramalingam had no idea where he went. He wondered if Samad still had family on the east coast. He had never asked, and anyway, Samad would never answer.

He perused the newspapers. A random article appeared, accompanied by a short profile of Ramalingam. He read it, against his better judgment:

> *Inspector Ramalingam was unavailable for comment, but it is believed that he still has the motivation to hunt down the gangs, particularly after the Bangsawan Heights murders that almost ruined his career...*

He tried to forget about it, but he was already falling, dragged back over twenty years ago.

>————<

He was a rising star then. Under Superintendent Kassim Muhammad's tutelage, he rose in the force. Supt. Kassim had been humiliated by the way Wong Kah Lok had simply walked out of the interrogation cell without punishment. He spent the remainder of his career preparing Ramalingam for the day he would eventually capture and bring the gangster to justice. And Ramalingam excelled at being a policeman.

Word began to spread, especially after a siege occurred at Pudu Prison. A group of ex-communists had taken over the clinic, cutting off electricity to the medical ward and threatening to kill everyone unless they were granted safe passage to Thailand. Ramalingam volunteered to join the special team assembled to rescue the doctors. They scaled the walls and stormed the ward. Smoke bombs and tear gas grenades were launched. The first few ex-communists raced out, choking and blinded by the smoke. But there was one more left who refused to leave. The rest of the team assembled, debating the best way to get him. He had a gun and gas mask and threatened to kill the last few hostages. But Ramalingam didn't back down. He entered, with only a pair of goggles and a wet cloth over his face protecting him from the smoke. He was almost blind, but he could make out the figure of a man with a shotgun, lit up by residual candlelight. He lunged once, taking the man by surprise. The gun went off and a bullet hit Ramalingam in the leg, but he managed to wrestle the prisoner to the ground.

HERO COP ALMOST DIES IN LINE OF DUTY—the newspapers proclaimed the next day.

And Ramalingam rose quickly in the force. The police brought him in each time there was a hostage crisis. He negotiated with the Japanese Red Army. He talked down a group of Vietnamese trying to smuggle arms into Indonesia. He helped to storm a warehouse on Old Klang Road, bringing a local kingpin to his knees.

"Don't you ever fear for your life?" a reporter from the *Malaysia Nanban* asked him once in an interview. And Ramalingam shrugged. "How could I die of anything but old age?" he said, a tad cockily. "It is not so easy to kill me."

He was feted by many politicians as a hero. One of them invited him to a Deepavali celebration in Port Klang. Ramalingam reluctantly agreed to attend, feeling uneasy as he entered the hall. He spotted several members of an infamous Indian gang and some of the minor Malay kingpins. They glowered at him but said nothing, placated by free food and the good graces of the politician who'd invited them. Then the politician showed him around the room, pointing out people whose names Ramalingam would never remember.

"There's Viranathan, the footballer, Datin Anita Sidhu, she's with one of the NGOs, and the young lawyer Karpal, I'm sure he'll be famous someday... Ah, Balasingam!" the politician shouted. "Stop lurking there, you rascal. Come and meet the young inspector himself! This is Inspector K. Ramalingam, you might have heard of him."

Balasingam reeked of toddy and some other drinks, but he was resplendent in a blue suit. "Inspector," he rasped. "It is a pleasure to meet you. We in Singapore have heard a lot about you."

"Yes ah?" Ramalingam said, taking Balasingam's sweaty hand and giving it a firm shake. "I am surprised. What do you do here?"

"I am a developer!" Balasingam beamed. "I'm building a place called Bangsawan Heights. Should be a nice place when it's done, eh?"

Both men smiled awkwardly for a moment. Balasingam looked around but the politician had deserted them to talk to the gangsters at the next table. Then he beamed.

"Ah, this is my cousin," he said, introducing Ramalingam to a young woman in a green sari. "Visanthi, Inspector Ramalingam is a big man in the police force!"

"Hello, Inspector, I have heard a lot about you from Datuk Thiru." She indicated the host. "He's been talking so much about the man who won't die!"

Next to her, Balasingam looked uncomfortable. He excused himself.

"Thank you," Ramalingam said, trying not to notice Balasingam's sudden disappearance. "How do you like the party? Are you liking your visit to Malaysia so far?"

"I am Malaysian," she said.

Ramalingam raised an eyebrow. "Forgive me, but your cousin is a Singaporean, isn't he?"

"Our families don't communicate much," Visanthi explained briefly. Ramalingam nodded, and he didn't ask any more. He looked up and noticed that one of the gangsters, a Punjabi with a cropped beard and an ill-fitting turban, had left too.

"Your cousin, is he all right?" Ramalingam asked. "He left so suddenly."

"He's probably not feeling well," Visanthi said. "Food poisoning maybe. He lived in Australia for a long time. He's probably not used to the food here."

"It's a shame. The food is very good tonight. Dato' Thiru knows how to throw a good celebration. You are here with your cousin, I assume. I don't see any other family around."

"Yes. It is not often that he comes all the way back to Klang, so he makes it a point of bringing me around," Visanthi said, but something lurked beneath her calm exterior, as though there was something she wanted to say but couldn't find the words for it.

So instead, they spoke about other things: politics (she was working for one of the opposition parties, trying to put an arts degree to some use), inflation (it's getting so much harder to get around nowadays, no?), and crime, which Ramalingam was able to talk about at greater length. He described some of the things he had seen, being careful not to give too much away, and once in a while the gangsters at the next table would look in his direction with suppressed annoyance, giving him the urge to laugh.

Balasingam still wasn't back after half an hour. Another gangster got up and left the table, the remaining men forcing themselves to talk about English football instead while a song from a Tamil movie blared over the speakers.

Suddenly Visanthi looked over to the table with the gangsters and turned back to Ramalingam. "Inspector, can I speak to you privately?" she whispered. "I don't want them to notice anything."

"It's better in here. If it's important, say it now. They won't pay you any attention."

Visanthi hesitated, but eventually she managed to whisper audibly enough over the music. "Bala is with them. He's been working with them for the last few months. He doesn't think I know, but it's obvious."

Ramalingam had suspected it from the start; that Balasingam, with his too-shiny blue suit and his slick manners, was in league with the murderers and racketeers who sat ten feet away from them. But he kept his nerve. "Thank you for telling me all of this. I am afraid we cannot talk here, it's too dangerous. But call when you can." He removed a name card from his pocket and handed it to her. "Tell them it's about Bangsawan Heights, and that I told you to contact me directly."

"Thank you, Inspector," Visanthi said. Ramalingam noticed how expressive her eyes were, how every emotional nuance shone through them. "I hope it won't be any trouble."

"Not at all," Ramalingam said.

Over the next few days, Ramalingam received calls from Visanthi. She spoke urgently, probably from a pay phone in her office, and Ramalingam put the pieces together from her story. Her cousin was running out of funds for his Bangsawan Heights project, trying to keep up appearances. He'd moved in with her and her family at Teluk Pulai, and his drinking had worsened. He would curse and talk about the project, about how his business partners were leaving one by one. She didn't dare to talk to him directly; the only chance for her to call was while she was at work.

"Please, if he gives you any names, tell me," Ramalingam said, gripping the receiver each time she called.

He had already launched investigations into Balasingam. The man hadn't done anything illegal, at least not yet. But the Punjabi and the other man who had disappeared from the dinner at the same time as Balasingam were definitely into the moneylending business. Ramalingam was tempted to call one of his counterparts in Klang to keep an eye on Visanthi's family, but there was no proof yet.

Amini, his secretary at the time, was watching Ramalingam. "That's three lunch breaks you've spent in your office, Tuan Inspektor."

"Well, I am busy. Lots of work being an inspector, you know."

Amini shook his head, clicking his tongue. "It's not just work, boss. You never skip lunch, even when you're stressed. You always try to be healthy. You can't fool me. It's the girl, kan? Why else would you be so dedicated over some loan sharks?"

"Don't make trouble; go back to work," Ramalingam reprimanded him. But he wondered if it was true. *Am I so interested because of Visanthi?* He'd had no close relationships with anyone, ever since his parents died of old age while he was in the Academy, and not since his older brother migrated to Baltimore. His world had narrowed down to his office and staff at the police station in Dang Wangi. But lately, he had been thinking of her. It scared him. He could lose his job. But he ignored Amini's teasing and kept on working.

"He's getting worse," Visanthi said urgently. "I don't know if we can control him much longer. He is just so angry about everything nowadays."

Ramalingam was stuck. There was nothing he could do to implicate Balasingam. *The man's just a developer, for God's sake. Not a very good one, either.* But Visanthi was getting scared.

"You should move out," Ramalingam advised her. "Get a room in Kuala Lumpur or something. Somewhere he can't find you."

"I can't leave. He will find me."

"If you leave, I can guarantee you will be protected," said Ramalingam confidently, although he could promise no such thing. "Please, Selvi. If he's unstable, you can't stay in the same house with him. Either you move or you talk to the Klang police."

"You've been too kind," Visanthi told him, her voice full of gratitude. "But I can't just go. It would be too dangerous for me."

When it came down to it, Ramalingam was a mere police officer. He could do nothing more but assure her that he was doing his best.

"He mentioned a Chinese name," Visanthi told him the next day, in what would be their last conversation. "Wong Ah Lok, or something like that."

"Wong Kah Lok? I know him," Ramalingam mused. He wondered if Visanthi, in her own office at the other side of the city, knew about the crimes the syndicate had committed. Ramalingam had watched Wong Kah Lok's ascent in the KL underworld, paralleling his own promotion in the police force.

He had been at Wong's wedding reception just a few months before, in an attempt to spy on him. It was at the Federal Hotel, an event so grand that rows of imported Mercedes and BMWs lined the streets, tussling with the Proton Sagas for space. He went discreetly, dressed in a suit, and the bellboys ushered him in, believing him to be another crime lord. He stood at the back of the banquet hall, watching as Wong, dressed in a slim-fitting three-piece suit, raised a glass.

All around, he saw familiar faces: Crazy Foo, the chief lieutenant, the brothers Feng of Limbang, the crooked contractors from Permatang Pauh, the head of the 228 Gang, surrounded by his female escorts, a representative of the Singaporean mafia. And in the corner, wasn't that the infamous Zahid, the son of Tan Sri Yunus Ishak? Ramalingam also saw Wong's new wife, wearing an imperial dress. The opulence astounded him as he saw men and women rising to their feet, yam-senging with their wine glasses. He imagined an FRU unit swooping in at that moment to arrest the gang leaders.

But that wasn't going to happen and he left Wong to continue with his celebration.

"Selvi, you be careful," Ramalingam finally said. "Your cousin is dealing with dangerous people. But he hasn't met anyone in person?"

"Only over the phone," Visanthi said nervously. "He's afraid. I can tell. But he hasn't done anything yet…"

"I suggest that you move out," Ramalingam said urgently. "Can you do that?"

"My parents are scared too, but there's nothing that we can do. Bala has nowhere else to go. We can try to talk to him, to make sure he won't do anything dangerous."

"Take care," Ramalingam said quietly. "Just call if you need any help. This line is always open."

"Thank you, Inspector," she said.

Ramalingam paced the office over the next few days, wondering if she would call. But for some time there was nothing. He grew so nervous even Amini noticed.

"Tuan, are you OK?"

"There's nothing we can do," Ramalingam said, shaking his head as he pored through files about the Bangsawan Heights project. "That rascal Balasingam, he hasn't done anything illegal. It just looks like he's in debt, but he can be dangerous. A broke man with nowhere to turn to is dangerous. Just like that case last time, what was it?"

"The Velanappan murder in Ampang, tuan?"

"Yes. How could I forget that? The old man killed his wife for her money. I'm getting bad with names."

"Well, I hope that you won't forget mine someday," Amini chuckled as he left the office.

The news broke. Ramalingam was summoned to the headquarters in Bukit Aman one afternoon, just two hours before he went off-duty. The IGP himself was there.

"Listen, Inspector, there is bad news," he said briskly. "We hear that a woman, Visanthi Veerasamy, has been communicating with you as an informant. She is now dead."

Ramalingam, his pulse racing, his head throbbing, forced himself to listen. Gunshots had been heard the night before in their house in Klang. The police had gone to investigate. They went in to find everybody dead. There was a safe in the bedroom that had been shot open; it was empty. Anything of value had been taken away from the house, and the assailant was gone.

"I know who did it," Ramalingam said, his fists clenching. "His name is Balasingam. A Singaporean. He's her cousin, he lived there… The bastard, the bastard!"

The IGP kept quiet for a moment as Ramalingam fought to control himself. "We can put out an APB for this man at once," the IGP said. "Are you sure it's him?" When Ramalingam didn't reply, the IGP sighed. "You may be wrong. But you know better than most. I'll send out the order."

Ramalingam could only wait for news. He was in his office every day. Sometimes he slept there, crazed with regret and fury. He could have stopped Balasingam if he had acted sooner. It was his fault, he realized. He wanted to talk to Visanthi, to keep her on the line, and now she was dead, along with her family.

"Tuan, please, get some rest," Amini insisted on the second day of his vigil. But Ramalingam refused to leave. He sent out his own officers to Balasingam's contacts, but nobody had heard from him since the murder.

In the end, Ramalingam picked up the phone, dialing the number of the one person he could bargain with.

"Inspector? This is unexpected," Wong said as Ramalingam entered the living room.

"You said you have records on Balasingam," Ramalingam said impatiently. "If they are satisfactory, I will leave you alone."

"He is a client of mine, yes," Wong said. "A despicable man. I loaned him money and he failed to complete his work. He was supposed to build a condo in Duta, you see. Some place for rich foreigners and businessmen. And nothing came out of it. He gambled his money away. I can't find him either. But I cannot simply betray a man. Trust is important in my work, you see."

"People have died because I did not act," Ramalingam said. "I intend to find this man and jail him, or…" He didn't finish his sentence.

Wong regarded him with a sad, almost pitying expression. "I understand how you feel. I have lost people I cared for."

"If you help me, you have my word," Ramalingam promised. "You're free to do as you like, provided you don't go too far. I will stop hunting you down."

Wong didn't say anything, lost in thought. Ramalingam tried to imagine the man before him ordering killings and vicious acts of torture. But perhaps everything had changed since his wedding.

"You have a wife now, don't you? Is she here?" Ramalingam asked.

"In Malacca, with her mother," Wong replied, looking out of the windows of the mansion. "She is expecting my first son."

"Congratulations. You are going to be a father."

"Thank you, Inspector."

Perhaps that *had* changed him. He wasn't quite the same man Ramalingam had pictured over the years. He seemed more contemplative now.

"Balasingam killed a woman, I heard." Wong gently turned to face Ramalingam. "Was she important to you? My condolences. I know why you are here now."

He disappeared for a moment and returned with a folder.

"Everything you need to know is here," he said. "But if you really want this man to be punished, listen to me. You know as well as I do that he will be extradited back to Singapore if you arrest him. But if you go by yourself, you can do what even the law can't give you. He's run afoul of all his backers. The Punjabi gangs have come for him. They came to me for advice only yesterday, after his funds were still not enough to cover his debts. I didn't tell them this, but he will be at the unfinished Bangsawan Heights. He has recruited a gang of Bangladeshis and Nigerians as his bodyguards. He knows he can't survive much longer, but he refuses to die. When a man is pushed into a corner, he will cling on to every chance to survive, even if it's madness. Go there. You'll find him."

"If you know where he is, why don't you go for him yourself?"

Wong chuckled. "He has nothing to pay me back with. Someone else will find him but the only satisfaction they will have is his death. I have no interest in what happens to him now. And after all, he already gave me this house in good faith."

Wong gestured at the spacious awnings and wide windows. Ramalingam, clutching the folder, shook Wong's hand and left the mansion.

"Listen, this man now has nothing to live for. He is armed to the teeth. We need to be careful," Ramalingam said to the five FRU men who accompanied him to the abandoned towers of Bangsawan

Heights, unpainted concrete and rusting iron joints ghastly in the evening light. He had read the file carefully before ordering the attack. "He has at least three bodyguards with him. The rest have fled. Two are Bangladeshis and one a Nigerian. They have knives and a submachine gun. But I am confident we can take him out."

He had discussed the plan with the IGP. The IGP hadn't even asked where he obtained his information. "Bring him down," the IGP ordered. "He's a murderer with bodyguards. We can't have him on the loose. This man has nothing to bargain with. He will fight to the death; he will try to take prisoners too if he can manage it. Do not negotiate with him."

The next day, five men were at Ramalingam's disposal as they crept up the stairs, Ramalingam in the lead. Balasingam had a suite on the tenth floor, and they went in silently.

Then the firing began from above, from all around them. Was it many guns or just one, echoing down the stairwell? Ramalingam hurried backward, under an awning, while the FRU men held their shields over their heads. But still the firing continued.

"Shoot back!" Ramalingam screamed. There were shots from his men while Ramalingam launched a flare. The flare illuminated the stairwell and the burly Nigerian with his gun two floors up. Ramalingam didn't hesitate. He took aim and fired. The man yelled and fell, slamming into the walls on his way down, hurtling past them to the bottom of the stairs.

"Move!" Ramalingam ordered. He raced up the stairs, the men behind him. *We're nearly there, aren't we?* Too quickly, two men emerged from the shadows; one of them punched Ramalingam and he fell backward, down the steps while the FRU officers charged past. One of them screamed as a blade went through his chest. More gunfire. One of the bodyguards landed with a wet thump next to Ramalingam as he hobbled to his feet, his knee aching from the fall. He clutched the stairs for support and his hands came away bloody. *Whose blood is this?* More firing and another FRU man was blown backward, while the remaining three held the bodyguard down, hands over his throat as he slowly went limp.

"Take care of them!" Ramalingam shouted as he hurried on. He would take care of Balasingam himself. He didn't care what happened next. He just wanted revenge. That was all, a glimmer of violence that crystallized in the back of his mind.

He found the door and kicked it open, gun aloft. Through the darkness he could see a dark shape, cloaked in the tattered remains of a blue suit.

"Inspector…" a hoarse voice said. Balasingam didn't even have a gun. He had a syringe next to him, as well as a tray of drugs.

"You murderer," Ramalingam croaked.

"You here to arrest me?" Balasingam sighed, the outlines of his face barely moving. "Well, do what you must. I'm safer in prison than with the loan sharks."

"Go to hell. You deserve to die." Ramalingam's hand was shaking even as he tried to steady it.

Balasingam just looked at him with disgust. "If I could shoot, I would have done so. You are just lucky," he muttered. "You know what it felt like, knowing that my own cousin was conspiring against me? I had nowhere to turn. Not the police, not my family. I have nothing left in this world."

That was enough. Ramalingam thought of Visanthi, who had so needlessly died, and he found a sudden cold-bloodedness. He squeezed the trigger again and again. He didn't stop until Balasingam's blood smeared his boots.

The truth of what he did never spread to the public. The newspapers damned him with faint praise:

INSP. RAMALINGAM'S MISTAKE:
POLICE RAID GANGSTER'S HIDEOUT, SIX KILLED.

They mourned the two fallen officers, and Ramalingam was there at the funerals, one in a Hindu temple and the other in a mosque. But people looked at him differently. Ramalingam understood why. The rumors had already begun seeping out: that he had made a deal with Wong Kah Lok, the man who controlled the city, in exchange for Balasingam's whereabouts. And those men in power who held the door to his future turned back to him and apologized; he would be passed over for promotion again and again. There was no way forward after Bangsawan Heights.

He began to neglect his health. He tried desperately to think of something, anything else, but his shattered mind brought him back to Bangsawan Heights and Visanthi's last words and him trudging up the steps of the Wong house, prepared to throw his own pride and integrity aside. He never quite recovered, shunted from station to station, finally ending up in Ampang Jaya. The aftermath of Bangsawan Heights never left him, trapping him even as his memory deteriorated, leaving him with nothing but the incident replaying itself.

19
SINS OF THE FATHER

One night, Gavin had a dream. No, it was more of a memory. It was of two years before, when he and Danielle were still together. It was at a church. They had driven down the coast after spending a night in Penang, where they had walked down the esplanade, watching the glow of the mainland like fireflies in the night. Gavin was driving, Danielle was asleep. He checked his watch. It was eleven on a Sunday morning. Gavin eventually pulled over in a small village, and from there he could still see the coast, sparkling under the scorching sun. He gently shook her awake.

"You should go," he said, pointing at the church opposite them. "It's a Sunday, after all."

"Sure you won't be coming in?" she asked, pushing back her bangs.

Gavin simply shook his head. "I'm not the religious type," he replied, as she slipped on her shoes and got out of the car. Instead of following her, he opened his door and stared as the ocean breeze wafted through the straits and stirred the waters, dotted with little fishing boats returning from a morning on the waves. He walked down to a stall where he bought some fruit from a woman who seemed to have wandered right out of the jungle, and eventually walked down to the beach, so far removed from the world his father occupied. There, he found himself remembering every detail that had happened over the past week.

When Gavin had first told his father about Danielle, Wong said bluntly, "You do know you cannot tell her anything about us, don't you?"

"Yes," Gavin said at once, over their breakfast.

He thought about it as he made his way to the church. He entered it, silently taking a seat in the last row of pews, while the pastor gave his sermon.

"...It has been repeated throughout history, that the sins of the father will be visited upon the sons."

Once the sermon was over, and the congregation offered up their prayers, Gavin walked to the pew where Danielle sat.

"I was there for the last part," he said. "What does it mean?"

She grimaced. "It means that the children pay for what their parents have done. There is no escaping your family or your past."

Gavin didn't say anything as they walked out. There were no clouds and the sea and horizon were indistinguishable, fired to a whitish-blue. They got back into the car as he tried to start up its engine.

"It was as if you were trying to tell me something back in there," he said at last, unclipping his aviators.

"No. Of course not. You're free to decide what your future is. It doesn't matter if your father is a street sweeper or a prime minister."

Over the next few days they talked at length about what it meant to make their own choices. He realized, too late, that he was in love. The reality was that he was trying to break away from the gang, at least for Danielle's sake, even if he had to give up working at Restoran Klasik for Crazy Foo. Anyway, it was what his father wanted, wasn't it? Old Wong had tried to keep Gavin out of the syndicate all his life. Gavin would do just that.

>————————<

Gavin now downed yet another drink at the bar. The Republic Club in Bukit Bintang, with its tall columns and minimalist furniture, had been open since late afternoon but Gavin had still not found the mood to join the dancers. Behind him, Boon waited with a worried glare. Gavin knew, as he called for another beer, that Boon was afraid Old Wong would find out about the meeting.

Crazy Foo was late. *What's happened? Surely he isn't dead or something?*

A girl in a tank top and cut-off jeans approached him. "I saw you sitting here, and I was wondering if you wanted to dance," she said, smiling coquettishly. She was slightly tipsy and Gavin shook his head automatically.

"I'm waiting for a friend, I'm sorry," he said. The girl looked disappointed and retreated to the dance floor while Gavin paid for his drink. Fuck it. He had to stop thinking of Danielle. He just couldn't forget her, despite everything.

Boon came over and whispered in his ear over the blaring of a Daft Punk song. "I received an SMS from Foo. He is arriving already. We'll go into the room first."

Gavin followed Boon to the back, where they had booked a private room. Ah Leong would probably arrive soon as well, and maybe even Gunner, back from a job in Teluk Intan. On the way, Gavin passed the girl who had invited him to dance. She was already in the arms of a tall Eurasian whose head was almost touching the lights. At least he wouldn't be missed.

They sat in a dim room adorned with stained glass and an aquarium filled with all manner of exotic fish. The doors closed and Gavin waited with Boon, who had drawn his gun. Boon's eyes darted back and forth quickly, like searchlights.

"What's wrong?" Gavin asked.

"This club, got something wrong," Boon said. "This is not one of our places. Cannot trust the people here."

"That's why we're here, because it's not ours," Gavin said resolutely. "My father cannot know about any of this."

Boon readjusted the sights on his gun. "Ah Leong and Foo fucking late."

"Ah Leong's coming too?" Gavin asked.

"Yeah. The whole leadership. Except your father."

Gavin felt a burning, simmering power inside him. "It's time we acted. I can't live like this. You're sitting outside, guarding me. We're scared; we can't even do anything without trying to hide first."

There was a knock on the door. Boon walked over, peering through the frosted glass. He opened the door and Gavin could hear dubstep pounding into the soundproofed room. Ah Leong entered, followed by Foo, who wiped his face with a greasy handkerchief. Boon closed the door, latching it.

"I booked the room for the whole night," he said. "The owner still owes us money from our job last night, so he doesn't have a choice."

Foo paced the room, silhouetted against the corals in the illuminated aquarium.

"We need to discuss things," he lisped. "I can trust all of you, right?" He tapped his Stechkin as he spoke. Gavin nodded and the other two men did the same. Foo, looking pleased, put his handkerchief aside. "Now, boss doesn't want to attack them. But I don't care already. We have no choice. How many people Chang's gang kill already? Last week, there were five men I know, good workers, very brave, and they work for the syndicate a very long time. All of them are in Hell now because boss is too scared."

"You are asking us to betray the boss," Ah Leong said sternly. "You know that boss has done many things for us last time."

"Last time!" Foo cursed. "But what is he doing now?"

There was a nervous silence, and Gavin felt the men looking at him, as if his response would galvanize them into action. "Foo is right," Gavin said, feeling much older than he was. "My father is too afraid. I don't know what he's thinking."

"You want to launch Day of Judgment, is it?" Ah Leong demanded.

Foo nodded vigorously. "You got read my mind," he said, his voice quivering in excitement. "We plan this for a long time already. We still got enough men to cripple all of them—"

The aquarium shattered. Boon immediately pushed Gavin down. He yelled as he hit the wet floor, shards of glass near his eyes and fish flopping around him. The other men ducked as well, fumbling for their guns, as another round of bullets came in. Ah Leong screamed out and fell to the floor, writhing.

"Fuck, fuck!" he was shouting over and over again, as a pale-faced Boon tried to staunch the spreading dampness on his shirt. Gavin was still gasping for breath when he saw Foo getting up, holding his gun. And he could hear screaming and stampeding from outside as well.

"Take boss's son away!" Foo screamed, pausing for a moment as his eyes adjusted to the glare of the exposed fluorescent lights behind the shattered stained glass, lighting up the room like an interrogation chamber.

Another blast of gunfire and Foo retreated behind the table, while Gavin crawled out of the way. Somewhere a fire had started, searing their flesh with its heat.

"Wait!" Gavin tried to call out to Foo, but Boon grabbed him and hauled him back to the exit while Foo cautiously approached the aquarium, clambering over jagged glass. Ah Leong held his own revolver aloft with another hand over his bleeding stomach, covering them as they burst from the door and into the club, where people were still trying to run, stampeding over upended chairs.

Gavin got to his feet as a fire alarm sounded belatedly. He turned back to the door, and he could see that Foo had disappeared behind the aquarium, and in the corner he saw the girl in the tank top. She was grasping her ankle, as if it was broken, and their eyes met for an instant, her tear-stricken face turning away as if she had seen into another world. Gavin wanted to run back and get her out but Ah Leong, his hands bloody, screamed, "Run, stupid boy!" and he turned from her and back to the exit.

They stumbled past the wrought-iron gates and Boon had already started up Ah Leong's car. Ah Leong stumbled into the back seat, grimacing and gasping, his revolver falling to the floor.

"Hide inside!" Boon ordered as Gavin scrambled into the front seat, while Boon ripped open a first-aid kit, dousing Ah Leong's fresh wound with antiseptic. The man screamed—surely he would attract the attention of the whole street. But people were running in the opposite direction, out of Bukit Bintang, and even the auxiliary officers in their beat bases were probably radioing their superiors for reinforcements.

Something doesn't make sense. Where's Foo? Surely we can't leave him?

"Dammit you fuck! Come back!" Boon screamed as Gavin plunged into a back alley after Foo. The gangster held up a bandage as Ah Leong spasmed feebly, life seeping from him.

>———————<

Foo was getting too old for running, and the gun was heavy in his grasp. The gunman from the Republic Club had run into the abandoned flat behind it. Four stories tall and currently occupied by drug addicts and other vagrants, he found an open door and raced inside. There were only lit candles and people were sobbing, moaning, or watching as he squirmed past them. He felt a sudden horror as he sidestepped broken needles on the floor and ran into a woman (or was it a man?) who clawed at him with a guttural yell.

"Where is he?" Foo yelled. When nobody answered, he fired at the ceiling. *Fuck these addicts!* Some people screamed while covering their heads and crying out to the gods they had forsaken long before, most people were silent, and a few pointed upwards.

"Thank you!" Foo took the stairs, gripping the rusted railings as he dragged himself forward. Where the hell was the man? The candlelight seemed to stop at the stairs. There was nobody on the second floor, or had they all run off or been killed? Foo raised the gun again. His breathing was heavy, and so was the gun. He was tired, and, for the first time, afraid. He was on his own now.

Then the firing began, bullets thudding into the wall behind him. The gunman had lured him there! He gasped as a bullet sliced through his wrist and smacked right into the wall of the flat. Then his legs gave out as his blood spurted onto the wall. He was screaming, sobbing, cursing in every dialect he knew as he sank to the floor. His gun was right there by his head, but his right hand was almost torn clean off, his brain fired by waves of pain.

The gunman approached him, stepping out of the shadows. Foo stared, the shape coming into focus. His eyes widened in shocked recognition.

"Maut?" he whispered. "Don't, please…"

Maut said nothing and fired his gun one last time.

>————————<

Gavin brought his knife out and crawled through the mess Foo had left behind in the Republic Club. He heard more screaming and the sound of police sirens. Then he was in the alley and the addicts and ancient trannies with their large Adam's apples had stumbled out into the lane. He stared at the decrepit apartment. *No, no, Foo isn't in there. How could he have gone in by himself? Or…*

There was silence as he entered. Everyone had either fled the building or was dead. "Foo?" he whispered. No reply.

A bloodied shoe had fallen down one of the steps, one of the loafers that Foo often wore. Gavin's heart was racing, trying to tell him it wasn't true, but he rounded the corner and saw Foo's corpse splayed on the steps, already congealing in his own blood. Gavin held the knife out, feeling unarmed. A sniper would be able to take him down, but he needed to check, just to be sure, that Foo really was dead.

He reached the top of the stairs and nearly retched. There wasn't much left to look at. Gavin turned away, the stench of death cloying, but he felt a terrible despair. *Foo's dead.* The man who taught him so much, who showed him how to use a knife and fire a gun, now lay dead in the rat-infested building. There was nothing he could do. Even the assassin was gone.

Then Gavin saw Foo's Stechkin lying next to him. He heard sirens from outside. Were the police approaching? He couldn't stay there, even if it meant abandoning Foo's body.

He saw the gun and took it. Without hesitating, he ran. He didn't turn back.

20
THE KING

Gunner was put on duty to protect Wong at the mansion that night. Maut hadn't been able to show up for some reason, and Wong made him stand by the front door with his safety catch off, ready to gun down any intruders. Eventually, he walked over the lawn to the Nepali at the gates. Old Wong was sitting at his desk in the living room, reading something. Gunner was in no mood to interrupt the old man.

"Quiet night for you, hah?" he said as he drew a puff from his cigarette. He stood by the open door of the guardhouse. He knew a bit of Nepalese and he often chatted with the guard, sometimes buying a chapatti for him.

"Yea," the Nepali said, glancing to offer a brief nod before turning back to the road. "Nothing ever happens here. Hard to believe that boss is a... crime lord."

"He looks like a harmless old man, doesn't he? But anyone can be harmless-looking. Politicians can look harmless, same with pedophiles and serial killers. Foo tells me that we should have seen him as a young man. They say he was the best."

A voice came over the CB radio.

"It's your friend Maut," the Nepali said, putting on a pair of headphones. Gunner smoked listlessly. The Nepali's head bobbed up and down before he put the headphones down.

"Gunner," the Nepali said, "Maut says to let the boss know he is coming. Says he has news."

Gunner hated being ordered around by the upstart assassin. Still, he had his orders. He turned back toward the house with a purposeful stride, ready to send the message to Old Wong.

><del>———————</del><

Retirement from crime didn't suit the young Wong well. He found that he was unable to concentrate as he worked at Muthiasamy Moneychangers in George Town. In addition to helping the staff with odd jobs, he sat at the front of the shop in uniform, with a shotgun loaded with cheap pellets ordered from across the Golok River. On weekends, when the moneychangers closed shop, he worked at a grocery store on Armenian Road.

In the evenings, he would walk over from the shop to the Chinese Advancement Society, where he joined a group of old men and women as they learnt, for the first time, to speak in faltering English. He struggled. He had studied nothing for years, and even those free lessons were difficult to follow, making him feel inadequate and out of touch. After dinner by the roadside, he would put on his other uniform and walk over to the E & O Hotel, where he opened the doors for well-heeled socialites. And after the same socialites left the hotel hours later, he would don a fresh batik shirt, one of those that Xue had brought for him from Malacca, before heading over to her house. She now lived on Cantonment Road with her grandmother, an ancient Nyonya whose Hokkien was laced with random Malay words, as well as other members of her extended family. Xue had moved there to work shortly after leaving school, and Wong, now freshly crime-free and trying to avoid the gangs of Kuala Lumpur, could think of nowhere better to go.

"Was your day all right?" Xue always said after letting him through the front gate, as they both sat on a cast-iron swing in the garden, facing the Japanese restaurant (and opium den) on the other side of the fence.

"It is fine," Wong always lied. "I like the work very much."

It wasn't, he thought as he left her at night, walking along Gurney Drive and staring at the dark straits. He was tired of his new life, even though his pay wasn't bad. The island felt like an illusion, too beautiful and welcoming. The idyllic place wasn't enough to make him feel safe. At night he could hardly sleep, wracked by the thought of Chang coming to the island with a machete, ready to slash him to death in the upstairs bedroom of his Victoria Street shophouse. He had brought his revolver with him; he wasn't free. Too late, he realized that there would be no escape from his old life.

With all those ominous thoughts, he wasn't surprised when Crazy Foo turned up one evening, unshaven and reeking of cheap beer, at the stall by the esplanade that Wong frequented before his night shift at the E & O.

"What are you doing here, brother?" Wong asked, embracing his old comrade.

"Ah Wong," drawled Foo. "Long time already. Come, I buy you a drink."

Foo had already brought some beer, and he handed a bottle to Wong.

"So why are you here?" Wong asked. "You have a dangerous reason, I'm sure."

Crazy Foo sighed. "Look, listen lah. There is problem with Chang; he is evil."

"We all know that already. Is he looking for me?"

"I told him you got killed by some Thais in a massage parlor. So you have no problem," Foo said. "But listen carefully first. There are a lot of people who are not happy with Boss Chang. Last week they plan to kill him already. I am supposed to help them assassinate him."

"What happened?" Wong demanded, gripping his chair. It was so surreal, discussing assassinations and crime in the capital while the sea breeze, smelling of salt and freshly grilled kembung fish, wafted through the air.

Foo pointed at his grizzled chin. "You think what? Boss Chang found out about us. He got some of his bodyguards to kill us. They attack us when we were having a drink in a kopitiam using a machine gun. Luckily I was in the toilet that time. I escape from the back door before they can find me. But everyone else is dead: Lucky Chew, Long Soong, Ah Niu, and even old Yew, the guy who own the coffeeshop. Where else can I go? I try to go back to my flat and I find out that Chang's bodyguards took all my money already. So I hitchhike here. It took me one week. And I also know you stay George Town mah. So it is very easy for me to find you."

Wong tried to think of something to say. "Listen, I will try to help you out," he said, feeling a stab of pity for Crazy Foo. "You stay with me first, like last time. I'll help you."

"Thanks, thanks. But I can only hide here temporary. Then I need to run away again. Chang knows where I am. I need to go and hide in Bangkok or something. Seriously, if I stay in Malaysia I will die for sure. He wants to find me. Last night, I was getting inside my bus at Ipoh station. I saw Chang's guys coming to the station. Lucky that my bus left and they didn't see me."

Wong was sweating now. "Are you sure you'll be safe? Chang's men are everywhere."

"Eh," Foo said, trying to smile. "I am Crazy Foo what! They cannot find me as long as I keep running."

Wong handed over the keys to his room. "Number 173, Victoria Street. Don't forget the address, OK? Go there and hide first. I have some food from lunch I didn't finish yet."

Foo departed gratefully, and left Wong sitting there. He didn't move for a long time. He was distracted all through his shift at the hotel, and during his usual meeting with Xue, he didn't speak as much as he usually did.

"What's wrong?" Xue asked as she walked him to the gate.

"I'm OK," Wong said, still trying to smile. "Don't worry about me."

He found Foo wide awake at the flat, polishing his gun with a fervor.

"Just to be careful," Foo said. "Dunno if can trust those fo-reign-ers outside. They might be working for Chang."

"OK," Wong said. He lay down on the mattress, while Foo lay on the thin blanket that Wong had given him, trying not to think about anything.

>————<

Maut arrived at the mansion on Cheras Hill. He had made his way back up the hill on a newly acquired motorcycle, past the Nepali guard who stared nervously back at the man with his hair freshly slicked back and his face impassive. His Glock still nestled in his holster as he limped up the steps of the mansion to brief Wong.

Wong was waiting for him inside, his hand twitching on his cane. Maut's eyes showed no emotion as usual and there was no telling what the assassin was thinking.

"I did what you asked," Maut said. "I went to the nightclub. Your son is alive. He is not hurt. Foo is dead."

Wong breathed in slowly. "So it is done. You're sure that Gavin is all right?"

"Only one man is dead."

"Thank you. I knew that I could trust you."

>————————<

Wong first saw the men two days after Foo arrived in Penang. Foo had been in and out of the flat frequently with a fake pair of glasses and his head shaved bald, making calls from a phone shop to Thailand, where he was trying to arrange for some of his contacts to take him in. Foo had assured him that he wouldn't be there long.

"If not they come and find you also," he said urgently. While Wong felt guilty about letting Foo go out on his own again, he assured himself that there was no other way. Both of them would die if Foo stayed in Penang longer than necessary.

The men were watching him from across the street at the E & O for the best part of an hour, trying not to be conspicuous as they sat at a construction site with other laborers. Wong tried not to look back at them. They were burly and burnt so brown from the sun that it was impossible to tell if they were Chinese or Malay. But that didn't matter. They were definitely killers. But would they hurt him? If they saw him with Foo they would, but if they didn't, they probably would leave him alone. He remembered Chang's widespread contacts, but the efficiency with which they hunted Foo down was terrifying. Did they recognize him too? What if Chang didn't believe that he was dead? He would be next.

He didn't visit Xue that night; he was too afraid. He jumped on a bus and left the stalkers far behind, and then he barricaded himself in the Victoria Street room. When Foo returned he looked at him in surprise.

"Our friends are here already," Wong said gravely. "You almost done?"

"Fuck," Foo said. "How the hell they find me? Never mind. I'll think of something."

"Foo," Wong said after a while. "Your friends in Thailand, they won't help you, will they?"

Foo laughed nervously. "I owe them some money for gambling. But we'll see. I think they don't mind helping me. Give me one more day. I try to settle with them first. After that, the stalkers won't disturb you anymore."

Two days passed. Wong didn't dare to see Xue and he was growing more frustrated and fearful. Foo was still at the apartment. One of Foo's contacts had refused to help and he'd turned to another one, bargaining with them in bad Thai. They were careful not to be seen together in public, but Wong had the feeling the stalkers knew exactly where he lived. Just the night before, he could have sworn he saw one of them walking outside the window, but when he checked again there was nobody in sight.

But he was prepared, just as he used to be. His revolver now nestled in a holster under his shirt. He thought of Xue. Was she worried? Would she end up going to the shophouse to look for him, only to run into the stalkers? Wong hadn't seen them that day, but he could never be sure.

He took the bus again and was deposited under a grove of casuarinas, where he walked down the alleys and toward the shophouse. He fumbled in his pocket for the keys. *Damn it! Where did I drop them?*

"Eh, you're back early," Foo said.

Wong turned around to see a bedraggled Foo limping down the street. "What happened to your leg?" Wong asked as Foo drew near.

"I saw the fuckers you tell me about," Foo said. "I was running and I fell down. Almost broke my leg. But they are gone already."

But Wong turned around. His keys had gone missing somewhere and they were out in the open. As if on cue, the two stalkers emerged out of nowhere on the quiet street holding out their guns. Wong didn't hesitate, dragging Foo down behind a flowerpot as the first shots whistled above them, smacking into the concrete. Wong reached for his gun but Foo already had his, crouching behind the flowerpot while firing wildly. Dogs barked and there were distant screams, but the silenced guns whistled again, the men coming closer this time. Wong managed to peer around the pot, and he fired carefully. One of the men shrieked, clutching his eye and falling to the ground. His cries distracted his partner for a moment, and Foo shot again. The second man hit the asphalt, a wound blossoming from his neck, next to his dying partner.

"Run!" Wong had finally found the keys and they hurried into the shophouse. Nobody was there, the landlord either out for drinks or cowering under his bed. But the police would be there soon. They took everything they had and were on the run again. Wong stopped at the end of the street, staring from behind a pillar as police cars drew up outside the shophouse, surrounding the dead killers. Then he turned away and continued walking again.

"Sorry," Foo said at last. "It is my fault."

"No," Wong said. "Forget Thailand." He shook with anger. "Boss Chang will come for us. We need to fight. If not, he will always hunt us down."

"How?"

Wong thought of all the people Chang had ever whipped or humiliated. "All of us," he said.

A day later, he was at the house on Cantonment Road. It was the middle of the afternoon and Xue would be at work, typing in the office. Wong stood there with his gun in its holster, ready to return to the place he had run away from only two years before. He would go back to Kuala Lumpur to fight Chang. But he felt a terrible regret. He had promised her he would leave the gangs behind, but his past had caught up with him.

The Cambodian maid eventually saw him and came out. "Yes, sir? So early today?"

"Please, take a message to Miss Xue," Wong said softly. "Tell her I'm sorry, and I will be back soon."

He left before the maid could say anything else.

>————<

Maut had been spying on Foo for some time, on Wong's orders. He had reported nothing unusual to Wong—until the week before. Foo had let slip he was unhappy with the gang and was planning to go ahead with the Day of Judgment, bringing Gavin with him. Old Wong felt a terrible anger at Foo's betrayal. Despite everything he and Foo had gone through for decades, he couldn't show mercy. It had to end before Foo ordered the men to attack Ah Fung II and his men.

Almost as soon as Maut left with a new payment for his services, Gunner re-entered the room, bowing to him. "Mr. Wong, what happened?"

"Maut was following Foo on my orders," Wong lied easily. "After what has been happening in the last few weeks, Foo is a big target for Ah Fung II and his assassins. So I sent Maut to be his bodyguard. Maut was following them secretly when he heard shooting from a nightclub that Foo and my son were in. He tried to follow Foo and found out he had been killed."

"Wait, what about your son?"

"Gavin is fine. But he's probably terrified. Go and contact Ah Leong or Boon, they should be with Gavin. Make sure he's OK. Guard his apartment as well tonight. Tell them I will call or visit soon."

"What about you, boss?" Wong could see that Gunner was shaking.

"Maut will be coming back later. It's supposed to be his shift tonight anyway."

A muscle twitched under Gunner's skin. "You really trust Maut ah?"

"Yes. He does exactly what he is told."

Gunner left Wong to his thoughts. Wong resisted the temptation to call Gavin. No, Gavin didn't need people to talk to him. He would settle everything on his own. Perhaps the next morning he would drive down to the boy's apartment to ask him if anything was the matter. But for now Gavin needed rest. So did Wong.

As he took to the stairs, he thought of Foo. Foo had been a good man, the bravest and best lieutenant. But he had gone too far. None of it would have happened if Foo hadn't been so stupid…

May Heaven forgive me, Wong thought bitterly. *I am sorry, my friend.*

>———————<

Wong waited in the back of a Mercedes lorry, along with ten of the killers from the gang who managed to escape from Chang. He and Foo had arrived in Kuala Lumpur the week before, staying in a seedy hotel called the Laksamana that some of Foo's allies owned.

Between them they had three hundred rounds of ammunition and five grenades in the truck, hidden under cans of rat poison. Foo was driving and they were near the gambling den in Cheras where Chang went for his weekly fix. One by one the men exited the truck, decamping in the alley. At that hour, the restaurants were closed and only the gambling den was still open. The gamblers had an unspoken agreement with the police: in return for keeping their own turf clean, the police would keep out. Perfect. Wong lined the men up. Chang's Alfa Romeo was down the street. Once Chang was done for the night, one of his men would drive it down to the back entrance, from which he would leave for his mansion in Seremban.

They waited, concealed in the crannies of the alley. The mosquitoes were out in full force but Wong didn't care, sweating heavily. He would put an end to everything that night.

At last, one of the men walked out of the den, swinging a bunch of keys in his hand. Chang would be out soon. Wong watched as the Alfa Romeo's headlights lit up and coasted toward them.

Chang emerged, surrounded by a knot of his most loyal bodyguards. Wong had heard rumors that Chang's most trusted men were paid in gold each month, and if they died in his service their families would receive a pension. Wong counted eight bodyguards flanking him. There were twelve killers that night. It was an equal match. He raised his gun and took aim at the nearest bodyguard's head.

On his cue, everyone fired. Shots were aimed at the bodyguards, and some of them fell instantly, while others bundled Chang out of the way, dragging him behind a wall. They unfastened automatic rifles from inside their coats and fired back. Wong ducked and heard screams as a barrage of gunfire raked his men. The Alfa Romeo had arrived as well and Foo led the attack, riddling the car with bullets. Three grenades were thrown. One bounced off the car and exploded in the doorway of the illegal casino. A second blew a bodyguard to pieces. A third failed to detonate and was kicked away. Then the shooters turned on Foo and his men cowered.

Amidst the smoke, Wong saw that the bulletproofed Alfa Romeo had been dented but not completely damaged. And he could see the last surviving bodyguards thrusting the door open and bundling Chang inside, where he took the wheel himself. One last burst of gunfire and the car was revving up, trying to escape. Another grenade was thrown, shattering the windows of the car, but it was still running, racing up the street.

Wong was already running. There was only one chance to kill Chang now. Their bullets were running out and the grenades were all but useless. He had to reach the lorry.

He found it in the alley and scrabbled up the ladder, getting into the front seat. The keys were still there and he turned the ignition. The machine roared to life and he reversed out of the alley. The Alfa would have to make a U-turn to get back on the road to Seremban, and he would be ready for it.

The car was coming down the street, its engine screaming. Wong turned the wheel and pushed the gear stick with all his might, his feet alternating between clutch and accelerator with little regard for the brakes...

The Alfa's horn was blaring and he could see that Chang was driving the car. Wong shifted to the highest gear and found himself on a collision course with Chang's car...

The next thing he knew, he was on the roadside, and Foo was there.

"Lucky you alive," Foo said, clutching a handful of bloodied bandages. "Serious."

"Chang?" Wong asked.

"Die already," Foo said. Wong looked up and could see the wreckage of the Alfa and the lorry. He tried to get up but could hardly walk.

"Come," Foo said. There were police sirens already and a Toyota was nearby, ready to pick them up. "We'll go back to the Laksamana and rest, huh? Congratulations, good job. We win. Now Boss Chang is dead."

>———————<

Maut was at the door when Gunner got his backpack, ready to leave. Gunner stared at Maut on his way out. The new assassin was unreadable. And he had been there when Foo died. Gunner felt a creeping unease. Maut had risen so quickly in their ranks. *Did Wong really trust him so much?*

"Make sure you take care of boss," he warned.

Maut said nothing and just watched Gunner leave the grounds. Gunner was tired and wanted nothing better than to sleep, to forget the fact that Foo was now dead. But first, he needed to find Gavin. The boy had insisted on going to the morgue at the police station to claim Foo's corpse. It seemed like Foo was more of a father to Gavin than Wong ever was. But who was he to talk? He had to go to the morgue to make sure the boy wouldn't do anything stupid.

Gunner got on the motorcycle, adjusted his helmet, and sped down Cheras Hill toward the police station.

>———<

Wong returned to Penang a fortnight later. He had a new shirt on and he was exhausted. A week had gone by with him hardly sleeping, as he tried to forge ahead with the newly established syndicate. Chang's remaining loyal men had been threatened at gunpoint and had left the city. There was a funeral in Seremban and what was left of Boss Chang's body was cremated, and chief among the mourners was the kingpin's eldest son, Kok Chye, back from his studies at the NUS in Singapore. Wong had read the news with interest, staring at the picture of the stocky young man in a black suit at the crematorium. Meanwhile, from the ruined ballroom of Hotel Laksamana he led the swearing-in of his new gang with Foo by his side. Wong raised a hand, making them swear allegiance. *No exploitation of the helpless. No killing without justification. No drugs and excessive alcohol.*

Foo was left in charge of the syndicate as Wong returned to Gurney Drive, walking toward the old house. He rang the doorbell. The Cambodian maid went to the gate at once, but she hesitated before opening it. It was as if something had visibly changed in Wong over the last month.

"Miss Xue told me to let you in when you arrived," she said nervously as Wong hurried to the front door, slipping off his brogues. He met the matriarch, an old woman who sat at the dining table with a porcelain teacup before her.

Wong bowed as she regarded him with an iron stare.

"You are Wong Kah Lok, aren't you?" she said.

"Yes, madam. Miss Xue has told you about me?"

"Indeed. Everything," the matriarch replied, staring him up and down. "You look like a respectable man, Master Wong. But we all know how men can hide their stripes. Treat my granddaughter well, do you understand?"

"Yes, madam." Wong bowed again.

"Sareiy, take Mister Wong to Miss Xue's room," she said to the maid.

The maid showed Wong up to the room while Wong heard the old woman coughing from down below. The maid eventually stopped at a room on the third floor, and Wong knocked. "Come in." He heard Xue's voice. He hesitated for a moment, afraid that she would turn him away, and entered, closing the door.

Xue was ill, and she lay on the bed under a thin blanket while an electric fan stirred up the sea air from the window.

"So you have come back at last," she said.

"Yes," Wong said, sitting next to her. "I… I couldn't leave you behind."

"I read the newspapers," she said, finally turning to him. Her eyes were wide with confusion, anger and fear. "They say there was a gang war in Cheras, and many people were killed. One of them was your old boss and they haven't caught the murderers. It was you, wasn't it?"

Wong told her everything. She didn't interrupt. "You should leave me," he said. His voice was wavering and threatened to break down. "Find someone else, a good man, maybe an honest businessman."

She didn't say anything for a long time as her fingers tightened around his.

"I will stay with you," she said.

Wong smiled, but he didn't know if he was happy or regretful. All he could do was stroke her forehead. She seemed so fragile under his calloused palms.

"You have a fever," he said. "You should rest for now. Tomorrow you will be much better."

He left after she fell asleep, dreaming of a world in which Wong was finally free.

21
THE CHANCELLOR

Chancellor Zahid was exhausted after spending the day meeting with reporters, corrupt politicians and Arab bankers, who all wanted his opinion. What was the meaning of the brazen assassination in Bukit Bintang? One Chinaman had been murdered, a girl was injured, and three drug addicts were in hospital. What did it have to do with the future of Malaysian security? How would the MACC tackle the corruption that was eating away at all levels of a government that allowed gangsters to roam the streets?

Of course, Ramalingam would be getting the brunt of it. The poor bastard had been raked over the coals so often in the last few days that Zahid almost felt sorry for him. He had gotten off quite lightly by comparison. They just wanted to know what he thought. Zahid was just a businessman and a minor official. They hadn't been able to dig much deeper yet, and he was grateful. There was still a lot lurking under the surface. The reporters had been on his father's trail for years. The old Tan Sri hadn't been very good at covering his tracks, unlike Zahid, and had paid the price with his own expulsion from Parliament while Zahid was still completing his studies at the London School of Economics. They only had to dig a little deeper and they would find out the things he'd done to pay his way into the government.

He sat in his office at Putrajaya, staring out of the window. There hadn't been much work that day, mostly supervising his subordinate clerks in the morning and returning to his desk to await further instructions from the higher-ups. But he knew they didn't want to push him too hard. After all, he was still the son of a Tan Sri, the chancellor of a local college, and a wannabe member of Parliament to boot.

He noted the date by when he had to submit his details to the Election Commission. That would give him four months. He cursed inwardly. Ramalingam wasn't doing a very good job of running things. Zahid was starting to believe that he had overestimated the man ever since he first met him during a reception on Independence Day.

>———————<

Zahid had been at another reception, a fundraiser for a politician. He mingled with the VIPs in their sharp suits and marveled at the congregation of gangsters in the ballroom of the Hilton. Damn! He never realized Datuk X consorted with so many gangsters. Zahid hadn't spoken to any of the men, preferring to nibble on the kuih after the main course. He saw Datuk X with the PM's aides and his latest wife, a former actress-turned-leatherback-turtle-activist called Erra. Datuk X had all the luck, while Zahid was stuck with a lowly position in the MACC and a third-rate college. His wife had left him the previous year after an argument over money, and then shacked up with a French racecar driver she met in Sepang the next month.

"So, Chancellor, why your face so sour?" the Datuk greeted him as he prepared to go home.

"It's nothing, Datuk," Zahid mumbled. "But how can you allow these men to come here? There are other VIPs around!"

Zahid was staring at the back of Hashim Samseng, head of one of the notorious rempit gangs that roamed the highways, their motorcycles speeding uncontrollably in the night. It was well known that Datuk X relied on Hashim Samseng to do some of his dirty work (such as beating up and threatening rivals), but Zahid hadn't expected Hashim to turn up at a political fundraiser.

Datuk X laughed. "We're all friends here!"

He gestured at the gangster, then at the PM's aides and the assortment of VIPs. "I certainly must invite all my friends. And nobody can touch us or complain. Bring one of us down, and all our friends will be out for your blood!"

That explained it, Zahid thought as his driver took him back to his house by the lake in Mont Kiara. *Friends and connections made all the difference.* Datuk X was like the Hydra with multiple heads—unlike his father.

Zahid remembered growing up in their house in Taman Duta. His father, Yunus Ishak, had been a rising star in the government. Yunus won seat after seat without having to mention his Indian wife, his occasional affairs, and his penchant for heavy liquor—all of that happened behind closed doors. He trusted nobody and refused to join the cliques that sprang up within the government. So when Yunus ran head to head against one of the big shots, the big shot's friends made sure to tarnish his reputation. They brought out all their ammunition and sent it to the press. Yunus Ishak lost the race and, with it, his reputation. The old man resigned, and halfway across the globe, Zahid, who was completing his thesis in a rented room in London, could feel the reverberations. He stopped working for a few days, wandering around Piccadilly Circus and Tottenham Court Road, drinking heavily while he followed the news.

Reporters hounded his father, standing outside the gates of the Duta manor. Zahid spent the winter alone in London, watching as his father eventually resigned due to the shame and refused to emerge from his own house, instead sending his servants to chase away the reporters at the gates. When Zahid returned to Malaysia, back to the desiccating heat and the oil palms, he chose not to live in Duta and moved to Bangsar. He couldn't risk being seen with the old man, whom everyone said was losing his mind. Those fellows in government had long memories and despised his father. It would be unwise to side with him.

Zahid didn't choose Ramalingam randomly. He had pored over a list of possible candidates. But Ramalingam was the most dedicated officer, with retirement scheduled and nothing left to lose. So he had hinted to the IGP on Independence Day that he wanted to meet with the old inspector. In the end, the frail man with his walking stick and patched uniform didn't exactly impress Zahid but he could see the fire still burning in the inspector's eyes. He invited the man to dinner at the Mandarin Oriental and watched him carefully. Ramalingam made only polite conversation, even as Datuk X and the other guests made crude and bawdy jokes.

"Hihi, hudud law!" Datuk X had hiccupped. "We can't possibly live like that, no! If so, I have to hide my whiskey here at the Mandarin Oriental!"

Later that night, after a cigar-smoking session which Ramalingam abstained from, a guest remarked, "Eh, Daud, take care of your kid. I think he's one of the delinquents going around with racist street gangs and bombing churches."

Eventually Zahid saw his cue. "Look at the crime in our country. We have an army, 100,000 police officers, the FRU, and they can't deal with gangsters? They are useless, only good for beating up civilians."

He saw Ramalingam looking at him curiously, while the other VIPs continued their childish posturing.

Ya Allah, thought Zahid. He hated all these men with their blatant lies and their ties to the underworld. They were mere parasites crawling under the nation's skin. But they still didn't trust Zahid enough to invite him to their private functions, their children's birthday parties or marathon golfing sessions at KLGCC. No, they still remembered his father. Damn them. If he could, he would have happily destroyed every man in the room.

After the VIPs left, Ramalingam stayed behind at Zahid's request. Zahid cut another cigar and offered it to Ramalingam, who once again declined.

"You are a man of principles, eh?" Zahid said, sucking on the Cuban. "I wish I could say the same for myself. You know all the news circulating about me? That they're calling me the Sheikh just because I went to a madrasa in Egypt for a year, and how I don't drink, at least not publicly? Nonsense! I don't care for any of that. I'm a rational man like you."

"What do you want me here for, Chancellor Zahid?" Ramalingam cut to the chase.

Zahid debated on whether to tell Ramalingam the truth but decided against it. Ramalingam would surely know, or would at least find out soon, especially with the services of the police force. They would dig up the entire invisible, unspeakable world that Zahid had kept hidden.

He was especially worried about Wong Kah Lok. Zahid first met the man more than twenty years ago, when the construction of Yohan Eng College started. Zahid had been involved in backing the project, his first big job. Upon returning from London and Egypt, there was little for Zahid to do in Kuala Lumpur. No political future beckoned, especially after Tan Sri Yunus Ishak's very public meltdown. There was still that psychiatrist visiting him once a week, for God's sake! Zahid was stuck on his own. He started out by bankrolling a printing agency that produced Qurans, but there was never much money in it. Later, he bought shares in some car companies with what was left of his father's money, and that went much better.

Now Zahid dreamt of starting a college. It seemed like a good idea, especially with the nouveau riche trying to send their pampered offspring to Sydney, London, New York and Toronto. But the construction ran into problems. One of the other financiers was bleeding the construction funds dry. At first, Zahid tolerated him taking cutbacks from his contractors, but the construction was running behind schedule and had exceeded its original budget. The worst part was that Zahid couldn't do anything about it. His rival was too well connected and a relative of Datuk X's.

Zahid met the young kingpin, Wong Kah Lok, at the Laksamana Hotel, and noticed the other Chinamen filing out, leaving him alone with Wong.

"So you want to kill him?" Wong mused. "That will be very difficult, and you're not the first to ask. He is very well protected and it's not worthwhile going after him."

"I will lose all my money if he's still alive! I have no choice."

"What can you give me?"

"Money. As much as you want," Zahid offered desperately.

"Money is not an issue," Wong said. "We have enough. But what you *can* give us is protection. There is a policeman rising in the force, his name is Ramalingam. He seems determined to stop my men and me for good. If we let him carry on, he will make a lot of trouble for us. What I need right now is an assurance. You will help me keep Inspector Ramalingam in check. Use your connections. Stop him from getting promoted and trap him where he is. Can you do that?"

"It will be difficult."

"But it won't cost you a sen," Wong said. "And right now you need your money, don't you?"

Grudgingly, Zahid agreed and kept his end of the bargain. He didn't know Ramalingam personally but a few coffee chats with the deputy IGP would keep Ramalingam in his place for several years. A week later, Wong's end of the bargain was fulfilled. The crooked financier was found dead while holidaying on an island. Official autopsy result: drowned in a freak accident.

From then on, Zahid returned to Wong whenever he needed help. There was a lot that he couldn't get done by himself, especially with no connections. But Wong and his assassins opened doors for him. Zahid realized that if anyone looked deeply enough, they would find out he was in cahoots with Wong. His political future would be ruined, especially since he intended to run for Parliament. Zahid's rivals and their friends wouldn't hesitate to bring him down, just like they had brought down his father. Perhaps he would even, God forbid, end up in jail or on the gallows.

Back in the ballroom of the Mandarin Oriental, he stared at Ramalingam, wondering how much to tell him.

"It's simple," Zahid said at last. "I need your help, Inspector."

22
DEATH WISH

Boon drove the Mercedes with Wong in the back seat, the car fighting through the traffic. He felt light-headed as they squeezed and inched along the rutted roads. There was some sort of event in the city but Wong didn't know what it was.

"Boon?" he demanded. "What's going on?"

"Demonstration, boss," Boon said, shrugging.

Wong stared ahead at the huge banners being held aloft, rippling like floating fish. A hundred thousand people were on the move, chanting for democracy and justice while the motorists in front had stopped, honking in jubilation, not caring that they were being delayed by the demonstrators. Those people didn't know that even if they succeeded in getting their message across, things would never change. People like Wong ruled the city. The police wouldn't touch them, nor would the law protect them from crime and violence. Things would continue as before.

Boon had received a panicked call from Ah Leong. Two days after Foo's assassination, Gavin snuck out of his apartment again and went straight to the hospital morgue. Crazy Foo's refrigerated corpse lay in storage like a hock of ham. Gavin showed up and demanded they return Foo's body. The desk sergeant at KLGH asked to see some identification. Gavin was on edge and the sergeant suspected something was amiss. He put a call through to Ramalingam, who ordered the desk sergeant to arrest Gavin at once.

"Bastard inspector!" Boon growled. "He think he so tough, is it? Can arrest your son?"

"Let him," Wong said.

Boon kept quiet, now worried he'd said or done something rash. It had been that way since he'd run away from Muar. He had challenged a small-town gangster, who was trying to steal his master's car, and they started fighting. The fight only ended after Boon slammed the gangster's head into a streetlamp, killing the man just as his boss, the big shot, arrived. The big shot looked at the body and laughed. "Luckily tomorrow is Cheng Beng," the big shot said. "Take him to the temple and hide him inside the big pit where they burn the offerings. Nobody will find him."

Boon was terrified by the big shot's callousness. Instead of driving the body to the temple that night, he snuck away from the big shot's house and left Muar on a late-night Transnasional, and then wound up in Hotel Laksamana. He ended up working for Wong, whom he regarded as a more benign gangster—a gentleman, really.

But now Boon saw the silent anger in Wong's eyes. He realized Wong wanted Gavin to be punished, and he began to sweat buckets. Did Wong know about how he, Ah Leong, and the late Foo had been conspiring behind his back?

Boon realized how Old Wong had known: Maut, of course. That dirty swine! Boon had heard rumors from Gunner that Maut went to the mansion on Cheras Hill once a week, ostensibly to report on things and run odd jobs for Wong. The old man must have been using Maut to spy on all of them.

An outrageous thought crossed Boon's mind: could Old Wong have ordered the hit on Foo for his disobedience? It sounded impossible but there was no black and white in Wong's world. Boon's hands were clammy and he gripped the wheel harder.

"You're sweating," Wong noticed. "Turn up the air-con if it is hot."

Wong knew everything, damn it! Now he was playing mind games while Boon trembled like a terrified rat in the storm sewers of the city.

"There's more news," Boon said, trying to change the subject. "Now that Foo die already, I will report the assassinations. Besides Crazy Foo, yesterday got five more of our men who died. Two were in a brothel in Ipoh and got stabbed, another guy got drowned in a swimming pool in a hotel in Kuantan, then got two more who die after their car got rammed off the road in Genting Highlands."

Their communications had been messy. The night before, Wong had summoned Boon and Ah Leong to his house. Since Foo was dead, Ah Leong would take over operations until a suitable replacement was found. Boon would assist Ah Leong as usual, but now he felt afraid. What if Wong tried to kill them all? If he was going to punish his own son, what would happen if (no, *when*) Wong discovered how they had all been betraying him?

"I think the highway is open," Boon said, breaking the silence.

"There's no hurry. Let's watch the demonstration," Wong said as the car ground to a halt again before the sea of men, women and children marching down the streets in defiance of the blue-suited policemen.

>———————<

Gavin's head throbbed. He had barely slept the whole night. Everything had been a blur since Foo's shooting. Ah Leong had got over the shock of being shot. Gavin stayed with him as Boon extracted the slug from under the flimsy padding that Ah Leong insisted was a bulletproof vest. Gavin hadn't winced while he watched the operation. He only felt the weight of Foo's Russian revolver in the pocket of his jeans. The horror of Crazy Foo's death unleashed something deep inside Gavin and he knew there would be no escape now. He had seen Foo, his only real friend and mentor, dead. Revenge, he needed revenge. He recited the words like a mantra. It wasn't a choice. Ah Fung II and his men had gone too far with the shooting.

As Ah Leong lay groaning and cursing in Cantonese, Boon took Gavin to the back of the Hotel Laksamana where they were out of earshot.

"Listen, you stay out of this," he said sternly. "You almost die, OK? If you die, then how? Think of the old man. You know why he hired me? To keep your family safe. Because I didn't do my job properly they are all dead. I was supposed to protect them last time. By the time I went inside the restaurant, Ah Fung II escape already and your mother and brother are dead. Your father also almost cripple. Now, before you get assassinated, I want to tell you first: stay out of this."

Gavin didn't respond. He stayed there all night. When morning arrived, Ah Leong was well enough to use a pair of crutches stolen from the crippled man who lived along one of the corridors in the hotel, and he went into the room Gavin was sleeping in.

"Go back home," Ah Leong croaked, clutching the wound under his vest. "Your father doesn't know about you. Pretend nothing happened."

"You know what we need to do," Gavin mumbled. "We need to finish what Foo started. The Day of Judgment."

Ah Leong was silent for a moment. "It is the right thing to do. But you can't be part of it. Think of your father. The pain will kill him."

But Gavin wouldn't listen. He was thinking of Foo, and how Foo was rotting away in a refrigerator in the morgue. The man had no wife, or at least none that Gavin knew of.

"Foo has no family, right?" Gavin mumbled as Ah Leong escorted him back to the Mercedes-Benz.

Ah Leong shrugged. "Not really," he said as he slammed the door of the car. The car made its way out of Pudu, past the empty chicken coops and grimy lorries on the potholed streets outside the public market.

"Foo has a daughter—dunno what happened to her—from an earlier marriage. The wife is dead. The daughter is in Hong Kong, I think? Working at a casino somewhere. They don't keep in touch."

Gavin returned to his apartment, knowing fully well that Ah Leong was keeping watch outside. Ah Leong had stashed a Chinese-manufactured copy of a micro Uzi in the glove compartment of the Mercedes ever since the assassinations had intensified. Gavin felt a terrible sickness. The same men who killed Crazy Foo would surely come for him next, or maybe his father.

He hadn't thought of his father since Foo's death. All he remembered was Foo's mutilated body. But he assured himself that Old Wong was perfectly safe in his mansion on the hill. It was gated, and guarded by a Nepali who had fought in the army. The doors were reinforced at great cost and Wong had a permanent staff of five men patrolling the house. And now there was Maut, going to and fro like a member of Wong's inner circle.

Gavin sprawled on the bed, frowning. *Something's not quite right with this picture.*

He dozed off again, neither asleep nor awake, and he was back in the train station with Danielle. He knew it was a dream because he couldn't remember that meeting happening in real life. But it felt so vivid. He was there in a gray jacket while the sky was choked with the smoke of a thousand fires from across the straits, waiting as Danielle's long-haul Intercity pulled into the station. They embraced on the platform of the old KL station, while diesel fumes merged with the haze around them.

"So you decided to leave after all," she said, smiling, her eyes wide and shining, betraying a sudden hope.

Gavin, in his dream, shrugged.

But he woke up again, drenched in sweat and hating himself for the dream. *All of it was a lie*, he thought, as he stared out of the stained windows of his apartment and at the blood-red horizon.

Eventually he decided to go to the morgue. He returned to the car park. No doubt Ah Leong would post a few men around the apartment block after his last escape. But there was always a way out. Gavin handed a bunch of notes to the old jaga, who gave him a lift out of the building in his beat-up Proton Wira. And then Gavin was once again on the streets of Bukit Bintang, but this time he roamed them alone. There was no Crazy Foo by his side any longer, no Danielle either. This time, he would retrieve Foo's body.

>————<

Gavin woke up in a cell the day after being arrested. He had never been inside a cell before, yet he was unafraid. He was angry because he had been nowhere near Foo's body before getting handcuffed and led away into a police car.

He heard a walking stick tapping the floor and looked up, not surprised to see Inspector Ramalingam on the other side of the bars. Gone was the shabby old Indian who greeted him outside the steps of Yohan Eng College. In his place was a man, enfeebled by age, who still wore his uniform smartly and looked at him with an iron stare.

"Good morning, Gavin," Ramalingam croaked. "I am sorry about the way we had to treat you. The desk sergeant was only trying to talk some sense into you when you tried to punch him. This is for your own good, you know."

"Where is Foo?" Gavin demanded.

"None of his relatives or next of kin showed up to claim him." Ramalingam wasn't leaning on his cane any longer. "Because of this, the hospital cremated him last night. That's what they do with all the dregs of society, you see."

Gavin felt sick to his stomach and an intense, burning hatred for Ramalingam. The inspector was old, yes, but there was no denying he was still out for blood. "You fucker!" he began.

Ramalingam listened as Gavin screamed and cursed, but he didn't flinch. "I had no choice, Gavin. That is the law. But understand this: I will not tolerate your father's crimes any longer. You know as well as I that the Chang gang is resurgent and picking your father's men off, one by one. I estimate that at least twelve of the syndicate's best assassins have been killed, as well as dozens of flunkies. Your father's top henchman is now dead. But there is a way out of this."

"What are you talking about?" Gavin asked, afraid for once.

"I can make them stop. I am giving you an ultimatum. Deliver this message to your father: if he surrenders now and goes to prison, all of this will end."

"You can't control Ah Fung II," Gavin blurted, unable to stop himself.

"On the contrary," Ramalingam said, his expression suddenly animated. "I have a friend, my Lieutenant Samad, a former conman and killer. He can be very persuasive. If I so wish, I can order Samad to make the attacks stop by tonight. But all of this depends on what your father does."

Gavin swore. He ran out of words to express his outrage and anger. Ramalingam was tired now, and he took a seat outside the cell.

"Let me tell you something," he said. "I am sick of the slaughter. I have the means to make these attacks stop. I made a deal with your father once. Somebody I cared for died because of me, and I had to take revenge, you see. I needed your father's help. Perhaps someday he'll tell you about it? I let him roam free in exchange, letting him do whatever he liked. He became the King of Petaling Street. He did what he wanted, building up his squad while I looked the other way. But now I'm old and losing my memory. I used to be known as the crimebuster of KL, but not anymore. I'm just a failed police inspector in an unimportant station. I've been content to let these attacks continue, because it has been the only way to cut your father down to size. But I've had enough."

Gavin spat. When he looked up again, Ramalingam had already left.

>———<

Wong's Mercedes pulled up outside the police station. His knee was weak and Boon helped him walk to the entrance, dressed like the old men he saw in the coffeeshops around the city. Wong had spent so much time inside his mansion that it had become his whole world. Boon didn't accompany him inside, preferring to wait in the shade of the meranti trees.

Wong entered the station and remembered the time he was hauled in for Ah Fung's murder, and how he was completely fearless back then. But now he was afraid.

"Where is my son?" he demanded to the clerk. He was directed to the cells at the back. At the doors to the lock-up, Ramalingam waited for him.

"Release Gavin," Wong said. "You have no right to detain him."

"We are Malaysians," Ramalingam said, shrugging. "Rights don't make a difference, Mr. Wong. But I will let him out now that you are here. He didn't do anything too bad. You need to sign some papers first."

There was something in Ramalingam's voice that made Wong uneasy, but he ignored the feeling.

"How do you like things now?" Ramalingam asked as Wong's trembling hand scrawled his signature on the forms.

"You know nothing," Wong shot back.

"But I do," Ramalingam said quietly. "I have a death wish, you see. My memory is fading. Only Bangsawan Heights comes back to me with perfect clarity. I see it every night in my dreams, when I forget my friends and my relatives and even the things I have done. I don't wish to live to the point when I only have Bangsawan Heights to keep me company. I don't want to be trapped, reliving that every night when I sleep… Do you remember what happened when you gave me information? I let you do what you wanted. The press vilified me. They said that crime was rising but I made a deal with you. There was nothing I could do to save my reputation. I hate you, Kah Lok. And I will tell you this: I won't hesitate to bring you down for good."

Wong saw the fury etched on Ramalingam's lined face, and understood how badly Ramalingam's life had fallen apart. "Here," he said, thrusting the forms at Ramalingam. "Let him out."

Ramalingam gestured to an officer, and a moment later, there was a creaking of rusty door hinges. Gavin, bedraggled and exhausted, was manhandled out of the cell. Wong reached out to steady Gavin, but his son pushed past him. Wong cast a look back at Ramalingam, but he had already left, hobbling up the stairwell to his office.

"Gavin, what happened?" Wong demanded, trying to catch up with Gavin as he emerged into the unfamiliar sunlight.

"Thank you for getting me out," Gavin said, not looking back.

"Gavin, please tell me," Wong said. "I'm not much of a father but tell me what happened. Why were you in lock-up?"

He knew why Gavin was there. He was furious that Gavin was part of the syndicate, against his direct orders. But he couldn't bring himself to curse and scream at Gavin. Without Gavin, he was alone in the world.

Gavin couldn't speak to his father. The old man's callousness, his pretending that Foo's death meant nothing, was enough to drive Gavin into a blind fury. Wong hadn't known that Gavin was there the night Foo died, barely escaping death, kneeling beside the lifeless body of his father's only friend.

"Gavin, please, come back to the mansion. It is not safe for you outside," Wong insisted as Gavin hurried further and further ahead.

No reply.

"Gavin!"

Gavin had almost reached the car without stopping when Wong felt something snap inside him.

"You know why I won't fucking fight back?" he shouted. "I don't want you to…" Wong couldn't bring himself to finish the sentence.

Gavin had his phone back from the police, and he was still upset. He didn't care what the old man thought. He had sent a message to Ah Leong and the swift reply came back with a surprising calmness.

`Tonight confirm. Day of Judgment.`

The thought had been burning away like a flame in the back of his skull. Foo wouldn't have died for nothing. That night, everything would change.

23
DAY OF JUDGMENT

"What is happening?" Wong demanded. "Where are all the men?"

He was pacing around the mansion. Only Ah Leong was there that afternoon, watching as Old Wong began losing his calm. Several of his usual guards had left their posts and he had no idea where they'd gone. He summoned Ah Leong at once. His new chief lieutenant arrived, blank-faced.

"Do you want to know what's really going on?" Ah Leong said.

"Everything," demanded Wong.

Ah Leong chose his words carefully. "Your son was with Foo when he died. He organized all of this. I worked with him. Me and Boon and Gunner and whoever was left. At the moment Gavin is sitting in your chair at the Laksamana, ordering the Day of Judgment."

"Foo?" Wong gasped. "Foo taught him all of this. And you were planning this behind my back all along?"

"No choice. Foo died. Ah Fung II and his men must be punished."

Wong pictured the scene. There were at least thirty assassins who were not yet incapacitated or killed. He saw them with their submachine guns in Semenyih, pulling revolvers from their holsters in the old town of Ipoh, unloading plastic explosives from the boots of their cars in Shah Alam, and loading bullets into well-oiled chambers in Tanjung Malim. That night, hell would be unleashed. In one synchronized attack, Ah Fung II and his men would be crippled once and for all. "Call it off! I order you, call it off!"

"I will not take orders from you any longer," Ah Leong said. "You are no longer useful as a leader. Gavin has given them permission to begin the killings. I must go now."

"Fuck you, Ah Leong!" cursed Wong. He hurried to the telephone. "I'll speak to him, talk some sense into the boy."

He dialed but there was no reply. He dialed again, to no avail. Gavin was on his own.

"Why did you let him do it?" Wong screamed at Ah Leong, who remained unmoved.

"Because you won't," Ah Leong said simply. "Think about it: we will end the war now. They will not harm our operation any longer, sir. Understand that. This is the right thing to do."

"You are a traitor." Wong sank into his chair, clenching and unclenching his fists.

"It is for the best." Ah Leong turned on his heel, leaving the old man in his mansion.

Wong realized that there was only one thing he could do. He had to send a warning to Ah Fung II, the man who nearly killed him so many years ago.

There was a painting on the wall of the mansion. A hajal bird was in full flight, escaping from a window and the jeweled hands of an Arab warlord, the desert mountains imposing yet indistinct in the background. The bird was enmeshed in the folk tales told by parents to their children in Syria. It was the symbol of the original Assassins, an order of killers who fought the Crusaders before being eradicated by their enemies. Who had told him the story? Zahid, of course.

>————————<

Zahid had invited him to a game at the Subang Golf Club. That was after he helped Zahid out with arranging the assassination of his rival, and just as Zahid was busy amassing his illegal wealth with the help of Wong's men.

"You know what they say?" Zahid mumbled as he teed off, his golf club tracing an arc in the air. "They told me these stories when I was in the madrasa in Cairo. There was an old man of the mountain, who commanded a group of assassins who terrorized the Christians during the Holy Wars. Are you familiar with it?"

"Unfortunately not," Wong said, feeling the weight of the 9-iron. "I am not a man who listens to stories."

"It is a good tale," Zahid said, grinning. "It could be about you: the old man living in his fortified mansion on a hill in Cheras, commanding Kuala Lumpur's most infamous assassins!"

"I have to admit that is interesting. But what happened to them?"

"They all died," Zahid said, walking to the buggy where his caddy waited for them. "The leader of the assassins made a mistake. He sent his men to kill Möngke Khan. The Mongols retaliated and surrounded them, killing them one by one."

Wong hesitated for a moment before joining Zahid in the buggy.

>————————<

Gavin waited in the Laksamana while dusk was falling. The hotel was preparing to open for business. Outside, the heat continued to rise. He could hardly stand it even with the windows wide open. Ah Leong had just arrived from the mansion and was smoking a cigarette. Gavin frowned, as Ah Leong rarely smoked.

"Any updates?" Gavin felt a sudden surge of power as he stared at the lieutenant from across the desk where his father used to sit.

Ah Leong shook his head. "They would have started the attacks already. We just need to wait for someone to report back."

The hotel was devoid of most of the usual gangsters who staffed the corridors. Most of them were out that evening, armed and on the streets. As far as Gavin knew, there were only a couple of guards on the lower floors.

Ah Leong's cigarette went out as they waited. He raised another one to his lips with trembling hands. Gavin stared at his phone. There had to be a reply, at least some news. The Stechkin in his holster was weighed down with an angry impatience.

Suddenly there was a splintering of glass, so quick that he didn't realize it until the first bullet smashed into the desk, inches from his face.

>————————<

"Ah Fung, get me Ah Fung," Wong demanded.

The gangsters at the other end of the line laughed. "You stupid old man," they said. "Don't you know that boss isn't well? One of your boys fired a bullet into his windscreen. Killed the driver and boss went smashing through the glass. Fella's almost blind now."

Eventually, Wong managed to get through and Ah Fung II took his call, his raspy voice speaking from a few states away.

"Yes, you tried to kill me?"

It had been so long since they last spoke that Wong didn't recognize Ah Fung II's voice, still bristling with menace and suppressed hatred, but now punctuated with shallow breaths due to his severe injuries.

"I tried to warn you," Wong said, sweating as he gripped the phone. "None of your men would put me through."

"It doesn't matter," sneered Ah Fung II. "We will kill all of your men now."

And he hung up, leaving Wong with the silent receiver.

>———————<

Gunner was at the Yew Hua Coffeeshop behind Jalan Masjid India. They waited at their table in the corner. He knew that members of the Chang gang's elite hit squad had booked most of the restaurant for some celebration. Only a few old men sat outside, almost out of sight, with their feet resting on their stools, chewing on roasted pork, their voices unheard above the din the other gangsters were making. Gunner and his men had their hands in their pockets, ready to draw their guns. He had a machine gun that would take down the assembled members of the Chang gang without much trouble, while his lieutenants carried sawn-off submachine guns. Their van and motorcycles were already parked in the back alley, ready for a quick getaway.

"Mr. Gunner," one of the men whispered over the loud cheering. "Where are all the waiters?"

Gunner turned around, frowning. As if on cue, all the workers in the restaurant had vanished.

He turned back and saw the gangsters at the nearest table looking in their direction, brandishing their guns. He tried to raise the alarm, but the silenced guns opened fire. Gunner fell to the floor, struggling for air, while all around him his men were dying before they had a chance to scream as the guns continued firing away. *It's a trap*, Gunner thought. *Ah Fung II's men knew about the Day of Judgment.*

Gunner shut his eyes. The floor was cool, calm and inviting. He lay face down until the waiters emerged to drag the bodies away. Outside, the old men continued eating, as though oblivious to the shooting behind them.

That wasn't the end. Up and down the peninsula, gunfire was exchanged but the syndicate's men were unprepared. They were cut down. Cars were set ablaze or veered fatally into plantations or ditches. Grenades were hurled and blew men to pieces. Concealed machine guns shot up illegal casinos, nightclubs, fortified apartments, and even Restoran Klasik was torched, flames licking its exterior while patrons ran for their lives. Men tried to call the Laksamana Hotel, crying out for reinforcements, but the calls never got through.

><

The gunfire was too loud and intense and Gavin could hear screams. *Where's the shooting coming from?* There was a dingy row of Art Deco-styled flats across the road from the hotel, where the snipers must have been stationed. Gavin clutched his Stechkin as he followed Ah Leong, crawling across the glass-strewn floor to the door.

"Out!" Ah Leong managed to turn the doorknob and they were through. People were racing out of the building. Obsolete fire alarms had gone off and sprinklers sputtered while Gavin smelled smoke. Someone bumped into him, and he stumbled and dropped his Stechkin. More screams were added to the din at the sight of the gun. Gavin dove for the Stechkin while the vagrants who inhabited the Laksamana ran past him. He grabbed the gun before it was kicked out of sight.

Ah Leong bellowed something, punching a man and sending him tottering down the fire escape.

"Gavin!" he screamed. "Get back! They are here!"

At the foot of the fire escape, more gunfire erupted around them. Gavin saw fragments of plaster fall from the ceiling when a bullet ricocheted off the fire escape. Now people were screaming and running back up.

Ah Leong crouched behind the railings and pulled out his micro Uzi, staring back at Gavin with a doomed expression. Gavin heard the clatter of guns, and men shouting in a dialect he didn't recognize as their footsteps approached.

When Gavin tried to take cover behind a fire hose, clutching the gun in his sweaty hands, Ah Leong leaned out from behind the railings and shot the assassins who emerged at the top of the stairs. With a click, Ah Leong's gun ran out of ammunition. Gavin struggled to his feet as his father's lieutenant tossed the gun down the stairs, turning to face him with a blank expression, as if all of Ah Leong's fears and emotions had been exhausted.

"Go out the back," Ah Leong said. "There's another fire escape outside. Go!"

Gavin hurried away, past the locked doors behind which the occupants of the hotel had barricaded themselves, while Ah Leong followed, leaving the stairwell behind with two dead men in his wake. Outside, the police sirens had begun wailing.

>———<

"How many are dead?" Wong asked as Maut entered the room. He'd summoned Maut immediately after learning from the Nepali that the assassin was still alive and was returning to the mansion.

The assassin's face was expressionless as usual, but there was a trembling in his voice as he spoke.

"Everyone," Maut whispered, standing disheveled in front of the painting of the hajal bird. His shoes were stained brownish-red and there was a bandaged cut on his face, the blood still congealing under it.

"The Chang gang knew we were going to attack them. They fired on us in Sentul, under the railway tracks. Everyone else is dead. Only I escaped."

"And the rest of the men?" Wong demanded. "What about the ones in Port Klang, Gombak, and Tampin?"

Maut looked at the old man and he knew that there was no need to answer.

24
I AM THE LAW

Ah Fung II wore dark glasses and gripped a walking stick as he limped out of the car and emerged outside Hotel Baladay. The conference in the ballroom of the hotel would still be going on. He pictured Ramalingam in his uniform and smiling as he faced the barrage of questions from the eager reporters. Ah Fung II's lieutenant, a man named Krishna from Terengganu, guided him into the hotel.

Ah Fung II stared out of his good eye, the other permanently scarred and sightless. The blurred outlines of the uniformed guards were opening doors and letting him in. Why wouldn't they? He looked just like another rich towkay suffering from old age, dressed in a sharp suit and stepping into a five-star hotel. The idiots! They hadn't even bothered to check for weapons. He heard Ramalingam's voice over the loudspeakers, coming from behind the teak ballroom doors. Ah Fung II licked his lips and thought of the gun concealed in the breast pocket of his jacket.

He had left the Yup Hoong mill only an hour before, against the advice of his men. Not that there were many of them left anyway. Most of Chang's original lieutenants had been replaced by Ramalingam's men. What was left of the gang's original membership was now rotting in shallow graves amidst the plantations or blown up in forest reserves. He was the last man standing. He had no choice.

>————<

Ramalingam had come for him the previous night as Ah Fung II lay wounded in the mill, among packets of Yup Hoong biscuits that had been tossed aside to clear space for a makeshift hospital bed. Krishna, who had trained as a nurse, was busy dabbing a sponge and antiseptic over the burnt remains of Ah Fung II's left eye while the assassin spasmed, cursing the member of the syndicate who had fired on him as he left the mill. Ah Fung II had been racing back to the mansion after receiving confirmation that the Day of Judgment would take place that night, only to wind-up half-crippled and almost blind.

Ramalingam's men were everywhere. They sat with Ah Fung II in meetings, watching his every move and reporting them back to the inspector. Now they opened the back door of the mill as Ramalingam hobbled in. Ah Fung II didn't open his other eye but he spoke into the darkness.

"How nice of you to come here, Inspector," he rasped. Even his throat burned, as if it was coated with sandpaper.

"Thank you for your help," Ramalingam said. "I got what I wanted. Most of the syndicate has been successfully crippled. I couldn't have done it without your help."

"You have what you want. Leave now," Ah Fung II croaked back.

"Not yet," Ramalingam said, and Ah Fung II detected a tremble of suppressed anger and triumph in the old inspector's voice. "Wong's gang is not quite finished. The old man has not surrendered just yet. I need your help, just for a while longer."

"And then what? You'll simply leave me like this? Look at me. Go on, look. I am a cripple!"

"Be grateful you're still alive. I could have let you die that night. But you're still here. You're even living in Chang's old house.

Don't complain. Get your men and order them to regroup. It won't be too difficult to attack Old Wong's mansion next."

Ah Fung II listened as Ramalingam turned and left.

Everything Ah Fung II knew had come crashing down on the night of Chang's death. He had watched, petrified, as Maut left Chang's room after the shooting. Maut hadn't killed him straight away. The bullet just missed his heart, exiting from beneath his ribs and smacking into the carpet. But minutes later Chang died, sprawled on the carpet, with only his body weight staunching the heavy bleeding from his wound.

The policemen came so quickly that even Ah Fung II was surprised. There was a medic there too, patching him up as he struggled to breathe. Then Ah Fung II was sent to hospital and Ramalingam was there. Of course he knew the old policeman. Everyone knew Ramalingam.

"We had men stationed outside Chang's house," Ramalingam said. "We knew something was going to happen last night. Once we saw a suspect fleeing, we went in. Now you are safe."

"What do you want?" Ah Fung II demanded. Damn. He felt exhausted, the wound still throbbing, as if about to burst open again.

"I want you to destroy the syndicate."

Ah Fung II laughed. "Chang is now dead," he said bluntly. "His gang will break into factions. They won't listen to you."

"That is why you must take over," Ramalingam said. "If you don't, I will hand you over to the magistrate. You will go to jail for the rest of your life, or be executed. Think about it. I am the law, after all."

What choice did Ah Fung have? He was discharged from the private hospital in Selayang and returned to the Chang gang headquarters at the Yup Hoong mill a few days later. But he wasn't alone. Several of Ramalingam's handpicked men were there as well. Ramalingam told him that Maut had killed several of the other lieutenants during Chang's birthday and had to be replaced. But Ah Fung II always suspected that Ramalingam had killed them himself.

Now Ah Fung II had no choice but to obey Ramalingam. He was alone, surrounded by a knot of undercover policemen watching his every move as he dictated suicidal strategies to his men.

"How can you do this to us, boss?" Krishna complained during a dinner at the Chang mansion, which Ah Fung II had moved into.

Ah Fung II pitied him. Krishna and the men had escaped their poverty-stricken lives for the allure of being a gangster. But their dreams were fading. Ever since the gang had begun its concerted attacks on the syndicate, they had been losing money. Men were mutinous or dying. They were being diverted from their usual haunts, and instead of supplying drugs to poor dealers and harassing defaulters, they were now being sent to the front line to gun down the syndicate's men. Guns were expensive and ammunition was difficult to come by. Ah Fung II thought of the hangman's noose and realized he was trapped.

Thoughts of murdering the inspector made Ah Fung II's pain bearable, keeping him awake at night.

When Old Wong struck back, Ah Fung II knew he wouldn't live for much longer. His injuries would take their toll. Krishna had told him all about it after Ramalingam left the Yup Hoong mill. He was bleeding to death, a hundred thousand tiny capillaries ruptured and losing blood. Within a week he would be dead. There was only one thing left to do.

So he ordered his suit to be brought over, as well as his gun. With Krishna's help, he raced toward Hotel Baladay, where Ramalingam was giving a press conference.

>————<

On stage in front of the reporters, Ramalingam looked uneasy as he struggled to answer questions alongside a group of inspectors.

"So, how do you explain the five murders, in five locations, which took place within your jurisdiction last night?" a reporter asked.

Ramalingam adjusted the microphone. "Sometimes these things happen. But take heart. No innocent people died—"

The door opened behind them but the reporters paid no attention, jotting down Ramalingam's answer.

Then the firing began.

Ah Fung II ignored the terrified journalists as he held the gun aloft, marching down the aisle in the center of the hall. TV cameras and DSLRs were pointed either at him or the floor as their operators ducked for cover. Reporters dove out of the way as security guards reached for their guns or ran out of the ballroom. Ramalingam stood up suddenly and Ah Fung II's first bullet struck the inspector. He approached the stage, shooting at the blurry outline of Ramalingam. Ah Fung II could barely see but that didn't matter—he had already hit his target.

Then someone raced out from behind the stage. Ah Fung II swiveled, ready to fire again, but he stalled. The person looked familiar, but before he could react he was already dead as the newcomer fired.

Samad stood over Ah Fung II's corpse, a Glock in hand while panicking reporters and TV crew jotted down notes or took photographs as more security guards rushed in with additional policemen. Samad raised a hand to cover his face as the cameras went off. He hated reporters, and he didn't want to be seen. He headed out of the ballroom. Ah Fung II's accomplice had already escaped but the new chief of the Chang gang was now dead. Samad turned to the stage, where paramedics were already attending to Ramalingam's still body.

"Hospital!" Samad screamed. "Get him to the hospital!"

Samad made a silent prayer. But when he saw blood pooling around the body, he feared the worst.

25
GAVIN II

On the night before Ramalingam's shooting and Ah Fung II's death at the Hotel Baladay, what was left of the syndicate regrouped at the ruins of Restoran Klasik. Gavin counted fifteen remaining men. Ah Leong was badly bruised and Boon was missing a few teeth after a narrow escape from a machete attack behind Low Yat Plaza. But they had lost Gunner and twenty-odd men over a period of one bloody night. It was the end of the syndicate.

Ah Leong barked out orders. "You three, tonight stay with Gavin in the corridor. You two, take the Honda Civic and stay outside. Watch out for anything suspicious. The rest of you, follow Boon. We need to protect boss."

"What about Maut?" one of the men demanded.

"He's already at the mansion," Ah Leong spat. "Old man Wong ordered him to go there after Maut's attack failed. Forget Hotel Laksamana, the police will be all over it by now. Forget this restaurant. They bombed the office already. There's nothing for us."

"What about our money?" another man called out.

"Wait," Ah Leong sighed. But Gavin knew there was no money for them. They had been promised a bonus for each man killed that night. But they were defeated and their laundered cash stored in Hotel Laksamana was now in the hands of the police.

There were protests, and another man shouted, "We are not fighting like this! I don't want to die, and if you want me to fight, I want money!"

Ah Leong had had enough and raised his gun, shooting the man right in front of everyone. Gavin had never seen Ah Leong lose his cool before. The other men drew back, suddenly silenced in the ruins of the torched restaurant. There was blood on the floor and on the walls behind them.

"Now, all of you, shut up," Ah Leong whispered. "The rest of you will be paid later. Get moving."

In the car, Gavin said nothing as Boon drove.

"Are you well?" Ah Leong asked as he sat beside Gavin. Ah Leong wasn't well himself. His hands were still shaking and he was trying to light another cigarette. "You will be safe for now. But tomorrow, after we make sure the house is secured, we'll take you to your father. We need to make sure you're both OK." Ah Leong accompanied Gavin up to his apartment. "You don't need to worry. There will be a few men outside the corridor. They will take care of you."

For a few moments both men looked at each other, unable to say anything else. Ah Leong managed to light his cigarette and blew smoke into the air, where it briefly caught the light of the crescent moon in the hazy night sky.

"You are my father's new chief lieutenant, you know." Gavin smiled for the first time since the attack on Hotel Laksamana. "You could lose your job."

"Perhaps I don't want it anymore," Ah Leong said. He flicked the cigarette ash over the railings and toward the mossy swimming pool below. "Get some sleep. We'll figure things out tomorrow."

"I miss Crazy Foo," Gavin admitted as he unlocked the grille door and locked it behind him again. "He was the only person who would teach me anything about the syndicate. He didn't deserve to die like that."

Ah Leong stared at him. "We all live and die," he said at last. "But not all of us get to choose our own deaths."

The two men parted ways. Gavin couldn't even bring himself to take a shower. He lay on his bed and stared at the ceiling. Why didn't his father pack his bags and leave the country for Vancouver or London or Canberra? But Gavin understood: his father could never fit into a proper life, and they were both destined to live in the shadows of the city.

>———<

Outside the apartment, Ah Leong sat in the car, adrenaline still pumping through his veins. So many people had died. The Chang gang would never stop coming for them. He would run until the day he was killed. He had a gun in front of him, and suddenly, a memory came back to him.

He was younger again, still a boy, and he was at a chapel in the grounds of his school in Malacca. He was reciting a prayer he could now no longer remember. Suddenly, uncontrollably, Ah Leong put his face in his hands and began to cry.

>———<

On the other side of the city, Wong watched as the men entered the house. They bowed to him but he could sense their anger. Boon was the last one through, and he stared at the old man.

"We are sorry, boss," Boon said, refusing to look Wong in the face. "No choice. If we didn't try to kill them then we will all die for sure."

"And in the process you have killed us all," Wong said.

"It wasn't just me, boss. You know your son Gavin, he is the one who order us—"

"Enough," Wong interrupted. "I don't want to hear excuses. Get me Crazy Foo. I need to talk to him."

"Boss?" Boon said nervously. "Foo is dead…"

"Just get him here," Wong said, repeating his words, unable to think straight. "Fetch Foo here, I need to talk to him…"

He thought of Gavin. *The poor boy, none of this was supposed to happen.* Now he was barricaded in his own house.

———◄

Gavin woke up the next morning. The haze was everywhere, almost blocking out the sun. He would need a mask. It reminded him of American movies, of assassins and mobsters hiding in the fog, and he knew on that day there would be a hundred of Ah Fung II's men combing the streets. He could no longer see the horizon from his window as the stench of burning wood filled his lungs.

There was a knock on his door. "Gavin?" he heard Ah Leong say. "It's time."

"Give me a minute," he replied. Gavin rummaged through his closet for his best clothes. They were crumpled but he didn't care. He looked into a mirror as he dressed. He had grown gaunt and thin over the last few weeks. At the last minute, he remembered the holster and the Stechkin and tucked both under his shirt. Gavin cast a lingering glance over his apartment, as if for the last time, and left.

"Your father is downstairs already." Ah Leong was wearing a dark suit, accompanied by a few haggard men as Gavin locked the apartment doors. "He came to pick you up in person."

"So what does he want to do?" Gavin asked as they entered the lift.

"You know what he is like; he doesn't even want to talk. The only thing he mentioned, besides demanding to come and find you, was your mother."

Gavin flinched. "I don't remember her anymore."

"You know you had an older brother, don't you?"

"Vaguely. He never talks about them."

"You can't blame him," Ah Leong said, staring at the changing numbers on the lift panel. "He lost so much. Perhaps that is why he wants to keep his distance from you. Maybe he doesn't want you to get hurt."

Gavin considered Ah Leong's words. "It doesn't matter anymore. Look what's happening to us now. But where will you go?"

Ah Leong permitted himself a sad smile. "I'm just like Crazy Foo. I have nothing but the syndicate. No family to go to. You are lucky to still have your father after all this. Take care of the old man, do you understand?"

"You still respect him after all this?"

"He was a good man once," Ah Leong mused. "Yes, I do respect him for who he once was."

Gavin was unprepared to see his father again. The old man was standing next to the blue Mercedes-Benz.

Wong made a move, as if to embrace Gavin, but his arms failed him at the last minute, returning awkwardly to his sides.

"I'm sorry about everything," Gavin said, looking down. And he meant it. He was sickened by all the deaths from the games he had been playing since Foo had first mentioned Maut.

As if on cue, the assassin appeared. Maut was standing in front of the car behind them, keeping his distance. Gavin stared at Maut, who looked at Gavin pointedly. He couldn't stand it and turned back to his father instead. The heavy haze rendered his father a silhouette against the stark grayness of the city.

The old man turned around to face Maut. "You drive," he said curtly. "Follow us from behind, understand? Don't get separated."

Maut nodded again and got into the Civic. Two other foot soldiers with automatic weapons under their raincoats entered the car as well. Wong gestured at the Mercedes.

"Get in," he ordered. "We have a lot to talk about. Ah Leong, you drive."

Gavin didn't look his father in the eye. He was angry with himself and his father. For the first time, he could tell from the bulge in Wong's pocket that the old man had his old .22 revolver on him.

The people who lived in Gavin's apartment block stared at the procession. Boon was on a motorcycle and he led the way. Behind him, Ah Leong put the car in gear and the Mercedes moved, tailing the motorcycle. Maut set off an instant later as they vanished into the haze.

In the Mercedes, the silence grew more strained as they drove past indistinct shapes and blurred images. Over the radio, there was news:

"Inspector Ramalingam of the Ampang Jaya police, who was shot two hours ago, is now in a critical condition. The gunman, believed to be a well-connected gangster, was shot dead by police operatives…"

"We all die, don't we?" Wong muttered to Gavin as Ah Leong turned down the volume.

"It's time for you to get out of all this," Gavin said.

"It's too late for me," Wong said quietly. "Now, if you hadn't acted so rashly last night…"

"Rashly?" Gavin lost his temper. "I did what I had to! There was no other way. We could all have died, Dad."

More silence.

"And you're telling me that I spoiled everything," Gavin said desperately.

"Yes," his father replied. "I've made some arrangements. You'll be going overseas; it is too dangerous for you to live here. I have some friends who owe me favors in Australia. You'll leave as soon as you can. They have a new passport waiting for you in Brisbane."

"And what about you?"

"I will stay here," Wong said.

A motorcycle raced past, so close that the pillion rider could have punched his way through the glass. A group of schoolchildren filed past in green sarongs and identical black songkoks. It was another Friday.

"Do something for me," Gavin said at last. "If this is what you want me to do, then promise me you'll stay away from me. You never talked to me about mother or about Gerald. You left me on my own all my life. It is easier that way."

Father and son said nothing as the car made another turn. This time they were turning into Brickfields, near the Hindu temples where carved deities and assorted gods reached for the sky.

"Go faster," Wong ordered Ah Leong. "We need to get to the house as quickly as we can."

It was a quiet hour. The faithful were in their mosques while everyone else took an extended lunch. For now, they were practically alone; two cars and a single motorcyclist in a quiet back lane in Brickfields, enveloped by the haze.

Then the firing began.

Bullets ricocheted off the chassis of the Mercedes-Benz before Wong or Gavin could react. In the same split second, the window exploded in their faces like a fireworks display. Gavin screamed, his face cut by glass fragments, and Ah Leong lost control of the wheel. Gavin clutched Ah Leong's seat as Ah Leong slumped forward, and the car skidded onto its side and plowed straight into the back entrance of a restaurant. Then their whole world was inverted as the car flipped upside down. Gavin and his father crashed against each other before the car righted itself and they were both sprawled across the leather seats.

Old Wong was gasping for air, his eyes shut, but Gavin had already kicked the door open, his head spinning as he tried to get his world in order again, despite the ringing in his sluggish brain. He peered out, trying to make sense of his world, with his blurry eyesight and blood running down his face. The Honda Civic behind them had already drawn to a halt and some of the men climbed out, firing their submachine guns into the haze. It was so thick that they could barely see anything. But more gunshots came back. Another man screamed and fell to the ground, clutching his thigh, and Gavin saw Maut with his Glock, leading the charge.

His father mumbled something but Gavin's mind went blank for an instant. He couldn't take anything in, not until he saw Foo's gun glinting next to his father.

"No, Gavin…"

"You stay here!" Gavin shouted as he reached for the gun. He crawled out of the wreckage and was gone. He was running after Maut into the haze.

Wong wanted to hurry after Gavin but he could hardly move. It had been a long time since he was out in the field. He screamed Gavin's name again.

"Stay there, boss!" Boon shouted from outside, as another round of gunfire started.

Wong, trying to reach for his own gun with his clumsy fingers, heard a click. He turned and saw Ah Leong feebly gripping a pistol. The lieutenant was slicked with his own blood, and his clothes were stained and riddled with bullet holes. The man was dying but a sickly determination burned in his eyes. For a wild moment Wong saw the gun aimed at his chest, but Ah Leong painfully turned it back on himself.

"No, what are you doing?" Wong gasped.

"I don't want... bleed to death," Ah Leong mumbled. "I will choose... how I die."

Wong closed his eyes but the gunshot was unbearably loud in the ruined Mercedes. It punctured the air and then Ah Leong moved no more.

"What the hell?" Boon had wrenched open the door in panic.

"Where's Gavin?" Wong shouted, trying to clamber out of the car, but Boon held him back. He shouted Gavin's name again and again but there was no reply. Police sirens were sounding in the distance.

"Faster take him away!" Boon roared at the rest of the men as they started up the Civic again. Wong was rambling, shouting Gavin's name as he fell to the potholed tar road, with Boon struggling to drag him toward the Honda. The syndicate's men had no choice but to run. Too bad about Gavin and Maut—someone would have to come back for them later.

By the time the police arrived, the gunshots had stopped. Only a ruined Mercedes-Benz and the corpse of a man riddled with multiple bullets remained.

Gavin was running. He was dizzy from the chase. Somebody was packing away a gun when Gavin saw him crouch behind a parked car. The man didn't see Gavin as he ran closer and screamed as he opened fire. The Stechkin recoiled as Gavin fought to control it, remembering everything that Crazy Foo had taught him. The man was hit and he was thrown backward in a spray of red mist, sending his assault rifle falling. Gavin didn't stop. He hated the man for what had happened. He emptied round after round until his hands shook and he fell back against the wall.

Gavin stopped. He felt sick. The gun was heavy in his hand and he tried not to vomit as he stared at the broken body of the dead man. He had killed him.

Something didn't make sense. Despite himself, he approached the corpse. It wore a police badge, almost torn off the blood-soaked uniform, and Gavin's skull pounded. Konstabel _____, he couldn't read the name but suddenly everything was thrown out of joint. The police had attacked them. He needed to get back to the gang at once.

Then he fell face down to the ground. There was a searing wound in his back but he was too weak to scream. His body throbbed in agony as he tried to turn over in order to see the shooter, and to grab his fallen gun. The shooter's footsteps echoed from behind Gavin and through his fear-wracked brain like depth charges as he turned to face the man.

Maut was standing behind Gavin as he reset the safety catch on his Glock. He didn't look down at him, but vanished from sight.

As the assassin vanished into the fog, nothing made sense any more to Gavin. He felt like he would die any minute now.

He needed to call his father to tell him about Maut... the dead police officer... and about whatever the hell he had just seen as he lay dying.

He couldn't reach the phone. He couldn't dial the phone number because his fingers were too weak.

"You're almost there," Gavin heard Danielle say. Somehow, she was now with him in that back alley. Gavin didn't understand but she was beside him, taking hold of his other hand as he tried his best to reach for the phone. Suddenly, he felt much weaker. He couldn't even crawl the last few inches to touch the cracked screen.

"I'm so sorry." He coughed up blood.

"It's all right," she said, with her hand on his. "It doesn't matter now."

26
DEATH OF A CHANCELLOR

Chancellor Zahid was tired. He was driving back to the office at Yohan Eng College. Things had rapidly spiraled out of control, and he blamed Ramalingam. How could the stupid man have trusted Ah Fung II? Zahid still felt sorry for the inspector though.

He had just left the surau in the MACC office in Putrajaya when the news came in. Every channel was tuned in, every office boy and girl was watching, transfixed by the TV screens. The television cameras had probably caught the shooting but the censors must have cut it. He watched the television silently as the dead assassin was carted out of Hotel Baladay and paramedics worked to save Ramalingam's life. They were sending him to KLGH, top priority, but Zahid knew that it would be too little too late. Ramalingam was old. He wouldn't survive the shooting.

More news came in. This time it was from Brickfields: there had been a shooting with no eyewitnesses. A boy had been found dead. Zahid knew instinctively it was Gavin Wong. The old man had survived but surely his time was running out as well.

Since Gavin Wong was dead and Ramalingam and Old Wong were going to die soon, that left only one loose end.

The reporters didn't come for him this time, but he couldn't concentrate on the paperwork filling up his in tray in Putrajaya. In the end, he left early. He was disorientated by the shooting and needed a rest. Everything was more chaotic than he had ever dreamed.

He remembered the night he first spoke to Ramalingam about his fears, back at the Mandarin Oriental.

>————————<

"What kind of help do you need?" Ramalingam asked.

Zahid explained everything. He talked about how he was in deep with Wong Kah Lok and some of the other criminal gangs. He had taken loans from Chang Kok Chye and hired Old Wong to kill off his rivals and enemies. They were not small fry. They knew all about the things Zahid did on his rocky ascent in politics. If he ever ran for office, his enemies would snuff him out easily. They had all the facts they needed. One word from any of the gang leaders and Zahid would be lucky to escape the death sentence. The thought terrified him every night, slowly driving him mad. In the end, Zahid realized the only thing he could do was to kill them all.

"What you ask is impossible," Ramalingam said when he first made the offer. "Take your sick fantasies somewhere else. Thank you for the dinner, Chancellor." But even as he turned to leave, he hesitated.

Zahid saw his last chance. "You could have done so much more," he cajoled. "Imagine, you could have been a hero. The man who took Wong Kah Lok down. Look at you now. You're just an inspector. You've been bullied by the IGP and everyone above you for the last twenty years, rotting away while Wong lives happily in his mansion. He runs KL, not you or me or the government."

"I'm not a murderer," Ramalingam said, his lips thin and stern.

"There is a Latin quote, which I learned from my days in England. *Pro bono publico*. We can interpret it as 'For the greater good'. Isn't this what you've wanted your whole life? To save the city? Think about it, Inspector. You deserve all of this."

Not long after, both men were working together. Ramalingam needed a team. Zahid paid for it himself, drafting in trusted police officers and retired army snipers to form the nucleus of a team that Ramalingam could use to covertly fight the gangs. But Ramalingam's first vigilante attack on a gang ended in disaster; three of his men were gunned down in their hotel room after giving themselves away. Ramalingam needed someone who had once been a gangster himself, who could guide their every move. Against Zahid's wishes, he ventured into Paya Besar Prison and emerged with Samad.

>————<

Zahid still felt uneasy as he drove. He didn't feel like going back to Duta that night. He finally managed to place a finger on it. Guilt. He was guilty because Gavin had been killed. He was afraid Ramalingam would die. He tried to distract himself. Within a few weeks, nobody would be able to link him to any crimes.

The Yohan Eng College was just up ahead. Zahid drove past the roads, congested with late-night shoppers and revelers, and into the main office where he went once a week to pore over the college's records. The guards had let him in unquestioningly and he was safe. He turned the knob on the door and flicked the light switch. The air-conditioner was still running at that hour—how strange.

Then the lights came on and Samad was there.

"How the hell did you get in?" Zahid asked, feeling the door shutting behind him.

The man's face was drawn, as if he was trying to hold back all his emotions. "Ramalingam is going to die," he said. "You were not there at the hospital. You didn't see everything."

"I'm sorry he's dying," Zahid muttered as he moved toward his seat, not taking his eyes off Samad. "I can see in your eyes that you are blaming me. But what can I do about it? That's life. He took a risk joining me. It's not my fault."

"He saved me from prison," Samad said. "A good man. And now dead because of people like you."

"People like me?" Zahid laughed. "Astaghfirullah! It is because of people like *you* he is dying. Scum, killers, criminals. I am doing what I must to survive."

His eyes never left Samad's. Beneath his calm demeanor Zahid was afraid. Samad had broken into his office. He knew, all too well, what Samad was capable of doing. He was a trained fighter, a killer by instinct. He couldn't forget the time when Ramalingam told him how Samad had calmly strangled a man on one of his jobs. Zahid was mumbling more nonsense, trying not to show his fear. He had installed a panic button under his desk in case of an emergency, and if he could just reach it in time…

"So what will you do now?" Samad said at last. "Almost everyone is dead now."

"Not yet," Zahid said harshly. "You are alive, and you hate me. That makes you a threat to my plans, Samad. I will have to deal with you."

"The inspector told me one of your quotes. 'For the greater good'. That is why I'm here."

Zahid couldn't react in time. Samad shot him with a silenced pistol.

He slumped back in his armchair in disbelief, fingers frozen just before he could sound the alarm.

"It's good that you told your security you would be here all night. They won't come running if you don't make a sound," Samad said.

Chancellor Zahid found himself staring as Samad left the office. There was a snapping sound from outside. He must have shot off the door handle. Zahid could no longer focus on anything.

A minute later, he was dead.

27
FUNERAL

Wong was trailing behind the black hearse that carried Gavin's casket. It made its way out of the specialist hospital where doctors had made a last attempt to save Gavin's life. But it was to no avail. Wong didn't shed any tears. He was just numb from shock.

The rain was falling and for the first time in days the haze started to clear. Cremations were arranged for Ah Leong and the other men killed in action. Boon was given the task of arranging Gavin's funeral. But first, Wong wanted the casket brought to the mansion. But just who would pay their respects remained a mystery. Gavin had always been a loner. There were no relatives who would visit. Only the ten or so remaining members of the syndicate, as well as Wong's most loyal business partners, would be there.

He walked with them along the street, the drizzle dampening his black suit. One of the men held an umbrella over his head but he waved the man away as they wound their way through the old streets. The men and women who lived and worked there, as well as the immigrants and luckless Chinatown youths, came running to witness the procession. The hearse advanced slowly, giving Wong enough time to follow, while all around them policemen kept watch. Despite the explicit orders of one of the few officers not intimidated by Wong, he had proceeded with the funeral procession. Traffic drew to a standstill as they marched on.

So many things went unsaid. Wong had wanted to tell Gavin all about his life in Chinatown, about how he met Xue and how they tried in vain to escape from his criminal life. And now it was too late.

>————————<

The last funeral he had attended was Xue's and Gerald's. Wong recalled being at the memorial garden, owned by a friend who offered him the grandest tomb— but Wong declined.

"Sorry all this got happen, boss," Foo said as they stood under the sweltering sun as the crematorium doors shut. All around them, other Chinese thronged the garden to see off their deceased relatives. But the double funeral was a quiet one. Gavin was still ill and was left in the care of the in-laws back in Malacca, who were too infirm to make it. Only Wong and Crazy Foo were there.

"What can we do about it?" Wong said. "We can't choose how we die. But this wasn't fair. Xue didn't… she…"

But he couldn't complete his sentence.

Foo was silent out of respect for a few minutes while the sun continued to scorch them. "And you won't tell Gavin about all this ah?"

"When he's older."

After the funeral, Foo drove him to Malacca. Wong found the in-laws house soon enough. They mourned Xue's death, and that of their grandson. They never blamed Wong, but he still felt immense guilt.

"I should have left when I had the chance," he told them. "I am sorry, Mother. I am sorry, Father. Please, forgive me for all of this."

He took the sleeping Gavin away. The in-laws watched as he disappeared with Foo. They knew they would never see each other again.

>————————<

Countless years passed. But no amount of good karma, generous donations to temples or prayers to the myriad gods in Heaven and Hell could prevent Gavin's death. Wong could no longer weep as they turned a corner and began the journey up the hill. The flags that the mourners carried, bearing a script so stylized and ornate that Wong couldn't understand it, fluttered in the wind as they entered the grounds of the house. Everyone was dressed in black as the casket was placed in the center of the living room. The lid was open and Gavin's pale body lay under a sheet of glass as if he was asleep.

"So what now, boss?" Boon asked as the prayers ended and the Taoist priests retreated to the back of the house for refreshments. The house felt empty and cold, despite the presence of the other gangsters, gazing at the casket as they huddled around in a circle. Wong and Boon walked away from the group. Wong could feel the stares of the men burning into him. He knew they doubted his leadership again. Sooner or later, someone would snap, and he imagined a man stabbing him to death to take over what was left of the syndicate while he joined Gavin in the hearse.

They were outside in the garden. The skies parted for an instant, and through the remains of the haze, he could see the Twin Towers jutting out of the crowded skyline.

"I don't want any more of you to die," Wong admitted at last. "We put an end to it all. I want to shut down the syndicate."

Boon stared at him. "This is our life, boss. Cannot be that you shut it down."

"If we keep fighting, all of us will die in the end," said Wong sternly. "Look at it: Foo is dead, Ah Leong and Gunner are also gone. Now it's Gavin…" Wong couldn't finish the last sentence.

When Boon spoke again he was trying to control his anger. "So we die for nothing, is it?"

"No, not at all. It's a ceasefire. We fought our hardest but it wasn't enough."

Both men were quiet. Then Boon turned around and so did Wong. A girl had just arrived, also dressed in black. She hesitated for a moment but approached them. Wong had never seen her before, but instantly he knew who she was.

"Please, are you Mr. Wong?" the girl asked. She reminded him so much of Xue that it hurt, and he gripped his cane a little harder.

"Yes, I am Gavin's father," he said. "Thank you for coming, Danielle."

Her eyes were moist with tears. "I had to say goodbye to him."

Wong was still in the garden when Danielle appeared again, exiting the living room. A few other mourners had emerged from their sports cars. Wong had shaken hands with forgers, businessmen and small-time politicians, all of whom voiced their non-existent grief. He hated them all and wished they had never come. But he had to keep up appearances. He was still the leader of what was left of the syndicate.

"I'm sorry," Danielle said respectfully, standing next to the old man as he stared at the city from the fence that ringed the garden.

"I'm grateful that you came," Wong said.

After an awkward pause, Danielle said, "He was very stressed about trying to lead a good life. He tried very hard, Mr. Wong."

Wong didn't tell her how deeply Gavin had been involved with the gang, but he suspected she already knew. "Please forget all of this. Live your life without knowing any more."

"It's not too late for you," she said gently. "I've been reading up everything that's happened in the last few days. So many people have been killed. But now you have to leave."

Wong shook his head. "Gavin's mother told me the same thing once. I have tried, but it never lasted."

There was a hint of rain in the air.

"I have to go now," Danielle said. "Please take care of yourself."

She shook his hand, and he felt worn out by all the deaths in the city over the past week. As Danielle left the grounds he saw her raising a hand to her eyes before she vanished into the dusk. Wong knew he would never see her again.

>————————<

Night was falling. Wong, still in his suit, hobbled back to the living room. He stared at Gavin's face, patched up by a surgeon at the hospital, and closed the lid of the casket with the Nepali's help. The next day, the hearse would return to take him to the crematorium. And only ashes would be left; all that remained of his last son, contained in a porcelain urn.

Caterers served dinner. But only Boon remained inside the house. A few of the other men had gone to their posts, guarding the mansion. Maut was still uncontactable and many of the men were spreading rumors about him. Some said he had been kidnapped by the remains of the Chang gang and tortured to death. Others said that Maut must have killed Gavin for some unknown reason before running away. Wong was too weary to care at that moment.

"Boss," Boon said, as Wong approached. "They say that Ramalingam dying wor."

"So I heard," Wong said, sitting next to one of the last few men he trusted. "KLGH, isn't it?"

"Yah," Boon replied. "My source in ICU, he say this morning Ramalingam in stable condition. But then his condition get worse. Now they say he will die tonight."

Wong looked at the casket for an instant, and then turned back to Boon, getting to his feet. "Take me to Ramalingam."

"But boss…"

"If he is dying, I want to speak to him one more time."

28
A GOOD MAN

Nobody stopped Wong as he approached the ward, his walking stick tapping on the tiled floor. Visiting hours were over but Wong only needed to mention his name and the terrified receptionists waved him through.

There were more policemen outside the ward, but all of them stepped aside as Wong approached. Wong recognized some of them. There was Corporal Harun of Bukit Bintang, SI Aminuddin, with whom he once had an uneasy tea while discussing an agreement to keep his gangsters from bothering the police, and Sergeant Pillai, who was nearly killed by Gunner during a shootout in Kerinchi.

Only Ramalingam's secretary, who wielded his own gun, stood in the way. "The inspector may die soon," he protested.

"Tell him that I want to talk to him one last time."

The secretary entered the room and emerged again a few minutes later. "He says to put your gun aside first," the secretary said warily.

"I don't have one," Wong said. He was admitted into the ward. There was no one there except for Ramalingam; the old inspector's tired gaze settled on Wong as the door closed behind him, leaving Boon outside in the corridor filled with policemen.

"I always had the feeling," Ramalingam wheezed, forcing himself to sit upright, "that you would be there at the end."

"No doubt you always thought I would kill you," Wong said, sitting beside Ramalingam's bed. Outside, the lights of the city came alive, flickering into the depths of the night.

"You have no family, do you?" Wong asked. "It must be painful. Now you are alone and there's nobody who will be with you. I am in your shoes too. Gavin is dead. We're both on our own."

Ramalingam shook his head. "I never recovered from Bangsawan Heights," he admitted. "That changed me completely. I didn't care about love or life. All I wanted was to work and forget everything. But now that I'm dying, the only thing that comes back with clarity is that day. Everything else is fading away. I'm sorry about your son. A good man always dies first."

"What does dying feel like?"

"I'm surprised," Ramalingam said. "I never thought about death until today. It is a sense of finality. This is the bitter end. But other than that, it's a quiet realization. Fear disappears and you begin to accept your fate."

Silence. The machines beeped in the ward.

"But…" Ramalingam said. "There's one thing that I do feel— guilt."

"Over what?"

"I have very little time left," Ramalingam said as if he had rehearsed it. "I have hated you ever since I first became a policeman. You could do anything you wanted while the rest of us slaved away. And when I had to make a deal with you, I was humiliated. None of the other policemen would dare to lay a finger on you. Either that or they were your friends."

Wong listened, strangely enthralled.

"I tried to kill you," Ramalingam admitted. "After Bangsawan Heights. I was mocked for so long that I started working with Chancellor Zahid just to find some closure. He wanted to kill you, to erase all the evidence of his crimes before he ran for office. He knew all about me and manipulated me. We took over the Chang gang. We used it as a weapon against you."

Ramalingam's voice wavered. He explained everything he had done over the past few months. The strain ate away at him, and on the rare occasions when he managed to rest, Bangsawan Heights returned to haunt him.

"In a way, I have been waiting to die," Ramalingam said. "I don't have to think about it any longer. I have done what Zahid wanted. I did what I thought I wanted. I'm no better than you are."

"Why are you telling me this?"

"I have nothing left to live for. I understand the despair that you must feel. I know you are thinking of your son, and how you are now alone because of what I did."

"Yet I'm still here."

Ramalingam chuckled softly. "You have lost Foo, Ah Leong, more than half of your gang, and now Gavin. It has been slow but there is a man who has been hunting you down all this time. He's been at the heart of your syndicate for months and he's been feeding us information."

In that brief instant, the confusing pieces of the puzzle slotted together.

"Maut. He was your inside man. Your spy."

Ramalingam nodded. "He was a simple killer when I first found him. He called himself Samad. I doubt that is even his real name. I rescued him from a prison in Johor. But he was a good lieutenant. He infiltrated the Chang gang. He tried to kill Chang but failed. What a stroke of luck that your men rescued him and took him in. He fed us information and we manipulated the Chang gang into exterminating you. The results were better than Zahid or I could have imagined. Within weeks both your organizations were crushed, and you were both killing each other, not realizing that we were pulling the strings."

The beeping intensified for a moment and Ramalingam took a deep breath, but the sound returned to normal and he kept on talking, as if rushing for time, using every last breath to tell his story.

"But the violence went too far. Samad is obsessed with killing you. He is like a machine. He has been taking orders from you and reporting to me. He is not a bad man, but he is determined to do what I have told him to. He came to see me this afternoon, you know. He promised to hunt you down for good, just like I ordered. I couldn't dissuade him. He's somewhere in the city now, waiting for you."

Wong was quiet for a moment as he regarded Ramalingam, whose face was drawn, counting down his remaining hours tethered to life. "I should have seen this. Maut was too good."

"Forgive me, please." Ramalingam stared at Wong. "We have both reached the end of the road. Now we are even. You and I will be forgotten. That is enough punishment for you. Now, I'm telling you to run. Get out of the city while you can, to where Samad cannot follow you. Don't trust anyone. Just go."

Wong stood up, head reeling from everything that Ramalingam had told him. "I wish you well, Inspector. I hope you have found peace."

Wong raised a handkerchief to his eyes as he turned away from the man whose life had been entwined with his. As he left the ward, Ramalingam coughed again. Bangsawan Heights was returning to haunt him, even as he lay dying.

He was alone and wouldn't last the night. Sometimes, in the days after his fall from grace, he tried to imagine a different future if he had acted earlier. He could almost picture himself: married and with a family, happily retired with his own estate, just like the one he grew up in before joining the force.

"Visanthi," he finally uttered her name after twenty years, "I am sorry."

29
SALAMAT

Wong hurried along the corridor, followed by an agitated Boon, leaving the policemen and the inspector far behind. "How long has it been since you last returned to Muar?" he asked.

"Why you ask?" Boon said suspiciously.

"I just want to know."

"Never went back since I run away."

"No family?"

"My mother. She still has a noodle shop near the market. I used to help her last time, before I become chauffeur for my old boss."

"Listen," Wong said. "Go back to Muar. I can do without your help. Thank you for everything, Boon."

"Huh?"

Wong couldn't even begin to look at Boon's confused expression. "I will be fine. Just go back to the mansion first. I'll take a taxi later. I just need some time for myself. Pack up your things and you can go in the morning."

Boon was unsure of how to react, but Wong wasn't joking. With a quick bow, Boon walked away, disappearing out of the front doors and out of sight.

Wong waited at the hospital for a long time. At midnight the staff watched him, still in his crumpled suit, wondering if he was suicidal or catatonic. Wong turned around as a team of doctors and paramedics hurried past him. They were probably going for Ramalingam. The inspector's internal organs must have failed him. Wong got up and dialed a number on his mobile phone. He waited, knowing that Maut wouldn't be late.

"Sir?" Maut picked up at last.

"Where have you been?"

"Injured," rasped Maut. "I went to a clinic. The gunman shot me. I escaped before the police came. But your son, he was killed."

"You never replied to any of my men all this time."

"I had no choice," Maut lied. "My phone was damaged. I only got it repaired this evening. I have just reported back to the Nepali and Boon."

"You're at the mansion now?"

"Yes."

Wong made his decision. If Maut was anything like Ramalingam described, he wouldn't do anything rash. He would still be waiting there, for the chance to kill him. Wong mulled over it. If all the men in the mansion took out their guns, Maut would be killed in an instant. Everything that Ramalingam, Zahid and Ah Fung II had conspired to do would come crashing down. And Wong would live.

"I'm here at the hospital. Ramalingam is dead." He imagined Maut shuddering. "I need you to come and fetch me. Now."

"Yes," Maut replied.

Maut arrived at the hospital in the Honda. Wong held on to his cane as he limped out of the hospital and toward the car. Maut opened the door to the passenger seat, his usually emotionless face regarding Wong with a sudden surprise.

"Why did you send Boon away?" he asked.

"I needed some time by myself," said Wong. He glanced at Maut's pocket, where the Glock bulged in its holster. "Were you injured badly?"

Maut nodded and winced, indicating his left shoulder.

"But you can still drive safely?"

"Good enough."

Wong clambered into the car, his plan already mapped out. "I will not be going back to the mansion tonight. I want you to drive me far away from the city. I don't want to go back to Cheras."

Maut nodded as he started the engine.

"I want you to drive to Johor," Wong instructed him. "But not on the highways. Just follow the coastal roads. Do you know the way?"

Maut nodded again. Leaving behind the slumbering city, they drove along highways illuminated by kilometers of sodium lamps. The lights thinned out as they turned into the old roads that wound past plantations and villages. When Wong was young, these were the roads loggers, adventurers, merchants and tourists took on their way to the south of the peninsula and Singapore. But now they were empty and lined with ghost towns, each with mainly elderly inhabitants.

As they neared Johor, Wong began to talk as Maut followed his directions. He told Maut about growing up in the hills of Johor, how he ran away to Kuala Lumpur, how his wife and first son died, and how he was alone. There was nothing left.

"Why do they call you Maut?" Wong asked at last.

"Death is all I know."

They left the roads behind and drove past the mangroves on the coast, where high tides sometimes submerged the tree roots, leaving the jungle stranded in the middle of the sea.

"Slow down. Turn left."

Now they were heading back inland and Wong continued to give directions. At one point the tar roads came to an end, replaced by narrow dirt tracks that were being reclaimed by the expanding jungle. Years before, the last people had abandoned the hills for Muar, Yong Peng, Kluang and Johor Bahru, leaving their old wooden houses to rot.

"Here," Wong said. The tracks had run out and the car was struggling uphill. Maut parked the car on the slope and they set out on foot for the rest of the way, past a few ruined houses and boarded-up shops, until they reached a clearing. In the center was a temple, flanked by the ghost town's remaining buildings. It was a small Chinese temple with protruding eaves and red paint, surrounded by a wire fence with a gate. It was seemingly hacked out of the jungle. They walked toward the padlocked gates.

The temple was closed for the night. But Wong turned a key and the padlock sprang open. He pushed through and walked through the darkness, illuminated only by the crescent moon. He walked up a short flight of stone steps and into a pavilion. There was a black marble headstone, devoid of statues or carvings, But Wong touched it with a reverence that Maut didn't expect.

"This place was called Salamat," Wong said, turning to face Maut, whose hands were in the pockets of his motorcycle jacket. "This is where I lived. It was abandoned in the seventies, I think. There was nothing left here. I came back after my wife died, trying to find some sort of meaning. There was nothing to do but to build something. I had this temple designed. The contractors and laborers thought I was mad but I didn't care. There are a few names carved on this stone here: my parents, my wife and my first son. There is room for two more, Gavin's and mine. I had this built as penance for the things I had done, and the people I lost because of my own actions."

Maut still didn't do anything as Wong approached him.

"I know all about you. You want to kill me," Wong whispered. "It is so easy. I haven't got a gun."

"Why are you doing this?" Maut asked. If there was any confusion on his face, Wong didn't see it. Maut was rendered temporarily invisible when a cloud obscured the moon.

"Because I have nothing left to live for," Wong said. "But I'm ready. Then you are free to go and do what you want. Ramalingam died in the hospital three hours ago. I was there when it happened."

Maut had already removed the Glock from his holster and disengaged the safety.

Wong stared back into Maut's eyes. "When you have lived as long as I have, you will understand how rare it is to have the chance to choose your own death. I could have ordered you killed. But I would only have an empty life after that, completely meaningless. I would prefer to go this way."

For a moment the assassin hesitated, and then he aimed the gun at Wong Kah Lok's head.

"I'm sorry. I killed Gavin," he admitted.

Wong said nothing. He had already turned around, staring at the headstone. Those names would soon mean nothing. The jungle would take over what was left of Salamat and there would be nothing left. The memorial would be meaningless, almost like the indecipherable carvings in the Bujang Valley, or the graffiti adorning the walls of old KL. All that mattered was that in moments, he would escape the pain that had gripped him for twenty years.

I'm sorry, Gavin, Wong thought. *Forgive me.*

Maut finished adjusting the silencer. He fired a single shot. There was a crack as the bullet smashed into the headstone. He replaced the gun in its holster and turned away from the lifeless body of Wong Kah Lok. He made his way down the hill and toward the car. Minutes later, the moon was blotted out again and Salamat returned to darkness.

30
HIGHWAY

Once past the mangroves and on the highway, he drove in darkness. He was alone on the empty roads that stretched from the south to the north, snaking from the old towns of the west coast to the quiet villages in the east. His expression was hardened by the countless times he had fired his Glock while taking in the final moments of his targets. In the end they were all the same to him. The hissing of the air-conditioner interrupted the quiet confines of the car. He looked up at the sign ahead: **Kuala Lumpur, 200 kilometers**. Behind him was a town that no longer existed. In the opposite lane a car screamed past. Was it one of the syndicate's men, searching for their dead leader, or just another young man bored with life as he raced as fast as he could go? In the end it didn't matter.

>————<

So, who am I? Maut or Samad, those names ran through his head, interchangeable like parts of a machine. He had another name once, but he had long forgotten it. He drove back to the city, past the mangroves. They reminded the assassin so much of the monsoon-drenched shores of the east coast where he grew up. He had lived there his entire childhood, his hands running over the knives and pistols in the house, all of which he had seen in his father's hands at some time or another as they crossed the Golok River and back again.

His father had also been a hired killer. That was in the badlands of the north. He had served in the army once, a fighter who attacked the communists under the orders of his superiors. Maut's father was an expert sniper who covered for his comrades as they raided camp after camp, watching with sadistic pleasure alongside the other boys—former farm hands from Pahang, Perak and Johor—holding polished carbines as their enemies burned.

There was no work after the Emergency ended. One fellow in the same unit as Maut's father had gone on to join the police, becoming an SI in Kuala Lumpur. Others joined the army, fighting in skirmishes against the Indonesians along the coasts. Some of them were too shell-shocked to lead normal lives, dumb and deaf as they tilled their farms or worked in the mines and plantations.

But Maut's father was different. He took the skills he had learned in the army and returned to the east coast. From their home in Tumpat, Maut watched as his father went out on jobs, working as an enforcer for the small-time gangs who roamed the porous Thai border. He sometimes followed as they entered villages where the people spoke a mix of Kelantanese and Thai, and where his father was a hero as he gun-battled bullies and corrupt policemen.

His father taught him how to fight. When Maut got older, he joined his father on jobs in the north. They were invincible together.

"Maut," his father said one day. "That is the name that you should use someday. One day you will do great things. Be a better man than me."

His father wasn't prepared for any other type of life. They were almost always poor. Maut never knew his mother, but he sensed from his father's fury when he killed his targets that she had been a victim. But who had killed her? The communists, the Thais, or some other Kelantanese? His father never told him and Maut never asked.

One night, everything went wrong. A corrupt imam in town had been stealing money from the faithful. Maut's father sensed the anger of the people and, without anyone issuing orders, he crept into the mosque where the imam preached and stabbed him as he was leaving. The killing provoked an uproar. Maut was hiding in the mosque and watched as the devotees fell upon his father in retaliation, never realizing what the corrupt man had done. They beat his father to death.

Maut knew they would be after him next. He packed up and fled, taking as much money and as many weapons as he could carry. He was seventeen and knew nowhere else except the coast, but he ran from the small town and into the wilderness that was the rest of the world. He caught the night train out of Tumpat and never returned to Kelantan.

In the years to come, and from town to town, he gained a reputation as a hardened killer. People never crossed him but watched in awe as he dispatched his targets at night, before joining them for breakfast in the stalls. He became an enigma. The man they called Death.

Yet he still went to the mosque, sometimes clutching prayer beads as punishments for vices and sins were solemnly recited. Sometimes, he was so fearful that he couldn't sleep. But he knew he was damned to Hell and could never escape.

He moved whenever the police began to suspect him. For a long time, he had no home and no family. He was nameless, drifting like a ghost.

Everything changed again in Johor Bahru, when he was tasked to kill a Singaporean businessman. Maut had waited for his target at the duty-free in a seaside hotel restaurant by the strait. He was there all day until the businessman arrived at the hotel, dressed in a Hawaiian shirt. As the businessman sat down to eat, the assassin emerged from the kitchen, dressed as a waiter, with a gun concealed under his jacket. He fired at the businessman but misjudged his aim; the bullet ricocheted off a platter and shattered the glass in the businessman's hand.

Maut fled without getting a second chance to shoot the man. Behind him, security guards with shotguns were already running out of the hotel entrance. One of them opened fire and shot him in the thigh. He managed to limp to his motorcycle and sped away, bleeding profusely.

He abandoned the motorcycle and tried to bandage his wounds in a hostel in Kuala Sedili, where he was the only occupant. But the Hainanese hostel owner had been suspicious of him from the moment he limped in, and he would surely call the police. Maut ran again, taking a succession of taxis further and further north.

He wound up in Kuantan, still unable to recover. He went to see a traditional healer he'd known in Mersing to get the bullet removed. But the wounds opened up again and he needed proper treatment. With no valid identification on him, Maut would get arrested if he went to a hospital.

For a few days he survived by going to small-town clinics, where the staff were too afraid of him and greedy enough to accept his bribes, while they tried to treat his infected leg. But it wasn't enough.

In the end he went to Hospital Tengku Ampuan Afzan. The doctors were reluctant to take him in, rejecting the forged identification card made for him in Jerantut. In desperation, he pulled out his gun and the police were called in.

They treated him before sending him to Johor to face the magistrate. There was suspicion that he was responsible for the attempted murder, but the businessman had fled to Singapore and refused to give evidence. The assassin, carrying the identification card of Samad Esmail of Johor Bahru, pleaded not guilty. The magistrate responded by sentencing him to ten years in Paya Besar for the illegal possession of firearms and threatening hospital staff.

He was offered the chance to escape several times, but Maut refused. He was tired of being on the run. All he could think of was leaving prison and settling down. A year went by in prison before Maut met Ramalingam, who offered him a way out. Maut accepted Ramalingam's offer and grew to develop a strong bond with the inspector. He was prepared to do anything to help, as Ramalingam had rescued him from destitution.

Time passed but Ramalingam didn't make any progress, even with his team of former criminals and rempits. An assassin who could blend in well with the gangs was needed. He was hesitant at first, still trying to escape from that way of life, but with Ramalingam out of options he volunteered himself. He would become Maut, the nameless assassin who emerged from the wilderness, the most skilled killer in the city.

Now that Ramalingam was dead, Maut would have to find a new life. There were still criminals in the city, even with the Chang gang and the syndicate crippled. He would continue to do what Ramalingam had struggled with his entire life. The only way to honor his memory was to keep the city in check. In the end, he would always be a killer.

He had abandoned the Honda Civic and set out on foot. He passed the nightclubs of Bukit Bintang, with people still unaware or oblivious to the madness of the past few weeks. He walked into Chow Kit, past the bazaar, the police station, the massage parlors and into the back alley where men and women did things in secret, where the Indonesian refugees from across the straits had come in the hope of work, and where the Nigerians and Sudanese lived as they feared arrests and police raids at night.

He climbed the rickety steps, past muffled voices and sounds, to the flat. He reached the stained worn-out door, where he turned the key in the lock. There was no noise from inside as he entered the living room, still bearing the aroma of gulai ayam.

He had a wife. Or at least that was how he saw her. She knew of his past as a hired gun but still chose to stay with him. He had met her before his incarceration in Johor. He had only mentioned his arrest to her during a phone call from the courthouse, refusing to give more details. After he left prison and returned to Dungun before moving to Kuala Lumpur, he found her with another man. The assassin's reputation was enough to scare the man off, and he took her away the same night. Together, they had boarded a Transnasional to the capital.

She wasn't at home that night. They had reached an unspoken agreement during their journey across the peninsula. As long as she continued to take care of their daughter, he would continue to provide for her. For a while she remained at the flat which the assassin had rented with his generous salary from Ramalingam. But eventually she left him, believing he wouldn't miss her. She was still young enough to be enticed by the bright lights of Bukit

Bintang, and he was sure that she was with some other man by now.

For a moment the assassin stood in the darkness of the living room. He laid the Glock on the table. Next to the gun was the only book he owned. It was an Indonesian translation of *Man's Fate* given to him by Ramalingam.

"Chen, the terrorist, only had one aim: to kill," Ramalingam explained as he pointed out the text while both men were waiting for transportation out of Paya Besar. "What else was there to do in life?"

The assassin had read the book many times. Perhaps, just perhaps, there was a way out. But he knew that he wouldn't follow it.

In the next room he heard his daughter stirring. He went into the room, where she lay in her bed. She looked just like her mother.

"Abah?" she said groggily. The assassin, with great tenderness, reached out to stroke her forehead.

"Sleep, sleep," the assassin whispered. "Tomorrow I'll give you a better life."

GLOSSARY, ETC.

This is not a conventional glossary. It not only describes Malaysian terms, but also goes over aspects of Malaysian life that might otherwise go unnoticed.

Ah Long – Loan sharks. Usually violent.

Alhamdullilah – In everyday speech it can be translated as "Thank God".

Blur – slang for an unfocused attitude or "not paying attention".

Bodoh – Malay word for stupid.

Botak Chin – Legendary gangster who terrorized Kuala Lumpur in the 1960s and 1970s. Regarded as a modern-day Robin Hood until he was arrested in an epic shootout and executed.

CC – General term for cybercafé, usually frequented by schoolkids and computer gamers.

Cheras – A district of Kuala Lumpur that draws its name from an ancient royal dynasty in South India.

Damn terror – Slang term for "very impressive".

Datuk – Honorary title bestowed by state and federal government of Malaysia.

Friday prayers – The cities shut down for 2–3 hours in the afternoon when the faithful go to the mosque for the weekly prayer.

FRU – Federal Reserve Unit.

Full Moon – The 30th day celebration of a newborn, usually with a huge party.

Gestapu – Not the Nazi Secret Police, but a reference coined by Malaysian journalists to describe the attempted 1965 coup in Jakarta allegedly masterminded by DN Aidit's Indonesian Communist Party.

Handphone – Local slang for cellphones/mobile.

Ham sap – Usually dirty old man.

Haram – Forbidden from a Muslim viewpoint. The opposite of halal.

IGP – Inspector-General of Police.

Jaga – A guard, or the act of guarding, depending on the context.

Jalur Gemilang – Malaysia's national flag. Translated, it means "Stripes of Glory".

Kan – short for "bukan", which means "no" or "not", depending on the context.

Kembung – a delicious type of fish.

KLGCC – The exclusive Kuala Lumpur Golf and Country Club.

KLGH – Kuala Lumpur General Hospital.

Konfrontasi (The Emergency) – A series of skirmishes between Indonesia and Malaysia in the 1960s, which ended after Suharto deposed President Sukarno to become the dictator of Indonesia.

Leng Lui – Cantonese for pretty girl.

MACC – Malaysian Anti-Corruption Commission.

Mak Nyah – Old slang term for trans women.

Memorial garden – Vast privately owned graveyards, usually catering toward Buddhist/Taoist clients.

Nyonya – a Peranakan lady. See "Peranakan".

Peranakan – Straits' Chinese; ethnic Chinese who adopted Malay cultural influences. Some families have been in the peninsula from the time of the Malacca Sultanate. The peninsula and the Indonesian islands traditionally had a fluid culture with no fixed boundaries until colonialization arrived.

Pondok – Hut.

RMAF – Royal Malaysian Air Force.

Salamat – A name derived from "Selamat", which means "safe" in Malay.

Samseng – Slang term for gangster.

Tan Sri – An even more impressive title than "Datuk". Bestowed by the federal government of Malaysia.

The Party – Which political party this book refers to is up to you to decide.

Tikam – a guessing game played in the old days. A bit like a downscaled lottery. The author's father used to sell it to Chinatown kids for extra pocket money.

Transnasional – A bus company with extensive coverage across Malaysia.

Tuan Inspektor – A common way to address inspectors by his subordinates.

Warung – A small shop, usually a café or restaurant.

Yam Seng – Chinese way of toasting.

ACKNOWLEDGEMENTS

A huge and sincere thank you to the amazing, tireless team behind Fixi London and Malaysia's own Buku Fixi – Amir Muhammad, Valisa Iskandar, and editors Eeleen Lee, Lyana Khairuddin and Richard Sheehan. This book has gone through a lot of changes from when I began the first draft in the fall of 2013, and to see it finally show up in London four years later is far beyond my wildest expectations.

Also, this would not have been possible without the help of my sister, Wee Nie Tham, for all her comments, criticisms, and witticisms. Thank you, really.

Richmond, Canada. December 2016.